Murder at the P & Z

by

Dorothy H. Hayes

Mainly Murder Press, LLC
PO Box 290586
Wethersfield, CT 06129-0586
www.mainlymurderpress.com

To [illegible]
Thank you for
coming! Love
Dot Hayes 4/13

Mainly Murder Press

Copy Editor: Jennafer Sprankle
Executive Editor: Judith K. Ivie
Cover Designer: Karen A. Phillips

Paperback ISBN 978-0-9881944-9-6
Ebook ISBN 978-0-9887816-0-3

Published in the United States of America

Mainly Murder Press
PO Box 290586
Wethersfield, CT 06129-0586
www.MainlyMurderPress.com

Dedication

To Arthur, my devoted husband, my constant friend and partner, you make my heart rest

To Carol McConway, my beautiful friend, who will walk every step with me

To my whole family, the best family a mother or father could ever have

~

"... Perhaps the larger portion of truth arises from the seemingly irrelevant."

Edgar Allan Poe

One
Maddy Trowbridge at the Planning and Zoning Department

It was business as usual at P&Z. Maddy was standing imperiously behind her desk in the receptionist's area straight ahead, about twelve feet from the front door. As always, she reminded me of Lady Bird Johnson, tiny with black hair and very white skin.

"Here," she said without looking at me as I approached her. She was peering down at her desk with her right arm extended, handing me a copy of this week's public hearing announcement. She continued to gaze down at her desk, strewn with stacks of files, notes and pink telephone message slips, as if I weren't there.

She was as terse as usual, I thought with a smile. Her actions told me once again that she preferred the young reporters, the ones she could mother.

Her black hair was combed straight back and obediently tucked into one tight curl that miraculously circled the nape of her neck from ear to ear. I couldn't help but stare at the curious curl and wonder how she managed to do it. She wore a beige wool coatdress, low beige heels and stockings. Neat and prim as usual, yet a pair of aluminum Christmas ball earrings, green, silver and red, hung from underneath the curl, clashing completely with her conservative style. On her desk sat a Christmas tree dish filled with the traditional hard candies. Three Christmas wreaths that she'd probably made herself adorned her desk, a window and the town planner's office door, leaving no doubt about her Christmas spirit.

Nothing subtle about Maddy. That's her major charm.

I scanned the public hearing notice with the Colonial Crest of the Town of Wilton, Connecticut, that listed the names of those who will appear before the planning and zoning commissioners on Wednesday night.

"Anything special I should know about?"

"No," she said, but then she glanced up at me with a doubtful expression. "The Stuart Island Condominiums again. They're requesting another special permit. He'll fix it," she said of the builder, Jack Manners, her voice deep and confident. "The feed lines to the underground storage tank have to be changed," Maddy rattled on without consulting any reports. "The developers applied for a special permit to change the UST as well." As she spoke her Christmas ball earrings swung back and forth under the curl. "They're going to replace the single-walled underground storage tank with a double-walled tank. The new tank will also get them up to speed with current leak detection measures." She was controlled as always, but her voice was growing in volume. "It's a more secure UST, since they're in the Aquifer Protection Zone. Knowing that they're in the APZ, why didn't they do that to begin with?"

She was talking about the precious pond of water, I told myself, that sat under the town and provided the majority of the town's well water, and the underground oil storage tank for the one hundred seven units of the condominium that could possibly pollute it.

The condos and their various problems were not news to me, but Maddy's worried expression was.

"Manners is here at least a couple of times a month for special permits, answering complaints from the DEP or to avoid legal problems with prospective owners," she said, her voice now resounding off the walls. "There's a mile high stack of DEP warning notices. If it's not about flooding in the basements, it's about what they're doing to avoid flooding in the basements. Then there's misplaced berms, railroad embankment erosion, parking spaces that direct rainwater runoff in the direction of the aquifer. And nobody has even moved into the condos yet. Wait until those complaints come in." She burst into thunderous laughter. "It's always something, but that's what we're here for."

She was like that person in charge of running a small shop, I thought, but the shop happens to be Wilton's environment. I glanced at Maddy's pictures of her ancestors, proudly displayed on the wall next to her desk.

"Jonathan Wood," I recalled her telling me, "built the first log cabin in Wilton. They were willing to die for the land. The least we can do is protect it," she said of the founders of Wilton. I remembered that from the first day I started covering P&Z, I got the feeling that her job was not just a job to her but a legacy.

I smiled at her robust laughter. It crossed my mind that she had not been herself lately. She had been uncharacteristically subdued, but I figured that was pretty normal under the circumstances with her boss of twenty-eight years retiring. Things were changing for Maddy. She had not only worked for Harrison, she had idolized him.

"The man wears seven hats," I recalled she said to me when I first met her two years ago as a way of introducing me to the functions of Wilton's Planning and Zoning Department and its town planner. I could still see the stars in her eyes when she listed Harrison's seven roles within the department. I wondered how the heck she was dealing with the new town planner. Timothy Esposito was a young man with a growing family and was a very different sort from

Harrison. Not the kind of person that Maddy could mother, that's for sure.

"You must miss Harrison," I dared to say as I glanced at her.

Her black eyes beamed back at me at the sound of his name, to my surprise. "I'm thinking of joining him in Bimini," she joked. She shot a look at her daughter's picture on her desk. "We got a couple of more years to go." I remembered that her daughter was a Yale student.

"I can't even imagine P&Z without you," I said.

"Right. No doubt I'll someday be pushing up daisies in one of the cemeteries along with my ancestors," she joked and let out another bellowing laugh.

As usual, I was in awe of Maddy's spirit, her sense of self and purpose.

I pulled my eyes away from her ebullient face to look over the public hearing announcement again and inquired about the proposed new preschool building. She frowned but shook her head, implying it was a regular application for a permit to build. I surmised that whatever perplexed her about this permit application was none of my business.

"The building site is on Route 7, just past Ridgefield Road, the west side heading north," she said, being specific, as usual. Her telephone rang. I waved a goodbye. She failed to notice. In her top sergeant voice and with her hand on her hip, she listed all the requirements necessary for a building permit to her caller.

I smiled back at her, grateful again for Maddy and her info. She never disappointed me. I headed toward the annex door. Whether she liked me or not didn't really matter. She was the source. The town planner seldom had time for reporters regarding routine matters.

As I turned to leave I recalled how she had softened up to me a little. The Professional Journalism Award is what did it.

That was almost a year ago, when I became a local hero, the reporter who is protecting everyone's well water. Ever since then we have a little more conversation. She also liked my two-part series on the aquifer. I loved writing it. I learned about the land, and so did our readers, which was the idea.

Yeah, great, I thought, but neither one of them landed me a job on a daily.

I caught myself reaching for the raspberry and mint green Christmas candy. You could get fat visiting town hall this time of year. I glanced at the file cabinets, but I was running short of time as usual. I would check the condos' and preschool files on Wednesday morning and ask Maddy my seemingly endless questions. I loved hearing her loud and jolly again, I thought, smiling. Maybe she was overcoming missing Harrison. I pushed open the annex's glass door.

A blast of cold air hit me in the face.

Two
Identity

The black ankle boots were so sensible, yet they were exactly where they shouldn't be. Only the poor woman's boots and a bit of her legs, clad in stockings, were visible. The rest of her body disappeared under the towering black spruce.

I checked my watch. In this brutal weather, at seven-thirty on Tuesday night, December fifteenth, I told myself, it appears as though I'm covering a murder. I shook my freezing cold head at my good fortune. My editor should be here. How lucky was I that he considered the telephone call about the body of a dead woman on School Road a crazy mistake of some kind?

Why would he think it was real anyway? Crime doesn't happen in Wilton. "There hasn't been a murder in eighty-six years," I recalled Evan saying as I beat it out the door while putting on my coat, thinking there is a murder.

This could be it for me, I told myself. The big one. At age forty-seven and about twenty years older than my fellow reporters, I needed this story. This is the one that gets you from a weekly to a daily.

I rubbed my freezing hands and estimated that I was about forty feet away from the murder scene. A screeching ambulance roared up Route 7, followed by a fire engine. They pulled into School Road and headed right toward me. I backed up to the road's far side. It came to an abrupt halt, parking in the middle of the road. A patrol car followed and parked across the entrance to School Road, blocking it off, while others raced up the highway to pull onto its shoulder. In seconds they lined Route 7 for about a block south of School Road.

The rush hour traffic that had been ebbing began to build up again. Commuters were rubber-necking, trying to figure out what crime had occurred on or near the otherwise sleepy suburban highway.

Meanwhile, Jerry squatted under the tree and leaned over the woman with a flashlight. Was he actually looking for signs of life? Someone lying that still on the snow-covered, frozen solid ground in this single-digit weather? His thick, black overcoat fanned out against the snow like ominous dark wings hovering over the poor dead woman. He finally crawled backward until he was clear of the lower branches and sprang up from the squatting position with his natural athleticism. In this cold weather I was impressed, even though Jerry at thirty-six had the slimness of youth.

He waved me forward with a quick gesture. He directed me to follow in his tracks by pointing to one of the two paths in the snow that led to the body. I followed his instructions and stopped about twelve feet away and next to the lead detective, Al Jenkins, who had just arrived.

I quickly introduced myself to Al and mentioned that Jerry had called me to help identify the body. I felt the need to explain my presence, since Jerry and I were seeing each other. Al just looked back at me from his puffy, cold, meaty face, saying nothing.

Jerry walked toward us with his head down. He seemed to be buying time to sort out the injuring moment.

"She's gone," he said, reaching us, his voice solemn.

Al and I exchanged glances.

"I know she looks like she's gone," he said with some impatience, "but I hoped." His near frozen lips and cheeks barely allowed him to speak. Each word was accompanied with puffs of smoke.

"A man walking his dog found her. He went into Cider Mill to call the station."

The lighted primary school building was about five hundred feet west of us and up a slight hill.

"There's blood behind her head. I only saw one entry wound to the back of her head. It looks like a single shot. A nine millimeter. It looks like death was instantaneous. So the one good thing, if there can be a good thing," he said, glancing back at the body, "is that by every indication she didn't see it coming. She looks peaceful."

Jerry's speech was clipped by the cold, and his breath was short and shallow from the stress of examining his first murder victim. He glanced at me and revealed his sadness. Then he quickly turned to gaze across School Road and about twenty feet up the spacious, snow-covered lawn to the shoveled cement walk. I followed his eyes. The walk led to the wide cement steps at the school's entrance. A dim lamppost barely illuminated the walkway.

"She was shot there," he said, nodding in the direction of the school's walkway. "She was about halfway up the walkway when she was shot, and then she was dragged back down here and shoved under the tree."

The drag marks in the snow were obviously drawn by the tips of the woman's boots. They ran from the walkway, across about twenty feet of the school's lawn, School Road's two lanes, and to the black spruce, which was about another twenty feet away. It appeared as though the murderer raked a branch or something similar through his footprints to obscure them.

The tracks in the snow, however, left no doubt about the pattern of the murder. Jerry revealed that the tracks began behind the mammoth trees that acted as a buffer to Route 7.

The killer's tracks led from the highway to the row of black spruces. It appeared as though he used the thick evergreens for cover while he waited for his prey. He then shot the victim and walked to the sidewalk to retrieve her body. He dragged her body from the shoveled sidewalk, down the hill, across School Road, and to the black spruce. In doing so, he retraced his trail in the snow.

Jerry's flashlight circled in on cherry red stains. The victim's blood marked her path of death in the snow as if she were revealing what occurred here.

The footprints of the man who discovered the body and his dog were also distinct. The man was obviously walking his dog down School Road. The road, having been plowed and sanded, was easily navigable, yet he and his dog stepped off the road to walk in the half a foot of frosted snow to reach the spruce. The only explanation for that, particularly on such a cold night, was that he wanted to investigate the object under the tree. After discovering the body, it was clear by the mass of churned snow that the man had been horrified by what he saw, swooped up his dog and ran up the hill to the school.

A thick cloud cover hovered overhead, turning the night sky pitch black. Al instructed three patrol cars to park in such a manner that they would illuminate the crime scene with their brights. One parked on each side of the area, and another cruiser parked across School Road. The beams crisscrossed and lit up the area like stage lights, illuminating the trees, the body and the police carefully picking through the area looking for clues. Two other cops were stringing crime scene tape.

Al was under the tree, examining the corpse, as Chief Dominic Romano arrived in his patrol car and parked in front of the fire engine. The Chief stepped out of the car, his huge belly protruding from his unbuttoned dark blue overcoat. No doubt he's worried about the politicians in town who will be breathing down his back, I thought.

Murder doesn't dare happen in conservative, safe Wilton.

I backed up and stood in the middle of School Road as Jerry filled in the Chief. Al clumsily crawled backward from under the tree. Al, thick around the middle, I figured was in his late fifties. He was off-balance, his shoulders hunched, and he seemed chilled to the bone.

The police cars now blocked Catalpa Road, one block north. This made sense because it led to the back road to the high school, which eventually ran into School Road. Barely illuminating the pitch-black area that led to the school building were two dim streetlights that resembled colonial lanterns. One light was halfway up the sidewalk to the school. The other was in the opposite direction near the four-car parking lot where I had parked my car.

The one car in the small parking area seemed familiar but I couldn't place it.

My shivering intensified. I tucked my stinging thumbs under my fingers. Jerry, Al and the Chief were now in a huddle. At that moment, the Chief retreated from the weather to his nice, warm patrol car with the motor running.

"Ros, think you can take a look?" Jerry finally asked. My chest heaved with anxiety. Jerry stood a few feet from the body.

Of course, the cops wouldn't know the woman, I told myself, walking toward Jerry. Most town employees can't afford to live in Wilton, the bedroom community to Wall Street. Al's in Norwalk, five miles down the road and several rungs down the economic ladder. Jerry's place is in Georgetown, the old manufacturing section of town, where house prices are lower, I recalled.

I stood next to Jerry and took a deep breath. I avoided looking at the woman's exposed legs and boots. He instructed me to follow his lead. I retraced his footprints in the snow with a bit of a stretch. We bent down before the spruce. The thick excurrent branches offered just enough space with a healthy squat. I managed to avert my eyes from the dead woman while I avoided getting stabbed in the face or back by the sharp needles or the piercing points of the lower branches. I couldn't see her face, at any rate, from this angle.

As soon as we were under the tree, the scent of evergreen engulfed us, and it was less bitter cold. The infinite shoots of the bilateral branches crisscrossed and wove an intricate web above our heads. My fingers touched the ground on either side for balance. The earth was so soft and spongy under my feet and fingers that it surprised me. I felt the thick padding of natural detritus of green needles, earth, crunchy snow and twigs that had collected over the years. I thought the tree had to be hundreds of years old. My skimpy gloves would be soaked in no time. I couldn't help but think of my warm, thick ski gloves going to waste in my closet.

Jerry stepped ahead and to the side of the woman. I was at once overwhelmed when I finally looked. It was my first sight of her full body. My pulse quickened. I felt the burn in my gut while adrenalin shot through me. Her face was still hidden from me. Her body lay on its side away from me. She wore a black woolen coat. The small of her spine was thrust against the tree trunk. The rest of her was deep under the tree toward the back branches. It seemed that a half-hearted attempt had been made to hide her. Her coat sleeves were jammed around her biceps. They revealed thin, bare forearms and ungloved hands. Her palms and fingers were outstretched in front of her as if someone had dragged her there.

Her head was between her outstretched arms.

I heard a heavy sigh and realized it was me. My knees were shaking. They sank into the frosty padding as I stretched and dared to get close enough to see the woman's face. A shadow fell across her face, obscuring it. Jerry focused his flashlight directly on it.

At the first glimpse of her face, everything changed. I saw the familiar profile, her bare cheek against the snow, her sharp nose. That black hair. A fist grabbed my stomach and tightened. Recognition was accompanied with a cataclysmic sense of dread, that sinking feeling as if everything worthwhile in life was gone. Fear shot through me.

I had seen this woman twice a week for the last two years at the planning and zoning department. I thrashed backward through six feet of evergreen branches, driven to get away from the scene and my own feelings. The sharp needles scratched the round of my back and dug into my quilted coat. Now out from under the tree, I attempted to stand. My fingers pushed against the hard snow, and I was standing. There were her sensible boots facing me. I shuddered with my eyes fixed on them. This is Wilton. Not the south side of Chicago. Not New York City.

She was shoved under a tree and left like so much garbage.

Once again, death had slapped me in the face.

I glanced at the two detectives who were at my side and reaching out to brace me. They were the picture of concern and curiosity, but I couldn't speak. I just stared down at the woman I had seen just yesterday during my typical Monday morning routine at town hall.

"Maddy Trowbridge," I managed to utter from tight, freezing lips. "It's Maddy Trowbridge. She's the town planner's secretary."

Three
Maddy Kept Us Honest

The tears of sadness and outrage sat behind my eyes, waiting for a chance to break loose as I told the detectives what I knew about Maddy. How her husband was probably at home and wondering where she was. Her daughter was probably also home from Yale for the semester break. Maddy's married son and a couple of grandkids lived out of state.

"She was a healthy, vibrant woman," I said, my voice sounding strange, "and you should know that she was a prominent figure in town."

The icy cold had tightened the muscles in my face and formed a thick elastic band that wrapped around my cheeks and jaw. Each time I attempted to pronounce a word, it barely allowed me to form the words well enough to be understood. "She showed me photographs of her ancestors who were some of the founders of Wilton. 'They were willing to die for the land, the least we can do is protect it,' she told me. I never forgot those words, basically because I agreed with her."

I stared hard at the two detectives as everything Maddy had told me in the last two years started to rush back to me. I gave myself a few seconds' break from talking.

"Our recently retired town planner, Harrison Hayden, ran around, and everybody in town knew it. But to Maddy, Harrison was George Bailey, keeping Wilton from turning into Potter's Field." Al's attention was periodically drawn to the uniformed officers, as if he were monitoring them. Jerry, however, stared down at me, seemingly enrapt.

"You should know that Harrison told me that Maddy kept us honest. He meant during the growth years of the town, Maddy kept the planner's department honest." I wiped my running nose with a crumpled tissue I was grateful to find in my coat pocket. "My story about Maddy will begin there," I said.

"Her bag is missing," Jerry said calmly, his intense eyes still on me. "and her hat and gloves. Her coat pockets are turned out, and she isn't wearing a wedding ring," he said. "She is still wearing Christmas earrings," he added, his voice flat. "So as far as we know, the mugger stole her jewelry and took her bag, hat and gloves."

"I never knew Maddy to wear a hat," I muttered, "but she always wore gloves."

At that moment a man in a thick red and black plaid parka, cap and calf-high boots trudged up School Road. Jerry revealed that he was the county coroner. The average sized man shook his head sorrowfully. With a flashlight in hand and without saying a word, he knelt down to examine the woman under the tree. When he stood up again, the medical emergency team placed the body on a stretcher and set it down in the open. A few minutes later the coroner pronounced Maddy dead from what appeared to be a nine millimeter gunshot wound to the back of her head. The bullet was lodged in her brain.

He estimated the time of death to be at least two hours ago, approximately between four-thirty and five-thirty.

"Death was instantaneous," he concluded. "The woman didn't suffer. I didn't see any other marks on her body except a few scratches that occurred most likely from being dragged." He looked up to the school as he spoke. "I don't think she saw it coming. I'll know more tomorrow."

Town hall closes up at four-thirty each afternoon. Maddy usually stayed a half-hour later, I explained to Jerry and Al. If she died a little after five, it appears that she had driven directly to Cider Mill from town hall. It would have taken almost a half-hour with the heavier than usual rush hour traffic on Route 7, given the Christmas shoppers.

The two medical emergency technicians delivered the body to the open doors of the hearse. With a sense of helplessness I watched Maddy's body disappear into the hearse. She'd be taken to Farmington to the medical examiner's office for a mandatory autopsy, Jerry explained. The coroner promised a full report the next morning. Her body would be delivered to Johnson's Funeral Home in twenty-four hours. As the coroner offered his observations to the detectives, I stood off to the side. With an awkward grip on my pen from frozen fingers, I took down every word.

With each shaky letter I inscribed on my yellow legal pad, I found myself promising Maddy that the truth would prevail. I vowed that we would find the person who had stolen her life.

Four

A mugging gone wrong?

Al Jenkins, as the lead detective, was the first to categorize the crime, calling it a homicide that had occurred in the progress of a mugging. "The facts we have to start with are that the victim was killed and then robbed," Al concluded.

The single car in the parking lot was Maddy's, Jerry had just announced. The tan Camry didn't belong to anyone in the school building, an officer discovered, so they broke into it and found two trays of Christmas cookies. They were giftwrapped and labeled with nametags signed by Maddy.

I took in Al's deep gray overcoat and a black wool cap and earmuffs as I steadied my nerves.

"Al, do you remember Liz Rossi?" Jerry asked.

"I know Rossi from the story on our strike," he said. "What cop doesn't know Rossi?" He was giving me some time to pull myself together.

"I know most officers by sight, if not by name," I said in return, still trembling, my voice shaking. "I can still see them as they surrounded town hall with the First Selectman hiding inside. I even met Jerry that day."

I recalled how easy it was to get the stats from local towns like Darien and Weston to prove that the WPD demands for one more paid holiday and insurance coverage for their families was nothing more than fair.

"I couldn't get a traffic ticket in town if I tried, not that I'm trying," I said jokingly, smiling back at Al but still trembling.

"Ros, want my coat?" Jerry asked. "Are you okay?"

"I'm okay," I replied. "I'm just a little shook. I'm fine."

Jerry agreed with Al's conclusion that this was a homicide that had taken place during a mugging. "We can't exclude any possibilities," Al added. "Rossi, you'll be reading this on the police blotter tomorrow. I don't want you adding anything else for the time being. Stick to the blotter."

"Of course," I said, realizing that Al was again thanking me for the strike story by including me, a reporter, in this conversation. Although Wilton being a small town, officials often worked openly with the influential *Wilton Weekly,* I reminded myself.

"It's Christmas," Jerry continued. "People are carrying around more cash, and the school's lights were on." He waved toward the lighted school building to the west of us. "The trees were good cover. Then there's Route 7 for a quick escape," he said, giving a nod to the jammed highway behind the trees.

"We didn't yet find any distinct tire marks," Al interrupted, his voice growing hoarse as if he were coming down with a cold, and the icy weather was affecting him. He talked while he rubbed his gloved hands and then put them back in his pockets.

"The crime scene is clean," he continued. "We could have covered-up tire marks. We'll know more in the morning. The mugger could have come on foot, for all we know at this point. Granted, nobody walks in suburbia. No other cars were parked in the small lot except for the victim's. The main lot is in the back of the school. From his trail, he had to park on the shoulder of Route 7 or across the road. He went directly from the highway to the trees. It was rush hour, so he might have parked on the shoulder."

Anyone in the school?" Al asked Jerry.

"A couple of teachers waiting for us," Jerry said, adding that a full list of teachers would be faxed to the department tomorrow. "It was parent/teacher's day, so the full faculty was present. It ended at six-thirty."

With his chin down on his chest and a steady gaze, Jerry invited me to offer my comments. He rubbed his gloved hands together and pulled his black knitted hat down to his brows. Al and Jerry, I knew, were listening because of my reputation as an investigative reporter and because my last exposé had changed the outcome of a recent election.

"I'll make this fast," I assured Al, who I knew wanted to get inside the school to question the teachers and then head out to the Trowbridge house. "I do have the advantage of knowing Maddy Trowbridge. She'd be quick to size up the situation. Given the chance, she would have just handed over her money." My words came in spurts and smoky pants as I attempted to talk and breathe in the icy air. "She was a sensible woman. I don't believe she would ever fight back," I continued, picking up the pace, "but if she did fight back, where's the evidence of a struggle? She was shot behind the head execution style. I know you are not ruling anything out at this point, Al," I said, shooting him a glance, "so let me offer this theory." Al's watery blue eyes were just inches from me. His jowls were hanging lower by the minute. Jerry was amused as if he knew I'd come up with something.

"It looks like an execution," I plowed on, "not a mugging. If it were a mugging, why would the mugger shoot her from a distance? Stalk her, more or less?" I glanced at one then the other, determined to drive home my point. "Wouldn't a mugger confront her for her money and jewelry? Aren't deaths in a mugging the result of a struggle for the most part? Something goes wrong during the mugging?"

"Maddy got out of her car parked in the small lot," I said, staring at the small parking lot to the west of us. "She walked up the sidewalk to the school entrance. The killer stood behind the spruce waiting to shoot her. Isn't that strange, to take the risk of killing someone for a few bucks in their pocket? If it were just a random mugging, the mugger wouldn't know who she was, right? Or how much money she was carrying. Then why would the mugger take her gloves?" I continued. "Wouldn't a mugger rip the gloves off her and throw them on the ground in his rush to get to her rings and escape?" I continued, surprising myself. "I believe the killer was busy trying to make it look like a mugging," I said. "The missing gloves prove the point. The killer must have taken the gloves by mistake while trying to make this look like a mugging." Again I stared at one detective and then the other, waiting for a rejection to my theory. I gazed at Al's puffy blues eyes for a second before continuing. "And why stake out a school for a mugging?" I continued. "It's not a likely spot. You can't say there's a lot of foot traffic this time of day or cash required to enter a school. Also, I don't agree that Route 7 is a good escape route. It's jammed at rush hour when this crime was supposedly committed, and it's five miles to I-95, which would give access to a quick escape. Of course, you can't rule anything out at this early stage," I finished up, still wondering where I got the nerve.

Jerry shook his head, staring down at me, and moved an inch closer. He gave me a compelling look. "A hit is possible. We have to keep our minds open, but we have to start with the facts. Her belongings were stolen. The mugger probably panicked. Victims of a mugging are usually killed because the perpetrator doesn't want to be identified. Maybe she spotted him in the trees."

"But Jerry, you said she looked like she didn't see it coming," I retorted.

Jerry never answered. Our time to chat was over. I gazed at the two faces with red noses and cheeks and watery eyes, and I knew I probably looked worse, at least worse than Jerry, since I was almost a dozen years older than he. Al turned to leave, heading toward the school's shoveled cement walk. Jerry followed with a high sign to me.

"Did the desk sergeant get the name of the man who discovered the body," I called after Jerry, "the man with the dog?" I wanted to interview him.

Jerry shook his head, stopped in his tracks and turned back to look at me. "Maybe he's waiting in the school," he said, looking at Al questioningly.

"Pete didn't mention," Al replied, referring to the officer who went inside the building earlier. Al was now rubbing his freezing arms. "If you two are finished," he added "we gotta get inside and then to the Trowbridge's."

Jerry offered a goodbye glance that indicated he'd get back to me as soon as possible, but that didn't help. I squirmed. I loved that I was so curious, I told myself. It was a reporter's necessary tool. But as I stood there, literally left out in the cold, my big toes almost not registering anymore, my curiosity was killing me. I knew I'd have to wait for hours for Jerry's call for an update, and I'd still have questions.

I didn't trust the two detectives to ask the questions I was likely to pose. It's a process. Usually the answer to one question raises another. The process continues until the answer to a question fails to prompt another question. Most people, for some reason, stop asking questions too early. I hold little faith that anybody else would plow to the bottom of things as I would.

Jerry and Al were good cops. This was their business, after all. I sighed and wondered again why I thought I could outthink two detectives. I thought of my investigations. That's why.

I carefully jogged the short distance back to my car, watching for black ice. I observed Maddy's car being towed away to the police station. I thought about how I had recognized the car when I had first arrived but couldn't place it.

I was grateful to get into my freezing car. I started the motor to allow it to heat up a while and heaved a huge sigh of relief, grateful to be alone with my thoughts. That puzzling sense of impending doom that had started at my first glimpse of Maddy clung to me like the icy air.

Then there was this strange sense of responsibility, which I recognized for the first time. Why? Why should I feel that I must find Maddy's killer? The burning knot in my stomach was beginning to subside; the adrenaline flow had disappeared. I reminded myself that sometimes there are no immediate answers to questions. If Dad hadn't gotten sick, I wouldn't be here, I thought. I'd be teaching English to high school kids in Wayne, New Jersey. A flashback of my mother, closing her eyes for the last time one year after my father's passing, flooded my mind. I took a deep, woeful breath thinking how fragile life was.

My parents' premature deaths could be the reason for the knot in my stomach, that feeling that everything worthwhile was gone. Good people just disappear forever, people you think you can't live without.

I turned on the wipers to remove the surface of frost that had settled on the windshield in the past half hour. It didn't work. The wipers just rolled over the frost without removing anything. I turned on the heater, knowing I'd reach the newsroom before it actually warmed up. I fished for the plastic scraper under the passenger seat, got out of the car and gave the windows a quick once-over. In the process, however, my eyes were drawn to the murder scene.

The cops were now placing crime scene tape around the school area, marking what was believed to be Maddy's route to the school door. They also roped off the route of the man and his dog.

I pretended to walk in Maddy's footsteps. Why was she here? Was she meeting someone? My theory that it was a professional hit deepened as I stared at the walk and the trees. Nothing else made any sense. History leaves its mark, and individuals sense it. Something was left behind, and I sensed it. I also knew that the first impression made at the scene of the crime is the strongest.

Al and Jerry had their first impression, I reminded myself. Motive. I thought for the first time of motive. A mugger's motive would be quick cash during the holidays, as Jerry had suggested. If a hired hit man killed Maddy, the man who hired him would also have to have a motive. But who in the world would want to kill Maddy Trowbridge?

I slipped back into my silver Nissan to head back to the newsroom, but I realized part of me was still very much in the dark under the ominous black spruce with Maddy.

Five
Telling Evan

I checked my cheap watch. It was eight-fifteen. I was impressed that it kept running in the cold. I parked my car in the parking lot that had only one measly lamppost in the middle of it. As I walked around the corner to the newsroom, I sucked in the bitter cold air. I thought of nothing else but breaking the news to my exhausted editor. Not only is this the first murder the town in eighty-six years, I reminded myself, but the victim was an outstanding and much loved citizen and close contact of his for the last fifteen years. His whole tenure at the newspaper.

Bitter cold as it was, I took my time climbing the flight of steep, wooden steps on the outside of the building. As I crossed over the threshold of the narrow doorway and entered the semi-finished attic apartment, I was again struck by my good fortune to be writing for the venerable *Wilton Weekly*. I was also struck by the paper's humble digs. At the far end of the dimly lit, unfinished, narrow room with its ninety-degree attic ceiling and open beams sat Evan hard at work.

"Well?" He raised his soft voice only slightly to be heard. His eyes remained on his computer screen, barely interested in my response as he continued pounding his keyboard. "Was there a body?"

Without saying a word I walked toward him, avoiding the black, thick wires strung along the wide planks of the creaky wooden floor. Too bad I couldn't have called him with this horrible news so he could have at least received it in private. No chance, I told myself, I couldn't risk leaving the scene. I needed to get the story. He'll know that. I measured his exhausted, pale face, his glassy hazel eyes, and the light brown hair flecked with gray that was bound to get grayer in a hurry. This quiet, patient man, so opposite to the macho, chronically irritated editor, was about to get the shock of his journalistic life.

If he thinks he lives in chaos now, wait.

I approached his battered mahogany desk, a beloved remnant of the newspaper's beginnings in 1937. The heavy Victorian desk reminded me that not even the *Wilton Weekly's* founder, S. Gilbert Taggard, Wilton's first historian, had been tested with a homicide.

My eyes, however, focused on the beat-up floorboards when I told Evan that Maddy Trowbridge had been murdered. His keyboard pounding came to an abrupt halt. I walked to the chair beside his desk and finally dared to glance at him. Our eyes locked in grief. I fell into the chair ungracefully, coat, gloves and hat still on, paralyzed by the moment.

Evan's crushed face forced me to continue to talk to allow him time to recuperate from the news. I described each detail of what had taken place on School Road. "Maddy didn't see it coming, Evan, according to the coroner and the detectives," I repeated several times.

Then I read the notes on my yellow pad, quoting the coroner's preliminary report. We both fell silent.

"Let's concentrate on the police report for this issue," Evan began after a few minutes had passed and he had cleared his throat. I was used to the Yale educated, soft-spoken Evan who chose his words carefully and pronounced each word distinctly. But now I found myself leaning forward in my seat and concentrating on his lips to make out his words that were no louder than a whisper.

"We'll offer our sympathy," he said as if he were talking to himself. "I'll write a few lines about Maddy's historical ties," he said, then stopped talking for a second to collect himself.

"I'll announce that a special insert regarding her contribution at P&Z, the historical society, and her family's full history will be in our next issue."

It was quiet for a second.

"Al and Jerry are probably at her house now," I muttered. "They were going into Cider Mill to question a couple of teachers briefly when I left. It was parent/teacher night. Most of them had gone home already."

"Will you be able to handle tomorrow?" He turned to stare at me, waiting for my response.

I looked blankly back at him. My editor asking me if I can do my job? I must look traumatized.

"You cover P&Z tomorrow," he said.

"Right." I hit myself in the head while I thought yes, P&Z tomorrow. It's Wednesday. P&Z tomorrow and no Maddy to fill me in. "I'll be fine," I responded.

"Our first priority will be covering the investigation," Evan continued. "I'd like you to continue to cover this. Since you were at the crime scene, I think it best that you stay with the story. Your contacts in the police department are valuable. I doubt Jerry would have called me tonight," he said, looking directly at me with assurance. "Stick to the facts of the police blotter tomorrow. For now just make the announcement of her death from a gunshot wound to the back of the head, which appears to be the result of a mugging. Then describe the scene. Add any other details that come to mind. I'll fill you in on whatever information I receive from the Chief or anybody at town hall as the case progresses. Oh, and call Clifford Trowbridge tomorrow morning. Set up an appointment with him for burial information and later for ceremonies by the town in honor of Maddy."

Funeral arrangements were usually done by our chronically late receptionist, Susanna Swank. I sat there, staring at Evan and asking, why me? The murder on top of covering my usual beat was daunting enough. I blinked my tired eyes at Evan.

"I want you to do it since a decision will be made as to where Maddy will be buried," Evan explained as if reading my thoughts. "The burial ground of Jonathan Wood was lost over the years, so that's out. You'll need to do a little history of the cemetery chosen. Several family cemeteries date back hundreds of years. Descendants of the founding families are scattered around town, including those of Jonathan Wood."

History would be my co-writer, Evan had told me when he had hired me. To what extent, I'm sure he had no idea. I stared back at him.

As Evan spoke I realized I'd been given the opportunity to meet with Maddy's husband tomorrow. Although my curiosity was being served well, I shifted in my seat, thinking of intruding on the fresh grief of the Trowbridge family. This is what reporters do, I corrected myself, but here's where covering a murder in a small town is different. Everybody knows everybody. Some reporters would sell their grandmother for a good story.

I never wanted to be one of them.

When Evan returned to his work, it was my cue to get back to mine. I could feel the usual tug of the weekly deadline exhaustion. I'd dig down and find enough energy left to do all the extra work with some kind of coherence.

After I finally slipped off my outerwear, I sat down in front of my cold computer screen. I was about to describe again the murder scene on School Road as I had for Evan, but I soon realized the embargoed tears were flowing down my cheeks, and a crushing grief grabbed hold of me. I was grateful Dylan and Frank weren't in yet. I tugged the tissue from my pants pocket, leaned back in my chair and sank into the comforting shadows of the old newsroom. But soon the sobs took hold, and I went to our small corner bathroom at the right of the front door.

I couldn't tell who the sobs were for—Maddy, my parents or both. Angry voices attracted my attention. Dylan and Frank must have come in, and they were talking about Maddy's murder to Evan. I was grateful to be sitting in the lavatory and not seeing the expressions of the two angry young men who had viewed Maddy as a mother figure.

Six
The Deadly Legacy of Jonathan Wood

I finally finished the piece on the murder scene. Dylan and Frank, who had asked me many questions and calmed down, were still feverishly writing their stories on either side of me. I sat there, staring at my blank computer screen. Something Maddy said when I first met her had begun to haunt me.

"Wall Street corporate executives didn't always rule," she told me. "Wilton wasn't always a bedroom community."

I had been struck then by her bold words. It was an honest criticism of the town she loved. I sat there, remembering how I had looked blankly back at her, unable to relate to her observation.

Why hadn't I asked her what she meant? I was busily filing what she said and impressed that she had said it instead of reacting to it. I'm so slow to react, too introspective. I shifted uncomfortably in my chair. The negative thoughts were building, which wasn't unusual either. Actually, my thinking of playing detective to find Maddy's murderer was a bit of lunacy. Yet I had promised Maddy. What was I thinking? I have investigated environmental controversies; I haven't solved a murder case.

I shook my head at my own audacity, my mixed feelings.

I got up and walked across the attic. Taggard's history books of Wilton, six little beige booklets tinged with brownish tones of age, sat on a library table under the slanted ceiling. I instantly felt a sense of security as my hands gripped the thin booklets. My investigations usually started at the library. I was so grateful for Taggard's books. They could possibly help me to understand Maddy and better decipher her cryptic words. That understanding might get me one step closer to fulfilling the promise I had no business making.

I brought the first history book ever written about the colonial town of Wilton back to my space. I was carrying a rare treasure. Its thin pages were glossy and smooth with generous margins that set off the block of printed words.

"Land was even more important than religious freedom to the pioneers," was written on the first page. The line brought to mind Maddy's words, "They were willing to die for the land, the least we can do is protect it."

In 1706 Jonathan Wood was apparently as outspoken as Maddy and as fiercely independent, according to the book. It indicated that Wood was a stubborn man of forty-eight who refused to live in "Norwalke" with the other English settlers. He chose instead to live in the relative wilderness of Wilton among the "uncritical forest" with his wife and five sons.

I raised my eyes off the page of the book to gaze out of the octagonal colonial window straight ahead, no larger than a ship's porthole.

Was Maddy's job as secretary to the town planner at the heart of this crime? My first instinct was that there was more to this than a random mugging.

I turned back to the book. Jonathan's log cabin was built on the east side of Wilton known as the Pimpewaug section. Maddy's home was in that same section of town. This was no coincidence, I concluded. The book revealed that Jonathan and his sons were the first to clear some of Wilton's primal forests to plant seed. His farm was later called Egypt because wheat that refused to grow in other sections of town flourished for him. He was "old and feeble," twenty years later in 1726 when he signed the petition for the Wilton Parish. This was the beginning of the town, since church and state, at that time, were one and the same. I recalled the pride Maddy carried in her bearing when she pointed out Jonathan's name on the copy of the church petition that also hung on her wall.

I scanned the pages of Taggard's book and spotted the name Arabella. That was Maddy's daughter's name. She had named her only daughter after one of the ships that carried Jonathan and other pioneers from England to this land. Her son's name was Jonathan. Jonathan and Arabella, the historic praenomens given upon their birth, were yet another act by Maddy to honor the town's settlers.

According to Taggard, in 1630 sixteen such creaky vessels sailed to New England. The exorbitant fee was a year's salary or more for a family of six for humble accommodations. The voyagers, for the most part tradesmen and then farmers, "were successful in their fields, and twice as literate as their contemporaries in England."

So upscale Wilton was upscale from its very roots, I thought.

I sat back in my chair, and my pulse raced from fear as I realized the full depth of Maddy's dedication to Wilton's land. Nothing was built in town without going through P&Z. Within her capacity at the planner's office she had done whatever was in her power to protect the character of the land, the town, the aquifer, the wetlands and the Norwalk River as if it were her duty.

I replayed Harrison Hayden's words in my head: "She kept us honest." I sucked in air. Hayden, on the other hand, was more invested in progress in his position as town planner. But the land was Maddy's identity, her precious legacy. I read it on her face whenever she spoke of her ancestors. Whenever she gazed at their portraits or the parish petition it was with some authority. Her spine became rigid, and her head was held high. She'd have no struggle putting the land first, I concluded.

Questions hung with some tenacity in the night air as I closed Taggard's book. In her capacity at the planner's office, had Maddy Trowbridge uncovered something illegal?

Had she put her life on the line to protect the land?

To be loyal to Jonathan?

Seven
Sugarloaf Drive

It was six hours and forty-five minutes since the discovery of Maddy's body, two-thirty in the morning, and I was finally leaving the newsroom. I shivered upon impact with the brutal night air. The temperature had dropped even more, and the dampness felt like crystals against my cheeks. I descended the steep flight of stairs that were barely lit. My right hand clung tighter than usual to the wooden railing while the raw cold seeped through my clothing, making me tremble.

My eyes searched the village center spread out below. The quaint ice cream parlor, the bike repair shop directly under us and the toyshop to our right bore large, multi-paned colonial windows. It was as innocent as maple syrup, but I was leery. The shops were closed up and dark. My eyes sought every shadowy portal. I was exhausted, I reminded myself, and still traumatized. A little PTSD, I thought, like a Vietnam vet.

I took hold of the satchel strap across my chest, clung tightly to the sturdy band and tried to calm down. I walked in the darkness around the corner of our building to the huge, square parking lot. It was lit by only one colonial lamppost set in the center of the lot. It was lined with shops, also all dark and locked up for the night. The sounds of my steps were magnified as I mapped my way through the minefield of black ice in the scant light. Only our four cars remained in the otherwise vacant lot. With relief I reached my silver

Stanza. The car key turned easily in the unfrozen door lock. I exhaled, carefully stepped into the car and locked the door in record-breaking time, slamming down the locks.

The driver's seat was a solid block of ice, but to my great relief the motor started immediately. As I pulled out of the parking space, tremors from the car's refrigeration shook my spine. Since I lived only minutes away, actually a minute or two past the police station and School Road, there was no need to turn the heater on, I told my spastic body.

I took a right onto empty Center Road. It runs the length of the village center. Just a half block away on the dead quiet street, I made another quick right onto Ridgefield Road. It was one of the oldest roads in town in a town of old roads, I thought, and was amused at the corny line. But it was true. Before Wilton Parish had been established, early settlers had used Ridgefield Road to get to the Meeting House in Ridgefield, I reminded myself, proud that I had learned at least that much history about the town. Come winter and the heavy snows, the Ridgefield Meeting House was a lot closer than the one in Norwalk.

Okay, great. I knew why the settlers used the Ridgefield Meeting House, but I didn't know why Maddy had been at Cider Mill School.

I drove over the railroad overpass to the traffic light a couple of blocks away and took a left, heading north on Route 7, also closed up for the night. It was lit by nonintrusive streetlights. The police station a mile down the road on the right seemed eerily quiet in a night of murder and mayhem. It was a discreet beige brick building within clusters of evergreens. The daily police blotter was typically nothing but traffic citations, auto accidents, an occasional domestic dispute, a rare case or two of exploding mailboxes, and all homegrown, I noted as I drove by.

Until tonight.

When I passed School Road on my left, there was the crime scene tape marking the murder scene. The vivid image of Maddy under the tree returned in all its gruesomeness. Two cruisers blocked off the School Road entrance. Another blocked Catalpa Road. Knowing that the cops were on the job around the clock was comforting. The Wilton cops weren't used to murder cases. Could they really handle this? Wilton's residents would ask that same question. I took the left onto Olmstead Hill Road and the first right onto Sugarloaf Drive. The overcast sky blocked celestial light. No glow from stars, planets or the moon broke the night's darkness. No lamplights, curbs, white lines or sidewalks marked the way on Sugarloaf or any other block in town. The lack of such modern features preserved the look of a country road in a small town. I loved this aspect of it.

Christmas lights gleamed brightly on the dark roads this time of year, but they were turned off by ten. The area was in total darkness. The Olmstead name is synonymous with the origins of Wilton, I thought as I drove up the short distance up Olmstead Hill Road, keeping my mind occupied. Evan had told me that Richard Olmstead and thirteen other men and women purchased the land that spreads across Wilton and Norwalk and parts of three other towns: New Canaan, Westport and Lewisboro, NY. "Olmstead paid fifteen pounds back in the summer of 1650 to another pioneer,'" he'd said. "The exact same price Chief Mahackemo got ten years earlier from the Connecticut Colony. The Chief got the same price for the land."

It was even darker on Sugarloaf since we were farther away from the highway. I started to think how Sugarloaf Drive was a giant hairpin curve. It traveled up a gradual hill about a half a mile hit some rocky land and made a hairpin turn to go back down the hill to Olmstead again. Sugarloaf was both the first and the second right turn off Olmstead, if I were heading west.

The land dipped and rose at will, and everywhere there were trees, lovely and innocent trees of all sizes. The red and white oaks, sugar maples, white ash, black birch, some graceful giants reached the open sky even when they were rooted in one of the many small but deep gorges and gullies. I smiled as I thought of the neighborhood squirrels, skunks, chipmunks, hedgehogs and the families of raccoons, opossums and the deer that often looked through my kitchen window.

Maddy never forgot that we all lived on well water. She started to talk to me more after she read my two-part series on the aquifer. Route 7 was a ribbon that wove through the river valley land, and some Wilton citizens fought to keep it a sleepy country highway because it was built over the great pond. The valley caught the precipitation that slowly made its way down the surrounding hills to the wetlands, the bogs, the streams and ponds, and finally to the Norwalk River and the aquifer underneath.

Since the precious wetlands filtered our well water, they and the birds were protected by local and state laws. All lay under the watchful eyes of the planner's office. For the last twenty-eight years one of the most watchful set of eyes had been those of Maddy Trowbridge.

"Maddy kept us honest," I could hear Harrison say.

Now Maddy's eyes were closed forever, and Harrison was retired.

I was approaching my dark, unlocked house. Tonight the Wilton custom seemed foolish. I pulled the car up to the door and parked, then stepped out onto the gravel driveway and the quiet, dark night. I walked to the front door and opened it, holding my breath all the way.

In the vestibule I opened the multi-paned inner door, stepped into the warm, comforting entry hall and closed the door, leaving it unlocked in case someone was inside.

I flipped on the entry hall light and kept my hand on the doorknob for a second. I listened for suspicious sounds from the foot of the stairs on my left that led to the three bedrooms upstairs, from the pine-paneled living room to my right and straight ahead from the dark hallway leading to the galley kitchen. I refused to progress any farther until I was sure I was the only one in the house.

Then I heard a high piercing sound. My bones were jumping. Then I realized it was the phone. Down the narrow center hall I ran to the wall phone in the kitchen and grabbed it as if it were a life raft.

"I called the paper; they told me you just left." Jerry's voice was anxious and his breathing shallow. "I'm a little worried about you, Rossi."

I heaved a sigh of relief. The extra key was hidden under a stone off the driveway, just below the smaller living room window next to the front door, I directed him. I locked the front door and charged upstairs for a most desired shower. Because Jerry was coming over, I could actually enjoy the hot water rolling over my exhausted body.

Another dangerous thought came to mind as I soaped up. I was actually encouraging the relationship with a handsome man eleven years younger than me. Had I lost my mind? In this youth loving culture, why would I make it so hard on myself? But then I recalled the soft brown eyes, the caring hands. I smiled and sighed.

Ten minutes later Jerry's red pick-up was in the driveway. I ran downstairs so he wouldn't have to fish for the key. When his large frame filled the doorway, I let out another sigh of relief. There he was with his smiling eyes, the amused gaze that told me he was glad to see me.

I was anxious to hear all about his visit to the Trowbridge house, but I'd wait before asking all my questions.

He took off his boots and entered the house. It was then that I realized we were being drawn together at warp speed by Maddy's murder, drawn beyond our chemistry and our many shared interests. While I was working at the newspaper tonight, I half expected him to show up to escort me home. When my parents had died, the thought of someone worrying about my well-being above all others had died with them. I looked at Jerry and realized how much I'd missed it and how Jerry had revived that feeling. He took off his black overcoat and knitted black hat and threw them on the cushioned chair next to the front door as if he'd done that a thousand times. We headed upstairs to the master bedroom for the night, leaving the downstairs in darkness and the outside lights blazing as if it were routine. Yet this would be the first time he slept over.

"My mother's at the house," he explained. "A local kid's helping her. I expect we'll be working almost around the clock."

He'd sleep a few hours and head back to the station. He usually reluctantly rushed home to his small farm to care for the animals. Tonight it seemed almost necessary to have him here. I couldn't shake the sense of impending doom that I had first experienced when I recognized Maddy's body under the black spruce, even in the safety of my own home.

We reached the second floor landing and headed toward the master bedroom. Jerry and I will take it as it comes, one instinct at a time, I told myself, and one question at a time.

For the last couple of hours one question had dominated my thoughts: What was Maddy Trowbridge doing at Cider Mill School?

Eight
Al and Jerry's Investigation

We sat side by side on the floral comforter on my queen-size maple bed. A single window was a few inches to our right, adorned with sheer cafe curtains. The transparency bothered me.

One candlestick bedside lamp on the nightstand cast a soft glow, but it was bright enough to highlight the grief and stress pulling at Jerry's face and shoulders. As he described what had occurred at the Trowbridges', his right arm hugged me to him as if he were protecting me and at the same time comforting himself.

"I began to reconsider your theory about a professional hit," Jerry said, turning to look at me. "Mr. Trowbridge said that Mrs. Trowbridge had been acting strange for the last two weeks of her life. Her daughter noticed it, too. She got back home from school on Saturday."

Jerry began flipping through his notepad as he spoke. "Mr. Trowbridge revealed that his wife was looking behind her as if she thought someone might be following her. She seemed afraid of something, but when he questioned her about it, she said he was being silly. Her daughter Arabella said that she thought her mother was not herself. She described her as jumpy. At first both of them thought it might be because of the changes at P&Z, but now they think it was more than that."

He hesitated for a second. "Mrs. Trowbridge was not going to be top sergeant in her office any more, Rossi. That must have been pretty upsetting at her age. Change at any age makes people nervous."

"Jerry," I said, "Maddy was afraid? That's so not like her. That's significant. She was a little dynamo at P&Z. If she were afraid, how can this be a random mugging?"

"Well, her nervousness might have been just about the changes at P&Z."

"Jerry, what was Maddy doing at the school?"

"Nobody knows," he said, shaking his head wearily. "Mrs. Trowbridge was supposed to go to her bridge group in Georgetown but never got there. It was their Christmas party. They were exchanging Christmas cookies. When Mrs. Trowbridge didn't show, the group called her house, but nobody was at home. They called an hour later, and the daughter answered. By that time they all thought that Mrs. Trowbridge might have been in a car accident. Arabella, the daughter, then called the station. When Al and I got to the house, they thought we were there to report a car accident. They were afraid she was hurt."

"Oh, brother," I said.

"To answer your question, Ros, nobody knows what Mrs. Trowbridge was doing at the school." He turned to stare hard at me. "This is an investigation. Just print what you saw at the murder scene and what is on the police blotter."

He stared, waiting for confirmation. "Of course," I said. "I realized this was all confidential material." Jerry hesitated as if he were lost in thought.

"The crime scene was clean," he said. "Nobody saw anything, the teachers we questioned never saw Mrs. Trowbridge. They parked in the main parking lot in the back of the school. They never even saw her car in the small lot. I went back to the station and called the new town planner, Timothy Esposito," Jerry continued. "He was shocked to hear about Mrs. Trowbridge. He said everything was operating smoothly at the planning and zoning department. He seemed surprised to hear me ask the question. I insisted he open up the annex so we could check for anything suspicious. We found nothing."

Jerry let out an exhausted sigh and gazed past me and out the bedroom window. A car was coming up Sugarloaf. His bleary eyes were mesmerized by the oncoming headlights.

A car traveling up Sugarloaf at this time? That was strange, but it sped by without stopping. I took a deep breath.

"If it isn't a mugging, the prime suspect would be her husband." He shook his head once more. "The man is so physically weak, I don't think he's capable of killing anybody. He looked like he was going to collapse. Both the father and daughter kept it together for each other. Did you know that he's recovering from a heart attack?"

I nodded. "Yes. It happened in early April. Everybody at town hall wanted to help Maddy through those days. Pots of soup flowed into town hall like a raging river, mine included."

Jerry chuckled, gazing at me in amusement. "He could never have killed his wife," he said. "The man was overcome with grief." He shook his head in sympathy. "I know it's possible for people to fake it, but it seems genuine to me. And he's not financially gaining from his wife's death, as far as we know. I took a quick look at their financial papers. She only had a life insurance policy that will pay for the funeral arrangements. We found nothing else."

He continued, "His alibi is solid. He and his daughter were out Christmas shopping. You know their daughter goes to Yale with grant money. They live in a small ranch, one of the ones built on one-acre lots."

Jerry shook his head in a youthful puppy dog way, as if trying to wake up, and his wavy hair swayed artfully from one side to the other. He grinned at me, laughing at his attempts to stay focused. For a minute he acted like the familiar breezy Jerry and seemed about twenty years old. Thanks to his vegan diet, people think he's about twenty-five, but he always says he didn't look like he presently looks when he really was twenty-five.

I thanked my Italian ancestry and being a vegetarian for my youthful looks, which helped to close the decade-plus-one-year gap between Jerry and me to some degree.

"Did you notice any anxiety in Mrs. Trowbridge in the last couple of weeks?" Jerry asked, bringing me to the present and turning to stare hard at me.

"I did notice that her answers to my questions were shorter than usual like she was preoccupied. This was out of character for Maddy. She took pride in sharing her knowledge. Come to think of it, I remember thinking that she looked nervous or worn recently, but I attributed it to the Christmas season, changes at P&Z and her husband's illness. Then on Monday she seemed pretty much her old self."

I had so many questions, but I knew I'd be at the Trowbridges' the next morning. They are the source, I told myself, not Jerry. I slipped under the quilt and was greeted by freezing sheets and a below-zero pillowcase. Jerry decided to take a quick shower. I reached up and turned off the lamp as he returned and slipped under the covers.

"Geez!" he exclaimed, shocked by the cold sheets.

I chuckled. He wrapped his arm around me and drew me to him.

I couldn't help myself, the questions were mounting.

"Jerry, I was thinking that Maddy's killer must have followed her to School Road. How else would he know where she was going if her phone wasn't bugged?" I stared straight ahead into the dark.

"You mean, assuming it's a hit," he continued, all business, as I moved close to him. "Any bugs could have been removed when they knew where she was going and planned the murder," he suggested. "Or maybe they just followed her from the town hall parking lot. If the perpetrator was waiting for her to leave work, with the fire department and town hall and the annex right there, where would you least want to commit a murder? But anybody could sit in a car in the town hall parking lot for a while without looking suspicious. Once Mrs. Trowbridge stepped out of the annex into her car, the perpetrator had time to pull out of the front lot, wait for her to come down the drive and easily follow her onto Route 7."

I loosened Jerry's arm so I could turn and look at him as he considered the prospect of a hit.

"And when she pulled into School Road and drove up to Cider Mill's parking lot, he must have parked on the shoulder of Route 7," he continued, "or someone dropped him off and parked nearby. By doing either he avoided leaving tire tracks in the parking lot, and it gave him some time to get out of the car and hide in the trees. He had time to do this while Mrs. Trowbridge drove down School Road, pulled into the parking lot, turned off the car and bundled up to walk up the hill to Cider Mill."

"Right, then he waited for her to walk up the path and ..." I couldn't go on. "What about the man walking his dog?"

Jerry shook his head, obviously disgusted with the sergeant at the front desk. "He didn't get his name. He thought the man was old and had too much sherry at dinner, that he probably saw a doll or something like a doll thrown under the tree by school kids. Basically he thought the old guy was seeing things, but at least he followed protocol and called Al and me. I ordered him to dispatch the squad cars to the area immediately. Al was driving home, and his beeper wasn't working for some reason.

"You know, Ros, murder just doesn't happen in Wilton."

"My editor thought the same thing," I said. I had every intention of interviewing the dog walker. If the man wasn't involved with the murder, he'd probably call the paper for answers tomorrow like half the people in town. I'd get his name.

I slipped my arm around Jerry's broad chest. Even Jerry is starting to think it's not a mugging, I thought. Hearing that Maddy was afraid of something or someone for the last two weeks of her life, well that just confirms what I suspected from the start.

Maddy's murder was a well-planned homicide.

Nine
Maddy and Harrison

The sight of the sensible boots worn by the sensible woman refused to leave my mind. Even lying in Jerry's arms, sleep escaped me. I tossed and turned and failed to get comfortable.

What was Maddy doing at Cider Mill? If she were afraid, like Jerry said, then why didn't she tell someone?

I tried to put the questions out of my mind and concentrate on another aspect of the case, Maddy and Harrison's relationship. Their story was emerging in my overworked brain from information I had collected during my two years on the job. The words in my head refused to allow me to sleep. They were nudging me, promising me that they would lead to some conclusion.

After being appointed Wilton's first town planner, Harrison Hayden had been in his office only days in November 1955 when Maddy Trowbridge walked through the door and applied for the secretarial position, Maddy had told me.

Maddy said Harrison was a handsome, charming man at age thirty-seven, recently divorced, with a head of thick black hair. He loomed before her as a dynamic leader, the man who would influence the development of the town for years to come. Along with becoming a consummate secretary, she immediately took him under her wing. His divorce had left him a bit vulnerable, one of the secretaries in town hall had revealed.

Harrison from the start had allowed her to be his official sounding board and in years to come promoted her to office manager, I recalled Harrison telling me. During the years he easily chatted with her about most growth opportunities in town. I got the impression that they both virtually helped to develop Wilton as it is today.

As the years passed and Maddy observed Harrison's efforts to protect the quality of life and the character of Wilton, her devotion to him grew into something near worship. Jonathan Wood and his offspring would have approved of Harrison and how he handled the population explosion after WWII. Wilton grew from the two thousand or so people who lived in town to approximately seventeen thousand in the post-war boom and beyond.

Wall Street got its grip on the town then. New York executives rushed to Wilton in hopes of finding inexpensive farmland on which to build year-round homes. Developers wanted to place subdivisions on land that had once been pastures. The advent of trains had changed the farming community forever, bringing in lower-priced produce that put local farmers out of business. The farmers and their children left for better job opportunities on the same trains that had stolen their trade. This was a matter of history.

Harrison fought the suburban spread, Maddy had told me with eyes beaming with hero worship. At highly attended meetings he was among those who urged the planners and the first selectman to expand the one-acre lot requirement for building private residences to two acres. He demanded a certain amount of open space for building permits.

As the number of businesses grew to provide goods and services in town, I recalled Maddy's telling me that Harrison campaigned to outlaw garish commercial signs, billboards and the like. He fought to prohibit fast food stands like

MacDonald's and Wendy's on Route 7, the so-called country road.

It was the street signs story that made my eyes pop wide open at God knows what hour. The signs in town bear the names of Wilton's early settlers. She explained to me that the very roads we drive on today were created in Jonathan Wood's time, plus a few years, about 1705 to 1738. On one Friday afternoon in October, 1963, Maddy told Harrison she was fearful that the contribution of the founding families would be lost in time, that new generations would forget the struggle of the town's founders. A couple of weeks later he introduced the idea of changing some street names and signs from insipid names to those of the founding families. The idea was met with wide approval at a town meeting.

I tried to remember all the signs and what families they honored as if they'd be signs that would lead me to Maddy's killer: the Woods, Olmsteads, Beldons, Cannons, Keelers, DeForests, Gummans, Sturges family, Dudleys, Kents, Middlebrooks, Lamberts, Merwins, Comstocks, Gregorys, and Gaylords, to name some of them. Then there's Chicken Street, named after Chief Chi-ken, a descendant of the Mohawk Tribal Nation.

Each Wilton generation had been confronted with its own particular challenge or threat to its way of life from several wars to the advent of trains. Did Maddy see something that she thought threatened her generation?

If she did, why wouldn't she do something about it? I again thought of her being afraid for the last two weeks of her life. She knowingly allowed the dangerous situation to continue. This was contrary to her character. Why didn't she go to the police for protection? It could have saved her life. Well, she didn't, I told myself. Why? Why would the sensible Maddy risk her life?

I sat upright as if a bolt of lightening had hit me. Jerry turned around in his sleep, disturbed by my jerky movements.

She had been protecting someone! That's the only reason she'd risk her own life by keeping her fears a secret.

But who was she protecting, I asked myself, staring at Jerry, who was again peacefully snoring. She'd risk her life for any member of her family, but her husband and daughter didn't know why she was frightened, according to Jerry.

Other than her family there was only one person that Maddy would risk her life to protect that I knew of.

I stared at Jerry, wanting him to wake up so I could tell him the one person that could be at the heart of all this, the one person besides her family that Maddy would protect with her own life.

Harrison Hayden.

Ten

Wednesday Morning, December 16th, P&Z

Arabella Trowbridge had answered the phone and agreed to see me at 10:15 a.m. Her voice was strong, I was relieved to hear. I checked my watch and realized that my lack of sleep was catching up to me. I wasn't moving as fast as I wanted to. It was nearly nine. I'd have just enough time to make it to P&Z to check the files for the hearing tonight and maybe drop in at the newsroom before heading to the Trowbridge house.

Learning about Maddy's fear had put a new light on my covering P&Z. Each trip there would be considered an active part of my investigation, I thought as I ate a quick bowl of oatmeal and headed out the door.

It was the kind of brilliant winter day that lifts New England spirits even in the worst of times. The temperature was a tropical thirty-six degrees. Snow was melting from everywhere. Ten minutes later I was staring at Wilton Town Hall, sitting atop a dazzling, snow-covered hill. I pulled into the wide driveway. With six white Ionic columns, a generously wide white front door, and three oval Georgian windows on either side of the entrance, I thought, as I always did, how it seemed like Wilton's very own White House. The suburban seat of government looked down upon the morning traffic on the very wet country road. I recalled how Route 7, or Danbury Road, had been labeled a "country road" by the original settlers because it brought them from one town to another.

I headed toward the town hall annex. It sat on the north side of the parking lot. I parked in the annex's small parking area a few feet from the front door and under a wispy cherry tree with limbs soaked black from the melted snow that had sat on its branches just hours ago.

The annex was a red brick one-story structure that had nothing to do with the classic design of town hall. It had a front window the shape of a half-moon. From her desk in the reception area, Maddy could look out that window. I pushed open the glass door as I had at least two times a week for the last two years, but this day the action delivered a hard punch to the gut.

The Christmas wreaths of pinecones, decorated with a red velvet bows, still hung in their places. The wall to the left of her desk still held the historic pictures. Her Christmas candy dish was still there. A stack of public hearing notices was sitting in the usual corner of her desk.

Everything was in its place except for Maddy. I was reminded once again how the absence of a person can fill a room.

The planner's office was in an alcove to the right of her desk. The public works director, the new town planner, Timothy Esposito, his assistant, a typist and the director of the environment were in attendance. I had no doubt about the subject of the discussion.

To the right of Maddy's desk was the familiar file room. A squat, square map file cabinet sat in the middle of the room. Behind it, lining the three walls, were the general file cabinets. I walked through a misty vapor, which I realized were my tears. I passed by the map files and headed to the general files.

In the "S" drawer was Stuart Island's familiar file. The manila folder was thick and even heavier this morning. I set it on top of the file cabinet and opened it up. The letter from the

DEP was on top of the thick stack of other DEP complaint letters that filtered in on a regular basis, as Maddy had noted. They seemed small problems, however, compared to building permits so I never paid them much attention as a reporter. At any rate it appeared that DEP was on their case. As I leafed through the files I thought of how I had driven past the condos often to get to Route 7 since they were directly off Center Road. The complex always reminded me of a small English village with its individual buildings and peaked tiled roofs. It also had the amenities of a large swimming pool, tennis courts and a clubhouse.

Maddy's Monday update about the "mile-high stack of complaints" was loud in my head as I read the top letter from the DEP about the replacement of the underground storage tank and the flow lines to the tank. The stack of complaint letters from the DEP was impressive.

I checked the preschool file and three more files for special permits that didn't amount to much. Those stories would be no more than a couple of graphs.

I'd be fine, I told myself with little conviction. The public hearing announcements were published in the newspaper. Most often if people had a problem with a project, they'd show up at the annex and talk to Maddy first, in particular on the Monday and Tuesday before the hearing.

Today, there was no Maddy to give me updates. I took another hard swallow.

I heard raised voices emanating from the planner's office. The meeting was breaking-up. I slapped shut the file folders, shoved them into the drawers and slammed them shut with a bang. Then I literally ran to the door to escape. I was relieved to step into the brilliant sunlight. The crisp air tingled my cheeks, utterly welcome and refreshing.

The last thing I needed this morning was town hall chatter about the murder, no matter how heartfelt it may be. I planned to interview Maddy's pals at town hall, but not this morning. No, not this morning. My first burning questions would be for Arabella and Mr. Trowbridge.

I jumped into my car for a fast getaway. It was 9:30. I had just enough time to get in and out of the newsroom for an update. I should just make it to the Trowbridge's by 10:15.

I arrived to find Evan still at his desk and rushed through the newsroom to him as if it were an emergency. He sat before his computer, so limp that I thought he was about to collapse into the screen. He gazed up at me with such exhausted eyes that I caught my breath.

"They made an arrest," he said in a hollow voice.

Eleven
The Arrest

Richard Freemont, 26, had been arrested late last night during a brawl at the The Benbow Tavern in downtown South Norwalk, Evan revealed. In Freemont's possession were a semi-automatic 9mm Glock 17, Maddy Trowbridge's wallet, keys, driver's license, wedding and engagement rings, a single pearl necklace and her Christmas tree pin.

Jerry and Al searched Freemont's Elizabeth Street apartment near the projects at about 7:00 a.m. They found Maddy's stolen black purse and red Christmas gloves.

"The Wilton detectives got the call about five-thirty this morning," Evan was saying. "I'm guessing it took until then for the Norwalk police to put it together that they had arrested the mugger who had committed the crime here. It was finding the gun that tipped them off. Freemont claims the gun wasn't his, by the way. The arresting officers realized the gun had been recently fired. That's when they started to call local stations. At least that's Jerry's story."

I continued to stand at Evan's desk, looking down at him. "So Al and Jerry went down to apprehend the suspect," I said. "Then they went to the South Norwalk apartment to search and collect evidence?"

"Right, with Norwalk detectives. They think it's very possible that the Glock is the murder weapon, since Maddy was killed with a 9mm. Now they're back on School Road with the help of daylight searching for empty cartridges and tire marks. They're also waiting for a ballistics report." With that, Evan sighed.

"Evan, usually you're home sleeping off deadline," I said, concerned.

"I did a little more than a quick history of Maddy's lineage. Who could sleep anyway?" He stood up, grabbed his black ski jacket off the back of his chair and prepared finally to leave.

While Evan spoke I was going over the facts of the arrest in my head. A man in South Norwalk, a Richard Freemont, had been picked up during a bar brawl last night several hours after Maddy's murder. He possessed the possible murder weapon and Maddy's jewelry, wallet, keys and driver's license. When the Wilton police had searched Freemont's apartment, they had found her gloves and handbag. Freemont was possibly Maddy's murderer.

Evan, finally exiting with ghostly eyes, hesitated at my side.

"Jerry says the suspect has a record of petty crimes, none of them violent." His haunted eyes looked down at me as if he were waiting for my reaction.

Freemont caught with the goods satisfies the police department's mugging theory, I thought, but I kept this observation to myself.

I followed the exhausted and lethargic Evan out the door. I had only a few minutes to spare to get to the Trowbridge's on time. We descended the challenging stairs slowly thanks to Evan's exhaustion. This gave me time to think, however.

This guy, Richard Freemont, sounded dirt poor with his living in or around the South Norwalk projects. Did he even have transportation? No buses go through Wilton. You have to take the train from South Norwalk. Right, I can see him boarding the train with his Glock and returning casually with his stolen goods after murdering someone. Did he have a jalopy that could get him to Wilton? Most likely he had an accomplice who owned a car. Was the man walking the dog another accomplice?

Is my theory of a professional hit just my ambition talking? My desire for a Pulitzer?

Maybe Richard Freemont actually did it.

Twelve
The Trowbridge Home

Although the temperature continued to climb, I found myself once again in the icy cold darkness under the black spruce. Not even my insatiable curiosity could act as a redeeming factor for being at Maddy Trowbridge's home to discuss her funeral arrangements.

I drove up to the modest ranch that sat on a little more than an acre of land on Pinetop Road. It was among similar homes in the Pimpewaug area. The pale green house with black shutters was on a slight hill. In the background were rolling hills that faded into the distance and were dotted with snow-capped evergreens. Perfect farmland. This was exactly where Jonathan Wood's farm, Egypt, had thrived, I reminded myself, as if this little bit of knowledge allowed me to know Maddy better. I pulled up and parked in front of the house, grabbed my yellow legal pad on the passenger seat and got out of the car. The dripping of melting snow seemed loud on the quiet block. I navigated the puddles on the stone path from the street, knocked on the white door and took a deep breath. Seconds later, the door opened as if they were waiting for me.

At the sight of Maddy's husband and daughter, I caught my breath for the second time this morning. The newly minted grief was etched on the craggy face of Clifford Trowbridge. It looked like a lead pencil had darkened each crevice. Although Arabella was beautiful, she seemed older then her years. Her face was tense and dominated by a new sense of responsibility.

It had been just hours ago, I reminded myself, that they had learned they would never see their precious Maddy alive again.

Mr. Trowbridge's framed glasses covered his red-rimmed eyes. Wearing a tie and tones of gray, he respectfully carried the burden of grief on behalf of his wife. Arabella, who stood behind her father, resembled her pretty mother. She appeared controlled, her every fiber focused on her frail father.

The trace odors of cinnamon and baked cookies, no doubt left over from Maddy's baking, seemed remnants of another time. On the living room wall to the right were the black and white photographs of Maddy's ancestors. The women were dressed in floor-length black dresses, and the men wore dark suits. The unsmiling, dour faces reflected the harsh times. Straight ahead was the sunken family room. In front of the sliding glass door was a fully decorated Christmas tree, its cheerfulness turned to melancholy under the circumstances.

They showed me to a deep-seated English burgundy sofa at the side of the Christmas tree. The father and daughter sat across from me in matching chairs. I offered my condolences and uttered words reflecting the respect I had had for Maddy.

"Mr. Esposito, the new town planner, called a few minutes ago," Arabella said calmly. "Mom's memorial service at town hall is scheduled for Sunday, January tenth, at 2:00 p.m." She was all business. Her dark eyes with sweeping black eyelashes were clear, her peaches-and-cream skin flushed. What a beauty, I thought.

"All the official bodies Mom associated with, like the P&Z, the Garden Club, the Historical Society and the selectmen, will be represented. The ceremony will be open and held in front of town hall to accommodate anybody who wants to attend. Mom wouldn't have it any other way. A tree planting ceremony at town hall in honor of Mom will take place in the spring," she said.

Arabella continued to talk with an official air, clearly keeping her own emotions under control while bearing the onslaught of new responsibilities. Her mother's wake and funeral at Johnson's Funeral Parlor were to take place Friday.

"Mom will be buried on Saturday," the young girl managed to say without tears and with a certain amount of pride, "at Hillside Cemetery on Ridgefield Road. It's where eighteen Revolutionary veterans are buried, so Mom will be given the burial service of a fallen hero."

I wrote this down on my yellow legal pad with a certain amount of awe, especially after the words, "so Mom will be given the burial service of a fallen hero."

When I looked up and gazed across at Arabella, tears streamed down her cheeks. She sat so proudly in her seat, staring blindly ahead through the glass doors to the rolling hills outside. She was holding on, attempting not to collapse into the bottomless grief in her heart.

I fully recognized that grief. I realized that witnessing Arabella's profound loss for her mother stirred my own agony. Maddy and my parents dying before their time made death doubly unacceptable. Helping to find Maddy's killer allowed me to do something while being otherwise helpless in the face of death.

Mr. Trowbridge fidgeted all the while his daughter talked as if his thoughts were elsewhere. It was as though he hadn't heard Arabella's words and didn't see her tears. He swept imaginary crumbs from the arm of his chair, concentrating as if he needed to ferret out each invisible tidbit. He seemed to want to say something but hesitated.

Did he know that the police had made an arrest? I didn't want to burden either of them with my usual questions, but clearly Mr. Trowbridge was troubled. I got the sensation that he knew something. What the heck was going on? What was he thinking?

"Mr. Trowbridge, is there anything I can help you with?" I prodded, unable to keep silent any longer. I leaned forward. "You know I worked with Maddy." I glimpsed at Arabella, who was wiping away her tears.

"Maddy spoke so highly of you," he began, "your beautiful series on the aquifer and the exposé on the Inland Wetlands Agency. That article changed the town's process by which it protects its water. Maddy had such high regard for your work. She and a few others in town see you as a bit of a local hero, someone watching our environment for us."

His sad hazel eyes were sincere and demanding, imploring me to understand to what extent Maddy appreciated my work.

"At those times, Ms. Rossi," he continued, "Maddy would come home from work and read your articles to me. Every word."

He stared at me, paused and shook his head as if he realized he was speaking of Maddy in the past tense.

"She had respect for you as an investigative reporter. You know she operated as if the protection of the land were her duty and an obligation to the founders of Wilton and the country. She didn't get paid much for that job at P&Z for all the work she did," he paused, "but she wouldn't miss a day. She didn't trust anybody else to do her job."

He stopped for a second, gazing down at his gray pants and raising his thin eyebrows as if trying to figure out a riddle.

"The last two weeks it was as though she were looking over her shoulder, as if she thought someone was following her whenever we left the house."

He hesitated and gazed at his daughter for confirmation of his characterization of her mother's behavior. Arabella gazed down and shook her head as if overwhelmed by the memory of her mother's last days.

"Mr. Trowbridge, here I go asking questions. You know I drove Maddy crazy with my questions." I looked at both of them for acknowledgment.

The two sad faces broke into smiles like the sun bursting through storm clouds. They exchanged knowing glances.

I raised an eyebrow. "I guess Maddy told you about all my questions."

They broke out into chuckles. I waited for a minute, having no desire to break the room's brief buoyancy. When they gazed at me with smiles, waiting for my questions, I began.

"Did you hear that the police made an arrest?" I asked Mr. Trowbridge.

"Yes, they called," he replied, but he seemed crestfallen. "For all we know this man could have been following her, and that's why she was looking over her shoulder. But why? She never carried large sums of money."

"Did you tell the police about your concerns, about Maddy looking over her shoulder?" I knew that he had, but I wanted to get his reaction.

"Yes, but I was vague. Maddy told me I was silly. I was imagining things," he said, perplexed. "That's what she said, that I was silly and imagining things," he repeated with more confidence. "So I had no concrete evidence to offer the two detectives. Then the detectives seemed so sure that they caught the right man." He gazed at me sharing his confusion. He hesitated, continuing to look at me intently.

"At first I thought my wife was jumpy because of the new town planner and all the changes. She wasn't going to be running the office as before, Ms. Rossi, so this was a tough adjustment for Maddy. She likes to be in control, you know." He sat up straighter in his chair, seemingly relieved by the conversation. "Yet when she came home for lunch just briefly yesterday to check on me since she had bridge last night, she seemed more like her old self."

"Do you know why?"

"I was so relieved I didn't ask. I didn't want to stir things up."

Silence fell for a second. I waited to see if he'd add anything more.

"Mr. Trowbridge, let me assure you that I'll employ whatever investigative expertise and whatever little influence I have."

I remained at the edge of the couch as I attempted to reassure him. I realized that he was turning to me because he believed that the detectives were not listening to him. He also thought my position at the newspaper allowed me to do some investigating on my own. As I had thought, the *Wilton Weekly* was expected by its readers to do its own investigation into the murder.

"I hear your concerns," I said, sitting at the edge of my seat. "Maddy looking over her shoulder is a major element to this horrible crime. I consider that a major clue, and so do the detectives," I lied. Although Jerry and Al considered Maddy's fear, I didn't think Al was giving it the weight it deserved. But Mr. Trowbridge needed reassurance, I told myself. That man looked deathly ill. Besides, it was partially true.

"Mr. Trowbridge, I think it would be a good idea if you were to repeat your concerns to the detectives." I sat back in my seat, attempting to calm down but staring firmly at Mr. Trowbridge.

"I had a heart attack a few months ago, of course you know," he said, his gray eyebrows knitted together a little more tightly. The creases in his brow deepened. "Everyone at town hall knew. But since then Maddy wouldn't let me comb my own hair, if you know what I mean." He gazed at his daughter fleetingly for affirmation. "I just learned that my son suffered a financial setback, and he borrowed some money. Maddy never mentioned it. If something were bothering her, I'd be the last person to know. So I never believed my concerns were silly or that I was imagining things. That was just Maddy protecting me."

Mr. Trowbridge's every word more than confirmed my original suspicion that Maddy's murder was not the result of a random mugging.

The doorbell rang. Arabella rose and walked to the door, and opened it.

There stood the two detectives.

Thirteen
The Primary Suspect

Richard Freemont was with his girlfriend, Janet Goldridge, at the time that Maddy Trowbridge was murdered, Jerry explained. Al and Jerry stood just inside the house and in front of the closed door, facing Mr. Trowbridge and Arabella. I stood to the side and took notes.

Goldridge was a nurse in good standing at Norwalk Hospital, Jerry revealed. They were both in her apartment in South Norwalk last night from 4:30 until 10:00 p.m. Freemont had a solid alibi. He also had a long rap sheet. At eighteen he had been arrested for carrying a concealed weapon and eleven pounds of marijuana. An undercover cop made the arrest. Freemont was found guilty of a felony and got ten years in a state prison. After being released eight years later, he was arrested for several parole violations, attempting to sell cocaine to an undercover Norwalk police officer and conspiring to sell a couple of pounds.

It was obvious that the detectives thought Richard Freemont a perfect suspect. They doubted his alibi because it came from his girlfriend. Jerry explained that Freemont's very respectable girlfriend lived several blocks from Freemont's apartment in South Norwalk. Freemont claimed he had found Maddy's handbag and its contents, the gun and jewelry in a shopping cart parked in an alley on Elizabeth Street at eleven o'clock last night. The alley was sandwiched between his apartment house and another building. At first it was his impression that someone left the handbag in the shopping cart by mistake. He took it inside his apartment and discovered the recently fired 9mm Glock. Freemont then surmised the goods were stolen and the firearm used for the robbery.

"So he went to a bar with the money and the gun and got into a brawl," Al said. "When the cops came, they found the gun."

"Well, Detectives," Mr. Trowbridge said, looking from one to the other, "where does this leave us?"

The two detectives glanced at each other, as if deciding who would talk first. Then Jerry began. "The case is still active. As far as we know there is no other reason than robbery for Mrs. Trowbridge's death. Why the stolen property was dumped is questionable. Freemont's alibi is less than solid because the nurse is his girlfriend," Jerry continued, "but according to the HR Department of Norwalk Hospital, Janet Goldridge is a reliable and upstanding citizen. So if Freemont's alibi holds up, and we accept his story, it could be that the mugger lives nearby Freemont's apartment. It's a tough section of town, and the police heavily patrol the area. It's conceivable that the perpetrator was on his way home with the stolen goods and was interrupted by a policeman. We think he might have stashed the goods in the shopping cart and parked it in the alley to avoid suspicion. He intended to return for the stolen goods later."

"But Freemont is still our prime suspect," Al added. His voice was heavy with exhaustion, but he stared with intensity at Mr. Trowbridge. "The story about finding the stolen goods in a shopping cart I consider far-fetched." He gave Jerry a look of skepticism. "We are considering the theory that Freemont had an accomplice. It could be that Freemont's job was to fence the stolen property. He might have been an accomplice to the robbery and then went to the bar to celebrate. He doesn't have a car. His girlfriend doesn't own a vehicle either or have a driver's license. Unless he stole or borrowed a car, he couldn't have committed the crime on his own. In any case Freemont will remain in custody."

Al's many years on the force accented his voice with assertiveness. "He's broken his parole by carrying a weapon. He'll be going back to jail for years one way or another. We think he'll ask for blanket immunity in exchange for information on his accomplice, not that he'll get it." Al darted a look at Jerry, and his puffy, exhausted eyes flashed back to Mr. Trowbridge. He looked like he had not slept last night at all.

"Right now we're heading to South Norwalk to question Janet Goldridge," he continued. "We've got a couple of senior Norwalk detectives also working on this case. Presently, they're questioning everyone in his and his girlfriend's apartment buildings."

Jerry offered a caring look to both father and daughter. "We thought we'd let you know the status of the investigation."

"I told you that my wife was acting strangely for the last couple of weeks," Mr. Trowbridge answered with a little impatience, "as if she were afraid of something or somebody. But everybody in our private life loved her. She had no enemies I was aware of."

"We questioned the town planner, Timothy Esposito, to see if any business at the planner's office might have posed a danger to your wife," Jerry said. "We asked him if he was aware of any business problems at the office or if he knew of anyone that Mrs. Trowbridge viewed as an enemy or suspicious regarding the business at the planning and zoning department." Jerry looked down at the floor for a second and then back up to Mr. Trowbridge. "He was surprised at that question. If anything, he said, the planner's office was extremely well run, thanks to the former planner and Mrs.

Trowbridge. And he said there was nobody in town who didn't love your wife, including the builders that were often at P&Z."

Mr. Trowbridge's gray pallor deepened. He seemed crushed by Jerry's response. He excused himself, saying he had to lie down. Arabella, standing at his side, assisted him by bracing his arm.

"Mr. Trowbridge," Jerry called after him, "we will question her colleagues at town hall and her friends. She must have confided in somebody. If she was worried about something, we'll find out."

Mr. Trowbridge stopped and turned around to stare at Jerry with an ironic grin. "You didn't know my wife, Detective. If she faced any danger, the last thing she'd do is involve someone else, but I guess it couldn't hurt."

Arabella ushered her father into another part of the house. When she returned she went to the kitchen. Jerry followed her. She wrote a list of Maddy Trowbridge's friends and included their telephone numbers. I stood at the door in anticipation, not wanting to miss anything. When the two returned, however, we just said our goodbyes. The three of us walked down the driveway to our cars in silence.

When I stepped onto the very wet street to the driver's side of my car, I heard the house door open. I looked toward the house to see Arabella running my way, putting on a sweater and calling my name.

"Ms. Rossi, can you wait a minute?"

Jerry and Al slipped into their black Ford at the bottom of the drive. Jerry flashed me a confident glance, knowing I'd get back to him later.

"Ms. Rossi," Arabella said, standing next to me in the street.

"Please, just Rossi."

"My dad thinks the detectives didn't take him seriously. You know, about Mom being followed."

I opened the car door and threw my yellow pad and satchel onto the passenger seat. I turned back to Arabella and took her soft, cold hands in mine. "Trust me. They are taking your dad seriously. Are your brother and his family on the way?" I asked, concerned. I was also doing a little fishing regarding her brother's financial problems.

"He and his family will be here tomorrow. They'll stay until Sunday," she shrugged. "He's a typical guy. They'll be gone by Sunday night, back to Georgia. He calls once a month." She shook her head and shrugged her shoulders. "We never even hear from his wife."

She'd be replacing Maddy as her father's caretaker, I thought. "When do you return to Yale? I know it's Yale because your mom did a little bragging."

She chuckled. "Yes, she was proud. Yale is the alma mater for many Wilton people, including many of my Mom's family, so it was kind of natural for her to brag. She couldn't afford to go, of course, but she made sure we'd get there. I have to see how Dad's doing."

She stopped and gazed down at the wet street as if to summon energy to divulge something to me.

"Rossi, I never saw Mom act—no, I'll come right out and say it. I never saw Mom afraid in my entire life." She gazed at me with youthful determination. "If anything, people could be intimidated by her. You probably know that better than I do. But I believe my father and I saw fear on my mother's face, and now I realize my mother was afraid for good reason. The last two weeks turned out to be the last two weeks of my mother's life."

Speaking those words shattered her frail composure. For a few seconds she struggled to hold back the flooding grief.

"Do you have any idea why your mother was afraid?" I said, stroking her arm.

"None," she said, shaking her head.

I took her by the shoulders and looked into her dark eyes. "I'll do my best to encourage the detectives to take your mother's fear very seriously."

"Ms. Rossi, I mean Rossi, Dad's right. If Mom felt that confiding in her friends would endanger them, she'd never do it. I think my mother was so afraid that she didn't dare tell us. She was protecting us."

"I will do what I always do," I assured her. "I'll work hard. They'll be no stopping until we get to the bottom of this whole thing." I gazed at her with assurance and brushed a strand of her black hair away from her face. "I've read that most cases are solved by seemingly irrelevant information, the collateral. That is exactly where I'm heading. I'll be digging deep into the muck and mire of trivia," I offered. She broke into a smile for the second time this morning. "You'll see," I continued, returning her smile. "I'll come up with something. I always do."

Where was this confidence coming from? I was asking myself as I stared at Arabella. Here I was again, vowing to come up with answers. Was I beginning to believe in my reputation as the local hero for saving people's well water? Actually, I didn't think the detectives would look in the same places I would. This somehow made me sure I'd find what we needed. Arrogance? Perhaps. If I believed the premonition under the black spruce that I was somehow in danger, then no doubt I probably already knew something that would lead me to the killers and, of course, place myself in danger. The detectives would do the police procedural routine. They might actually find something, but I seemed to believe that my information would solve the case. My award for investigative journalism flashed before my eyes.

"We will keep in touch." I said. Arabella offered a conspiratorial grin, and I reciprocated as I climbed into my car.

Fourteen
Panic

The news of the murder had made the twelve o'clock TV and radio news shows. I headed to my computer. Evan, back at his desk again, manned the ceaselessly ringing phones with the help of our receptionist Susanna, Dylan and Frank. Their four voices created a cacophony as they informed a hysterical public.

I cowered in my little space in my own personal panic. I needed yet to drive to the preschool location just around the block and take some notes. I also told myself that food and a catnap were absolute necessities if I were to survive the late night meeting in the overheated P&Z hearing room without falling asleep. I scrutinized the public hearing announcement sitting on the side of my computer one more time and reassured myself that it boiled down to the issues I'd checked out in the files. Nothing to worry about.

In the midst of the panic surrounding me, I launched into typing the information I needed to give Evan before I could escape. At the top of the page in bold were details for the Friday wake to read to callers. I printed several copies and dashed around the attic and handed them out, leaving a few extras on the corner of Evan's desk. In bold letters I also mentioned that the Saturday funeral was private.

It was 4:30 p.m. when I managed my escape without being asked to help with the phones. The setting sun lit up the horizon with dazzling orangey pinks and yellows. The scalloped edges of the many layers of clouds glowed silver, like the embers of a fire. At top speed I descended the stairs, my right hand clinging to the railing for support as I stared straight ahead at the setting sun's brilliance. In midflight a crystallizing thought brought me to a standstill.

If Richard Freemont had told the truth, and he'd found the stolen items in a shopping cart on Elizabeth Street, wouldn't that be a perfect cover-up? Dump the stolen goods in the drug-ridden, poorest section of town and wait for some poor sucker to take the bait?

Fifteen
The Public Hearing
Wednesday Night, Dec. 16

Maybe it was the drop in temperature and the bitter cold night and being dead tired, but I realized as I climbed into my cold Nissan that I was uneasy about going to the hearing. The arrest of Richard Freemont didn't offer me any comfort. I thought again about Maddy being frightened of something or somebody. I felt vulnerable again, as I had under the tree when I first laid eyes on her.

I pushed open the P&Z's glass door that seemed like lead and avoided looking at Maddy's empty desk. I settled on the hard benches in the overheated hearing room and thought that fear might actually keep me awake tonight. During a typical hearing when applicants droned on, it was like a lullaby.

A stocky gentleman sat a couple of rows behind me and several feet to my left. He caught my attention. He wore a black suit and white shirt. People generally don't come to these meetings dressed in black suits. He glanced at the woman approaching the podium regarding the new preschool, Frances Carter. I got the impression they were together. She appeared as wholesome and cheerful as you'd want a teacher to look in a burgundy wool suit and crisp white blouse. The man in the black suit looked on the tough side.

The Stuart Island builder, Jack Manners, sat on the far right side of the front row. He wore a black turtleneck and jeans. Rolled maps were tucked under his arm.

"Terrible thing about Maddy," a voice behind me whispered.

I turned to see Christine Moore, a reporter from the *Norwalk Hour.* She was a wispy, beautiful young woman with blonde hair.

"It's hard to believe," Christine continued, "in conservative Wilton yet, a town that doesn't allow controversy."

"Right," I whispered back. "The first murder in eighty-six years."

"Maddy had a few words with Frances Carter," she whispered, referring to the woman at the podium. "She gave Maddy a hard time. She didn't think an EIS was necessary because of the location of the preschool, just the aquifer assessment."

Christine's clear green eyes looked worried.

"I guess Maddy told her in no uncertain terms," I said.

"Oh, for sure," Christine chuckled, "but this woman is aggressive. So Maddy had to lace into her. Don't fall for the wholesome pedagogic demeanor. She's out to make a buck. I bet she builds preschools all over the country. Maddy told her, 'You want your school? You get an EIS, or DEP will shut the project down.'"

Maddy's reluctance to mention anything about the little altercation came to mind, but loyalty to her customers kept her from gossiping. In twenty staggeringly long minutes we processed through the typical questions. The preschool building plans were expected to move ahead.

I caught Frances Carter on the way out the door and spoke to her in the entryway.

"It'll benefit the town," she said, all smiles. "We expect to open next September."

With that, she left. She'd return to answer questions from the Inland Wetlands Agency when they began in about a half hour.

I rushed to the water fountain down the hall, passing Maddy's desk, and carried a cup of water back to my seat. I caught the man in the black suit and white shirt checking me out. Not in a flirtatious way. It was like he was checking my movements. I took my seat and ignored him.

Stuart Island was next. Dean Peterson of Peterson, Myers & Sheen, Inc., dressed in a business suit, took the podium along with Manners. The discussion concerned the special permit and the timing of the replacement of the flow lines to the underground storage tank. The builders were to pour the cement for the vault that would hold the oil tank this week or the next.

The Inland Wetlands Agency took the stage and continued to question the Stuart Island representatives. The six agency members asked questions regarding the impact that the condos would make on the aquifer and the Norwalk River.

Mr. Manners, a slight man and a likeable builder, went into detail on the superiority of the new material. He assured the agency that the changes would protect the town's water system from oil leakage far beyond the town's demands.

"Why didn't you put this quality into your building material in the first place?" asked Commissioner Rolland Sykes.

Dean Peterson took the question. "We're replacing any material that we consider problematic." He was a tall, thin man and looked seriously concerned. "It was the oversight of our purchaser, to answer your question."

"Well, it seems there are plenty of problems to go around on this project," Sykes continued with a smile. "You're a regular around here. I hope you anticipate the next problem and take care of it before it has to come before us in a letter from the DEP."

"Yes, sir," Peterson responded.

Frances Carter, who had just slipped back into the hearing room, followed. She told of the community need for a preschool. They discussed the EIS, and the Inland Wetlands Agency delved into the concerns regarding rainwater runoff because of the property's proximity to the aquifer.

At 9:30 on my hasty way out, Maddy's empty desk haunted me. I caught it on the periphery of my vision as I flew out the door, determined to avoid it. I was too tired, I told myself. I fell prey to the empty desk and all its implications.

I stepped into the cold night and gazed around the parking lot, thinking that I should be alert as if someone or something may be out there. Compared to the hot hearing room, the temperature seemed below zero. It had dropped to below freezing once the sun went down. With all the melting we had during the day, I reminded myself to watch out for black ice. I hoped we didn't get any snow; that would make it even worse. A fresh coat of snow over the black ice was winter's greatest trick. I stepped carefully to my car. It was in the annex's small parking lot to the right of the front door, only several feet away.

I slipped into the freezer of a car, slammed my door and locked it. The stress in my body was rising. I could even feel adrenalin flowing, but I didn't know why. It was instinct again. I turned on the ignition and hoped that the wipers would scrape away the building frost so I wouldn't have to get back out of the car to do it with the hand scraper. I also turned on the heater, although it was blowing in cold air and I'd be home before it actually worked.

The wipers weren't handling it. I fished for the scraper that had slipped under the passenger seat, as usual, and got out and scraped the windshield. I noticed a black four-door sedan idling across from me in the major parking lot, but I couldn't make out the figure behind the wheel. I scraped a bit of the rear window and a little on the passenger side and the driver's side, just enough to see, and hopped back into the car, shivering.

I pulled out of the town hall driveway and made a right onto Route 7. Black ice was again on my mind. It was predominantly on the sides of the roads. Virtually nobody else was on the road. If I hit a patch of black ice, at least there were few cars to skid into. I turned off the heater. It was just blowing in arctic air. I looked at my rearview mirror. The black sedan was right behind me, unusually close, almost at my bumper.

A few minutes later I passed School Road on my left. The crime scene tape was still up. No cops were there. My stomach did an obligatory turn or two, thinking again of Maddy under the black spruce. Her boots. The sense of doom I had experienced under the black spruce gushed back in full force. A burning knot gripped my stomach.

I glanced at my rearview mirror. The sedan was still way too close. A fresh wave of fear rode through my body. I gratefully took the left onto Olmstead Hill Road, so relieved to get there. Once I got home, I'd relax, I told myself. Fear and paranoia are bound to flourish when you've been traumatized and you're exhausted. It's only been one day, about twenty-six hours.

I glanced out the rearview mirror. The sedan had taken the turn and was again hugging my bumper. I wondered who at the meeting lived in this area. Yet this was not your typical Wilton driver, where everyone is polite. I started to get a bit concerned about the black sedan. I took the turn onto Sugarloaf Drive with my eyes on the rearview mirror. The car followed. Everything changed at that moment. Fear flooded my system as fast as the gas accelerated my car.

This was just what I had anticipated when I identified Maddy's body, but without knowing why. That sense of doom was more a forewarning than anything else.

"Concentrate," I ordered myself aloud.

Then I remembered the dead end street and hit the gas. Yes, I thought, I could use that road to hide. Whoever is following me would not know this road. Nobody knows this short road to nowhere except those who live on Sugarloaf, and nobody on the block has a black sedan. I'll park there and turn off the lights. He'll never notice it because of the hairpin curve. He'll be concentrating on making the turn and pass me right by, I calculated.

I turned off my headlights halfway up Sugarloaf. I stepped even harder on the gas and depended heavily on luck to prevent me from skidding on black ice. I sped past my house. No way I was going there. I raced halfway around the hairpin loop. I took the sharp right onto the dead end road just past the loop and came to a dead stop without skidding into the thick trunk of an oak that towered over the road. I turned off the motor. My car and I were swallowed up by darkness.

You had to live on Sugarloaf to know the little dead end road, I assured myself once again, but I did slip out of the car and was ready to run in case the sedan pulled in.

The sedan took the hairpin curve on two wheels as if it were trying to catch up to me. As it sped by the car's dash lights allowed me to catch a glimpse of the driver. The thick black form and the white shirt stood out. I had no doubts. It was the man at the hearing, the one I thought was with the owner of the proposed preschool, Frances Carter.

Carefully, I treaded down the icy cement road, walking on the snow-banked side, and onto Sugarloaf, making as little sound as possible. I headed to my house, again walking on the left on snow plowed to the side of the road. My heart pulsated in my throat. I passed three houses, all dark for the night. When I walked up my driveway, my house seemed the darkest. I entered the vestibule. I heard no sounds coming from inside the house, but I cursed at myself when I realized that the door had been left unlocked.

I entered the entry hall and waited, listening for alien sounds. The telephone rang as if on cue. It was probably Jerry. I ran to the kitchen and picked up the receiver. The silverware drawer was opposite the phone. I opened it to retrieve a cutting knife and gripped it in my left hand. My eyes were on the front and back doors. I was looking for the sedan, for the tough man in the black suit and white shirt. The multi-paned back door was to my left and off the kitchen dining area. I saw nothing but darkness. My stomach was clenched as I prepared to spring.

"Hey, Rossi," a tipsy voice greeted me.

"Dylan?"

"Yeah, it's me. We gotta talk."

I issued a sigh of relief. "Great, come over."

As I calmed down I was impressed with my resourcefulness under stress, how I had turned off my headlights and thought of the dead end road. Given my curiosity, given that I've been covering P&Z for two years, given my reputation for investigative reporting and the fact that I was at the crime scene and am covering the murder, fear was the appropriate emotion, I told myself.

I also have no doubt that I'll know, sooner or later, exactly what Maddy knew when she was murdered. "To thine own self be true," I thought. From the moment I laid eyes on Maddy's dead body I had known that my curiosity and sense of obligation would lead me right down the dark alleys of her mysterious death and into danger—and here I was.

I grabbed my coat and the steak knife and headed back to get my car. I had enough time to drive it back into the driveway before Dylan got here. Something told me the sedan wasn't out there, but I emerged slowly from my doorway to view the empty, dark street. Not a sound could be heard except the hooting of an owl off in the distance. It made sense that the man following me must know where I live. He knew who I was, after all, but whatever the chase had been about, it was over for at least the night.

Would Frances Carter really kill for a preschool? Now, that did seem a little extreme, I thought as I climbed into my car and backed down the short road and onto Sugarloaf. Maybe I got it wrong. Maybe the man in the sedan wasn't with her.

As I pulled into my driveway I wondered what was on Dylan's mind. Why did we have to talk?

Sixteen
Still Wednesday night

Dressed in jeans and a P-coat, Dylan held a Budweiser in his hand as he swayed in the doorway. Drink helped ease the grief, I thought. Maddy was a mother figure to him, I reminded myself, and he was Maddy's favorite reporter. This has got to be hard. He took off his boots, and I showed him to the couch. He managed to slip out of his coat. Then he stared at the empty fireplace as if there were a fire in it.

I drew the cream-colored linen drapes to cover the wall-to-ceiling windows that overlooked Sugarloaf opposite the couch. I ignored my racing heart and sat on an overstuffed chair across from Dylan. The periphery of my vision, however, was fixed on the windows. Although I thought my pursuer was gone for the night, I found myself waiting for unfriendly headlights that would penetrate the drawn drapes.

"I'm not buying this mugger thing, Rossi." He formed the words with difficulty, then took a sip of beer. "Rossi, something strange was going on with Maddy. I know it," he slurred.

My heart was starting to calm down as I listened to Dylan. I was taking deep breaths and sighing and attempting a little meditation. It would help me to sort out what had just happened.

"A couple of things, Rossi," Dylan slurred getting my attention. "Maddy told me she was worried about that idiot son of hers," I heard Dylan say. His blue eyes darkened as he stared off into space as if thinking about how much he hated Maddy's son. "Anyway," he said, bringing himself back to the conversation, "she told me she called that idiot and talked to him about something very important. Very important," he repeated, dragging out the words. "I think he was supposed to get back to her, and the jerk never did. At least, I think he never did. She kept jokingly saying in a nervous voice that he had to figure out a few things." His face was animated, full of concern for Maddy.

I took hold of his arm to help him focus. "Dylan, it's not strange for a mom to talk about her son."

"Yeah, yeah," he drawled, "but that's when she changed, you see." His voice rose with growing tension. "She was so anxious about everything, everything," he repeated, shaking his head. "After he talked to her. You know her Christmas spirit? It died. It went right out the window." He waved his left hand like a bird flying away. "She had her little candy canes for us, Frank and I. But after she talked to her son, she was nervous, so nervous. Didn't want to talk to us. You know that's crazy. Maddy always liked seeing us."

He took another sip of beer while his blurry eyes kept staring at me. I decided then that Dylan was not driving home. "Some crazy financial scheme, that creep got himself mixed up in some crazy scheme," he said, repeating himself yet again. "That's what I thought."

Mr. Trowbridge's words about his son borrowing money jumped to mind. "When was that, Dylan? When did Maddy speak to her son? Do you know?"

"About two weeks ago, I think." He sat silent, thinking for a second. "You know, Rossi, you said we took the place of her son a little, just a little. I know we didn't really take his place, but Maddy confided in me, yes, she did," he said, drawling out the words. "Last year or so, I don't remember when. She told me her son got into trouble at Yale, something about borrowing money and cheating on a test. That was it. He cheated. He bought the answers to some test. The answers were sold to a lot of the students. Remember that scandal? That highbrow scandal? I do. It was great," he chuckled.

Dylan went to Western Connecticut State University, I recalled.

"They suspended him. He graduated, though, yes he did. He graduated from Yale." He raised his beer as if to congratulate the graduate.

"What does he do now?" I asked.

"He's an accountant, I think. He's got a couple of kids. Got married in college. That's the trouble. But, well, anyway, she was worried about him, I could tell. Rossi, you know you're a good investigative reporter," he drawled, "a damned good reporter, and I'm thinking you know something about what's going on at P&Z with that creep Harrison. Do you, Rossi? Was Maddy worried about something, something about Harrison? Did she tell you anything? Rossi, was something going on at the planner's office?"

I shook my head. "It was business as usual at P&Z yesterday, Dylan. I was shocked. I still am. Maddy murdered? I don't think it's a mugging either, but believe me, I know nothing."

"You sure, Ros?" he said, leaning forward with a scrutinizing expression as if grilling me. "Are you really sure you know nothing?"

I heaved an impatient sigh. "I'm sure. I know nothing." He gave me that drunken, faraway stare for a few more seconds.

"Rossi, another strange thing. Again, her son whats-his-name, Jonathan, named after her ancestor, the guy who built the first cabin? Him. He came into the planner's office that afternoon. I saw him. That was strange, too, Rossi, because he lives in Atlanta, and I could tell that Maddy wasn't expecting him. She looked surprised when he came in the door."

No, I thought, I'm not going back to the son thing while Dylan is in this condition, although it is a genuine lead. But the idea that Maddy may have been killed by her own son and left like garbage under a tree is so unlikely, I thought, knowing what a caring mother Maddy was.

"I want us to talk about this in the morning, Dylan," I said. "I have some ideas about how we can get to the truth of this." I turned his handsome young face to mine. "Dylan, will you stay? I'm a little nervous tonight."

"For you, Rossi," he said, with great magnitude, "I'll do it."

Dylan's car in the driveway was some insurance against the return of my potential assailant. Besides, Dylan wasn't going to drive home drunk. It was at least ten minutes to his dirt-cheap studio apartment in Georgetown. It needed to be dirt cheap because reporters were paid a paltry sum for the privilege of writing. I recalled thinking that once I was hired as a stringer, I seemed to be in my element for the first time in my life. The staff writer's job followed three months later. I considered myself lucky to be paid peanuts to write on a full-time basis as a staff writer for the *Wilton Weekly*. Now for the big leap to a daily.

I relieved Dylan of his beer. I got a red fleece blanket from a pine chest sitting against the paneled wall of the dining area in the kitchen and spread it over Dylan. Watching him sleep, his car in the driveway, I was beginning to calm down somewhat from the 007-like experience.

But the final days with my father flooded back to me, because the couch had been his favorite place. When I moved from Wayne, New Jersey, for the last few months of his life, time was the most precious commodity of the day. He was patient with my mother's difficult personality and with my bumbling with oxygen tanks, and wires. Only one year later, while my mother grieved the loss of my father, she had a fatal heart attack, purely unexpected. They both died in their early sixties. After they were gone, sometimes I'd return home from work and the house seemed to glow with a superhuman velocity. My parents' furniture and my grandmother's rocking chair seemed to glow with their love.

I sighed as I stared at Dylan sleeping there, realizing my longing for them.

Headlights coming up Sugarloaf drew my attention. I exhaled when I recognized the sound of Jerry's red pick-up. I was still pretty much unhinged. Jerry's headlights lit up the drawn drapes as he pulled into the drive. I met him at the door, anxious for that puppy dog grin of his that lets me know he's glad to see me. The car chase was going to remain a secret from him as well, I decided, without knowing exactly why.

Jerry stepped into the doorway of the entry hall. He chuckled with relief when he saw Dylan sleeping on the couch. Although the word "commitment" was not yet in our vocabulary, I guessed that Dylan's International Scout parked in my driveway posed a bit of doubt for Jerry. He hadn't called to let me know he was coming over. After he threw his coat on the corner chair, we crept upstairs to the master bedroom again as if it were routine.

"You'll be happy to know," Jerry said as we climbed into bed and slipped under the comforter, "the man with the dog called back to get an update on the case. The guy lives on Catalpa and walks his dog on School Road every night. I still can't believe the sergeant didn't get his name."

I put my head on the pillow and stared at him. "Well, I still want to interview him. Will you?"

"His wife was with him, but it was so cold she turned around and went back home."

His strong arms wrapped around me, and I felt the terror subside. I didn't know I had been holding my breath until Jerry's arms slipped around me. I rested my head on his chest and felt his soft breathing. It was like being in a heavenly incubator. But then I realized that I was breaking the law. I was withholding information on a homicide case by not informing Jerry about the car chase. Obviously, the car chase had to be connected to the murder. Or did it?

Then there were Dylan's doubts about Maddy's son and Arabella's and Mr. Trowbridge's pleas regarding Maddy's fears ... but Jerry already knew about that, I reminded myself with a sigh of relief.

I required time to put things into perspective before I revealed everything to Jerry. I shifted my weight to get a bit more comfortable. My neck was getting stiff

It was only twenty-seven hours since Maddy's murder, and someone was intent on terrorizing me. Why? What do I know, or what does he, she or they think I know? I am a reporter investigating a murder, I reminded myself; reporters have been killed in similar circumstances. So it's not unheard of, but what is the source of it? That ignorance will keep me silent. I couldn't talk to anybody under such circumstances. I had to make sense of it first.

Seventeen
Flowers for Maddy

The phones were ringing nonstop as I entered the newsroom the next morning. My body felt like lead. Susanna was late as usual, probably getting fourteen hours of sleep. The callers told me that they couldn't get through to town hall or police headquarters, so they called us for information. I cursed Susanna under my breath as I attempted to quell the pandemonium.

At 9:30 a.m., Linda Carson, the first selectman's secretary, telephoned to announce a noon press conference on the police investigation into the murder of Maddy Trowbridge. "It'll quiet things down," she said. "The phones are crazy."

The conference would be open to the public to answer all questions, she informed me. The local TV networks and radio stations were reporting on the Wilton murder every hour. The New York press and network TV crews were expected at town hall, too. Evan had received calls late yesterday from *The New York Times,* the *Daily News* and others. The story was hot because of the sensational 1897 murder. Maddy's murder had been the first one in the eighty-six years since.

"There's a phenomenon going on," Linda said in a strange voice. "Rossi, it looks like spring here. The front lawn is blossoming. People put bouquets of flowers in front of town hall during the night. They were sitting on the snow when I came in this morning, surrounding our lighted Christmas tree. It is also a black spruce like the tree, you know, where Maddy was found. It's like people want to remove the violence from her death by showering her with flowers. You know how we all loved her. Well, I never saw such a quick reaction to anything. People from all those organizations Maddy belonged to, and all the ones Maddy invited to dinner over the years. They must have been busy on the phones yesterday."

Just when I put the phone down to answer another call, a posse of bundled-up Wilton citizens with anxious expressions invaded the newsroom, looking for Evan and demanding answers. As they surrounded me I stood up and quickly called Evan to alert him about the noon conference and the newsroom invasion.

"I'll have to dig up information about the David Lambert murder of 1897," Evan remarked.

"I can look up the basics and write it up for you," I offered.

I was attempting to calm the worried eyes that impeached me and smiled good-naturedly at the pink-faced elderly people waiting impatiently for me to hang up. I put up an index finger, indicating that I'd only be a minute. I got a couple of nods and smiles back.

"You've got copy to write," Evan's soft voice reminded me.

"Good thing I've a few seconds to play around with."

He chuckled, knowing we were all working more than our usual long hours.

"Let's put off that John Cummings profile 'til next week. We're not going to need it."

"Good." That P&Z commissioner profile was on the bottom of my To Do list anyway. It was three-quarters finished.

The worried faces surrounding me fell into categories: worried mothers and fathers, several grandmothers and grandfathers. As I spoke with Evan I overheard them talking about the treacherous steps to the newsroom and why didn't the paper do something about it. "You could get killed climbing those steps."

After I hung up, a gentleman spoke for the group. He urged me to give them an update about the murder investigation. I informed them about the press conference at noon at town hall and said it would be televised on Channels 3, 12 and 8. I advised them to go home and to wait to see it on TV.

"There has been an arrest," I continued, "a person from Norwalk. The police chief will address this at the press conference."

"Then I don't have to worry about my wife going Christmas shopping?" one elderly gentleman asked. He wore a wool cap, earmuffs, a red plaid scarf and a gray wool overcoat. His face turned pink from cold, the temperature hovering just above freezing.

"Sir, you are welcome to attend the noon press conference to ask questions. It'll be in the main hearing room in town hall."

Susanna came in and cowered past my desk, as well as my accusatory glance. The phones continued to ring as I spoke. I summed it up for the group surrounding me by repeating the announcement about the noon press conference. As they turned to leave, another wave of citizenry entered. I pointed them to Susanna. As the first group left, I overheard them saying they were headed for town hall. They'd wait there for the noon conference. They advised each other to hold on tight to the railing going down the treacherous stairs.

I slipped into my coat and put Taggard's book back. I grabbed another that would include a description of the 1897 murder. My pulse quickened. Why didn't I think of comparing the two murders like every other reporter was in the process of doing? Because I was investigating this one and seriously sleep deprived, was my answer to my own question.

I stomped down the stairs to head for the quiet of my car. I passed a new group of determined Wiltonians climbing the steps and clinging to the railing with two hands, grumbling and shaking their heads.

Eighteen
The David S.R. Lambert Murder

On the evening of December 17, 1897, two masked men barged into the home of David S. R. Lambert and wound up gagging his wife and killing Lambert when he arrived home, the account of the murder in Taggard's history revealed. The two killers had once been students of Lambert. Although they were bent on robbing the couple, one student held a grudge, and it could have been a revenge murder.

The two convicted murderers were later hanged.

My car was beginning to warm up, but even in the cold I was grateful for the refuge from the nutty newsroom.

The Lambert murder had dominated New York newspapers for two years because one of the two robbers, Ben Willis, had a father who was a wealthy, respectable New York broker, Taggard noted. His mother, incredibly enough, was a madam in a New York house of ill repute. She had hired lawyers to save her son from the hangman's noose to no avail.

The broker and the madam made great headlines in New York papers. Their coverage of murder in an upscale, conservative town swept most everything under the proverbial rug. To add another layer of sensation and tragedy to the Lambert murder, the Lamberts had lost two babies in their infancy.

The car was getting warm as I closed Taggard's history book and thought about the similarities of the murders. Maddy Trowbridge and David S. R. Lambert were both honorable members of society, hailing from prominent founding families. They were both murdered in December, just two days apart on December 15 and 17. They both appeared to be homicides that had occurred in the course of robberies.

Jonathan Wood built the first cabin, and the first David Lambert, 1700-1784, built the oldest house still standing in Wilton. Lambert Corners holds several buildings, including the Lambert Tavern, the first tavern in town. Maddy regularly volunteered at Lambert Corners, thereby physically connecting the two historic families.

Willis obviously hated Lambert for the whipping he had taken as a boy when he was Lambert's student. For that reason Lambert's murder seemed more a crime of revenge than part of a robbery.

After comparing the two homicides it seemed even more apparent to me that Maddy Trowbridge was a victim of circumstance.

But what was the circumstance?

I gazed at the Christmas shoppers walking by with someone staring at me every once in a while. Perhaps the circumstance was connected to her son's financial problems, I thought, or the preschool permit about which she had expressed some irritation, or another real estate deal that went through P&Z that compromised the environment in some way. From the start I suspected that Maddy's murder could be connected to the business at the planner's department.

I shut my eyes to think. The car was at least comfortable. About five or so building permits are presented to the commissioners each month, and several permits are presented each week that include special permits to change the structure of standing buildings or sites, I considered. In about fifty weeks that's two hundred fifty a year, at least. It could possibly be a permit issued years ago.

Perhaps something in Maddy's files would tip us off. I certainly could get access to her files as a reporter covering P&Z, but the possibilities were almost mind-boggling. I decided to start by investigating the most recent prominent permit applications that came before the planning and zoning commissioners.

I was sure of two things as I sat blindly staring ahead at the window of my car. First, Maddy must have a copy in a file somewhere of all the official public hearing announcements that she handed out and submitted to the newspaper. Second, as a reporter covering P&Z for the last two years, I know that no building permit was more prominent than that of the Stuart Island Condominiums. When it was issued three years ago, I was just stringing for the paper. I'd start there, I decided.

I returned to the newsroom with more confidence, a lot calmer and with an investigative plan. As I stepped through the newsroom's narrow doorway, I saw that young Susanna was on the phone and frazzled. Her light brown, curly hair actually stood on end, electrified. She'd been answering calls nonstop for an hour while periodically surrounded by panicking people.

Dylan shook his head at me, indicating that conservative Wilton had gone berserk. "People want to know what we're doing," Dylan said, putting his hand over the receiver to let off some steam. "They're calling because they're afraid to let their kids out. Husbands want to know if it's safe for their wives to go Christmas shopping. Several mothers called. They don't want to send their kids to Cider Mill. The crime scene tape is still up, and their kids are scared. They want us to tell them when the crime scene tape will come down."

He took a breath and went on. "Don't they know this is Christmas? Did the police make any arrests? Was it a mugging? Were there any clues? It must have been outsiders who did this because everybody liked Maddy Trowbridge. Do we know anybody who didn't like her? If the town hasn't had a murder for eighty-six years, shouldn't the cops ask for help? Hire private detectives like they did years ago? What's being done about that? What is the paper doing to help the community deal with this?

"Rossi, they're calling the cops, too, but they're not getting any answers. They're calling town hall. They're going to town hall. They're told there will be a press conference at noon, but they don't want to wait that long. In fact, there's a traffic jam getting to town hall right now, and the main hearing room is already full." He paused to look at his watch. "It's 10:10, and they're going to wait at town hall until the noon conference."

With that, Dylan stood up. "They want answers, and they want them now!"

Dylan's animation made all of us laugh. I was absorbing the life of a small town weekly in the middle of a murder case. When I sat down to write a few basic facts about the Lambert murder for Evan, my phone rang. I cursed Susanna for transferring the call, and I actually stood up so I could glare at her. Then I heard the trembling voice of a young woman. It was Arabella.

Nineteen
Still Thursday Morning

Thursday morning Arabella went to her mother's dresser, she was telling me. She opened the top drawer to look for an undergarment, a slip. Her mother always wore a slip, so she wanted to include one with the rest of the outfit to be sent to Johnson's Funeral Home. She fingered through some satin half-slips, neatly folded, when a note marked "For Rossi, Private and Urgent" fell out of the pile.

"The police searched her dresser but missed it," she told me. "It was hidden, Rossi. She bothered to hide it. "

Arabella waited for my comment, but I was too busy taking in the information to say anything.

She continued, "What should I do, Rossi? Should I open it up and read it to you?"

"No," I managed to say calmly while alarms went off. The images of the black sedan with the man in the black suit and Maddy under the tree flashed before my eyes.

"Arabella, please give the note to the police," I said. My nerves were jumping inside of me. I had to control my raging curiosity and my desire as an investigative reporter to read Maddy's note. Uppermost was the car chase and the notion that I may be a target, so I didn't want Arabella and I to seem connected in any way, thereby making her a target.

"But Mom wanted you to have it." Her voice was a desperate entreaty. "Why don't you read it first? Then you can you give it to them if you think you should. It's your note."

I was surprised at the tenacity and confidence of such a young woman. Who was I to deny her request?

"Where are you calling from?"

"I'm next door at my friend's house. Alison Munroe. I know the police checked our phones, but I'm still nervous." Her labored breathing intensified.

"Okay, I like that. Keep being nervous until this nightmare is behind us. Let's agree that I'll call Alison's house and ask her to get you. Then I'll call back. I won't use my business or home phone. I'll probably call from Orem's."

"Okay. I've been researching at the library," she offered. "I could leave the note at the receptionist's desk for you."

"Tuck the note in the first book of Taggard's history of Wilton. There's a whole section about Jonathan," I added.

She chuckled. "Don't I know that. My mom has her own set; she copied every page. I'll go to the library in a few minutes. I'll pretend to do a little work, and then I'll leave about 10:30. Is that okay?"

"That's perfect. Arabella, do you mind my asking if you found out why your mother was at Cider Mill School?"

"Of course not, but I have no idea. Neither does Dad. Tuesday night is bridge night. They were going to have their yearly Christmas party. They rotate houses, and this time it was a house in Georgetown. They swapped Christmas cookies. Mom had two big trays in the backseat of her car. I noticed because she usually only has one tray. Anyway, when Mom didn't show, her friend called here, but nobody was home. They thought maybe she was just late, out Christmas shopping."

"I'm so sorry," I offered, trying to find the right words. "I'll call you later and let you know I've got the note. I'll be at the library at about 10:40."

"Thanks for listening to me, Rossi, and not treating me like a kid. I don't feel like a kid anymore."

The library in the village center had a cathedral ceiling. It was expansive with large windows that filled the spacious area with morning light. A thick cloud cover blocked out the sun, and the temperature dropped to freezing during the night, leaving the day gray and cold. Several oblong walnut tables, perpendicular to the windows, allowed visitors to read, research and gaze outside at the sweeping trunks of the sleeping elms, oaks and maples.

The woman at the reception desk looked the quintessential librarian, calm and tucked in. She offered a smile as I rushed past her. I barely noticed. I was obsessed by my mission to reach the Wilton history books in the back row of the deep room and read Maddy's revealing note. I realized that it could be Maddy's last note to anybody.

There on the next to last shelf at the bottom was Taggard's series of history books. My hands trembled as I bent down and grasped the book I needed. Tucked into the pages was the business-size envelope, right where Arabella had left it.

"For Rossi, Private and Urgent," it read. I turned the envelope over to see Alison Munroe's telephone number on the opposite side.

My eyes scanned the library. No one was in sight except a relaxed gentleman reading a newspaper around the corner in a comfortable chair, but I was uneasy. I retraced my steps and rushed out of the library to the privacy of my car. I drove up Center Road with my eyes on the rearview mirror, then headed north on Route 7 toward Cannondale Train Station, where I usually jogged.

Snow had covered the roof of the red building that originated in the 19th century by the Cannon family and was later sold to the railroad. The station's parking lot was fairly full. I walked carefully out of the parking lot onto the road and over the bridge. The Norwalk River gurgled over the snowy banks. My right hand trembled as it held Maddy's last note to me or perhaps to anybody. Arabella, her dad, her brother, her niece and nephew and their broken hearts seemed right here with me as I held the note.

I stood on the side of Pimpewaug Road in the cold. I finally lifted the flap of the envelope and pulled out the piece of white notepaper with a message written in blue ink. I recognized Maddy's handwriting.

"Rossi, look at the original map of Stuart Island. Compare it to the new map they used at the hearing for the Stuart Island Condominiums. I placed a copy of the original, done in 1955, in the Holcomb Island map in the map file cabinet for safekeeping. Remember the 1955 flood. Maddy."

It was dated December 15, 1983. She had written the note on Tuesday, the day she was murdered.

Why didn't she just call me with this? I thought with my eyes on the note. Why not leave a copy of the original map in this envelope? I wondered as I gazed around at the woods on either side of Pimpewaug Road. The bitter air bit my cheeks.

Obviously, Maddy believed herself in danger and didn't dare remove even a copy of a map from her area, I answered my own questions as I gazed back down at the note. It was damp, cold and sunless, but I didn't want to go back to the car yet. I had to think. What the heck did this note mean?

Maddy's desk is the focal point of the P&Z department. It's open on three sides in plain view of routine traffic. Maddy obviously thought herself the subject of nefarious eyes, or maybe time and opportunity expired. A couple of cars came over the bridge as I stood there. I turned my head to hide my face from them. I didn't know why, but I felt I should.

What drove Maddy's suspicions? What led her to compare the two maps? Why did she feel it necessary to hide a copy of the original map? Obviously, she had hidden the original map because she thought it might be destroyed, I reasoned.

I turned the envelope in my gloved hand over to reread it. "For Rossi, Private and Urgent." It's hard to believe the opportunity to copy the old map didn't present itself, I pondered. Of course, if she thought there were spies watching her every move, and she felt in danger? Spies right there in the planner's office? That may help to explain Mr. Trowbridge's comment about the change in her mother's behavior for the last couple of weeks, why Maddy thought she was being followed.

The permit to build the first condos in town was passed by the planning and zoning board in December, 1980, I recalled, just one month before I was hired as a stringer for the newspaper. Dylan covered P&Z then. The condos were a high profile project endorsed by Harrison Hayden and the first selectman, that much I remembered.

I found it impossible to believe that Maddy wouldn't have told Harrison about discrepancies between the old and the new maps, assuming they're there.

Maddy's note only asked me to examine the two maps without giving me the benefit of her opinion.

Harrison's comment about Maddy's keeping them honest grew more significant by the moment. I took a heavy breath. Was I flying off into the wild in my thoughts? She just asked me to compare the two maps, nothing more, but under the circumstances it seemed pretty ominous. Maddy was murdered that very day she wrote the note, and I know that it was Maddy, in her capacity as manager of the department of planning and zoning, who made damned sure the DEP was informed of all building plans near the Norwalk River

But the woman had one glaring blind spot: Harrison Hayden.

I started to shiver as I thought of how Maddy had dismissed as malicious gossip Harrison's well-known womanizing exploits. He was still handsome with a full head of silver hair. My first impression of Harrison was that he was a consummate flirt. I recalled overhearing him tell a colleague about his retirement plan.

"My idea of retirement is to drink Mai Tais in Bimini, look at beautiful young women in bikinis and date two at a time, if possible."

He was married at the time. He retired in July. Rumor has it that he left for Bimini about three weeks ago, and he was in the throes of a divorce.

What has Harrison to do with all of this? I remained standing at the side of Pimpewaug Road, turning away any time a car approached. I gazed at the river once again. The cold was getting to me, but I remained stationary, thinking.

Dylan's doubts about Harrison sprang to mind, his suspicion that Maddy's last days were full of concern about Harrison. I recalled him telling me that in his drunken stupor.

I stared at the woods on both sides of the road but found little comfort in nature. It only chilled me to the core. I finally tucked Maddy's last message into my coat pocket and headed back to the car.

On the last day of her life, she hadn't found the opportunity or the privacy to call me. But had she wanted to?

A revelation began to dawn as I crossed back over the bridge and took another glimpse at the gurgling water. I stopped halfway and stared down at the river that was little more than a stream at this point. Maddy was her old self on Tuesday, according to Mr. Trowbridge—and yes, Dylan. Even I noticed on Monday that Maddy was more herself.

To whom did Maddy always turn with issues at P&Z? Harrison. If Maddy thought she'd be able to discuss her concerns about the maps with Harrison, she wouldn't have told me anything. In fact, I thought, there would be no need to call me and no need to give me the note. But why did she hide it? Why did she keep it?

I thought a little more, knowing Maddy's work habits as I did. Then I realized what might have gone through her mind. Maddy was thorough. If she found something wrong, her first instinct would be to check with Harrison; but if things went awry for some reason, she'd have a backup plan. That was Maddy. She was sensible and cautious. So the hidden note could be the backup plan. She'd give me the note if things didn't get ironed out with Harrison.

I concluded it was a logical explanation. I stared at the Norwalk River as I took a couple of deep breaths and meditated on my logical conclusions. My convictions only grew stronger. Maddy was going to meet Harrison at Cider Mill School. Even though it was a guess on my behalf, it was a good guess, under the circumstances. So far neither the police nor Maddy's husband or daughter had offered a logical explanation for her presence at the school. There seemed to be no apparent reason for her to be at the place where she had met her death.

Then there was the extra tray of Christmas cookies sitting on the back seat.

Twenty
Spies Everywhere

Maddy's note raised a new generation of questions, but it at least justified my investigation into the dealings of the Stuart Island Condominiums. I again questioned my conclusion that the man in the black suit and white shirt with whom I had enjoyed a car chase had been connected to the owner of the proposed preschool.

It now seemed more likely that he was connected to the Stuart Island Condominiums, which were also represented at the public hearing.

I grabbed the stinging cold car door handle and surveyed the rows of parked cars at the train station suspiciously. As I was slipping into the driver's seat and turning on the ignition, I had another revelation, astonishing me.

The Stuart Island Condominium project was the first major development approved by the brand new Inland Wetlands Agency and the first that didn't go before the state's Department of Environmental Protection.

Dylan was covering P&Z when this change took place in 1981.

My thoughts were coming fast and furious. I recalled that until that time, like every other town in Connecticut, Wilton's aquifer, wetlands and water systems were monitored by the Department of Environmental Protection. The new agency inaugurated a totally new monitoring system. It placed most of the responsibility of local water systems into the hands of town officials.

I sat staring blankly at the windshield, putting it all together. As town planner, it was up to Harrison to organize the new process. What did Harrison do? He anointed the P&Z Commissioners, who were builders, developers and real estate agents, the new stewards of the land, by placing them on the Inlands Wetlands Agency. So after every P&Z meeting the commissioners switched hats and became members of the Inland Wetlands Agency.

This worked for Harrison because the planning commissioners were interested in so-called progress. The land was an afterthought. Not one conservationist was on the panel.

I recalled how a conservationist commented, "It was the like the fox guarding the henhouse." I'd quoted her often in the last two years.

When the P&Z commissioners changed hats, as a reporter I witnessed their detachment from environmental issues. The commissioners as members of the Inland Wetlands Agency asked few or no questions on behalf of the land or watercourses. They displayed no knowledge of the potential environmental problems. Such insouciance offered rare opportunities for unscrupulous developers.

Even as a reporter new to P&Z, I could feel an exposé brewing from my first day covering the public hearings. I thought that this new and somewhat murky process of protecting the environment in Wilton was fertile ground for corruption.

Apparently some aspects of Harrison's job got by Maddy, or she turned the other way. It was a new process, I reminded myself. Besides, Maddy may have focused on the steps Harrison took to preserve the quality of life and secure the character of the town. She was a realist, as well. She knew that as town planner Harrison's top priority often was required to be progress.

I don't believe she thought Harrison would break the law. I thought again how star struck Maddy was about Harrison. It could be that Maddy was not aware of all negotiations before the town planner, I thought. Every once in a while, I found that she was mistaken or had omitted aspects of a building application. That's why I found it necessary to check the files. Besides I was always on the lookout for that story, looking for shadow negotiations.

That was another reason I irked Maddy, I realized, still staring blankly at the windshield. I was grateful I didn't have time to check the files Monday.

If the new map were bogus, one that didn't honestly represent the land, it would be a criminal offense. There were high fines for ignoring environmental laws, steep enough to bankrupt a company and put those at fault in jail for years. If Harrison were in on this, he'd be joining them.

Which led me to my next question.

Who owned the land? Are the developers and the landowners one and the same? What would the original maps show me? Every aspect of this project needed to be investigated.

I finally started driving out of the parking lot. I turned right onto Route 7, my eyes frequently flashing to the rearview mirror. We were talking about millions of dollars here, and "follow the money" was a mantra to journalists for good reason.

As I merged with the morning highway traffic, I wondered if the forged map was the motive behind Maddy's murder. From the beginning I knew that motive was the most puzzling aspect of the crime. I remembered asking myself who would want to kill Maddy Trowbridge, and here was Maddy, feeding me information as usual, I thought, shaking my head at her thoroughness.

Her last bit of information for me may very well supply a motive for her own murder.

Twenty-One
Why Me?

I gripped the steering wheel, and continued to glance at the rearview mirror, looking for a black sedan. One nagging question presented itself: why me? Why did Maddy endow me with this note? Why not one of the minions whom she considered her friends? Loudly repeating itself in my head was Mr. Trowbridge's significant comment about the inland wetlands exposé and Maddy's insistence that he listen to her read each word.

I stopped for a red light at Ridgefield Road. Sitting there, I couldn't help but think my role in this murder began with the exposé that made me something of a local hero. I was again in the overheated hearing room on that Wednesday night in late March of last year. The Planning and Zoning Commission was considering a permit to build a house in a hundred-year flood zone. After the P&Z meeting the commissioners changed their hats and became commissioners of the Inland Wetlands Agency.

I chuckled when I thought, that was the story I had been waiting for. Commissioner Albert Reynolds, a realtor in his late fifties who bore a fine old name, fell asleep. His elbow was on the table, and his head rested on his fist. He nodded off to sleep in the middle of the hearing and became a metaphor. What could prove the lack of concern about the environment better than a sleeping member of the Inland Wetlands Agency during a public hearing on building in a hundred-year flood zone?

I had dropped my yellow pad, raised my camera and taken a photograph of the snoozing public servant. The next day, I had photographed the pristine wooded area and the wetlands with the potential to flood. Evan ran the photos side by side. The story took up the whole front page. The thought of it made me smile.

I recalled how it had shocked the town. It was a conservationist's dream come true, but I remembered that the political wagons had circled around Reynolds. The first selectman, Samuel Hemming, refused to change the composition of the Inlands Wetlands Commission, thereby denying hundreds of calls for change.

"If it ain't broke, don't fix it," Hemming said to Evan, who was quick to report the quote on the front page.

The cliché proved to be political suicide. Hemming lost the November election. In January the board of selectmen and the new first selectman, Hudson Smith, reconstructed the Inland Wetlands Agency. Three conservationists and three planners were to replace the board that once had consisted of only planners. The Director of Environmental Affairs, a professional environmentalist, would guide them.

Soon after the exposé I was at town hall when one of the selectmen whispered to me, "We couldn't have done it without you." I recalled how for years many in town, Republicans and Democrats, wanted to place the Inland Wetlands Agency into the hands of conservationists but failed because of political pressure.

The traffic light turned green. I stepped on the gas and recalled how after that story Maddy's attitude toward me had changed. I sensed a certain amount of respect from her and also from total strangers in town. From then on I was commonly called "the environmental reporter." In a town dependent upon its well water, this was no small matter.

There was no traffic jam when I reached town hall. Everybody was already inside, waiting for the press conference. Hundreds of bouquets blanketed the sloping, snow-covered lawn, transforming it into a field of flowers with a glowing Christmas tree in the center of it all, a cheerfully bedecked black spruce. The town was mourning Maddy on its own terms.

It didn't wipe clean the memory of the darkness under the spruce on School Road for me, though. Finding her killer will be my first step towards recovery, I thought as I pulled into the wide drive.

As I drove towards the annex's parking lot, the answer to the nagging question of why Maddy had turned to me popped into my mind: Maddy trusted me to protect the land, not her conservative friends at town hall. They, for the most part, sided with the former first selectman.

As I pulled into the small parking space by the annex, I realized once again that change comes hard in this conservative town. Maddy had known this better than anybody. I turned off the ignition.

From the horrifying moment when I recognized Maddy as the dead woman under the spruce, I had been puzzled by my reactions. It seemed to me that my emotions exceeded my distant relationship with her, but it was crystal clear now. We had bonded in our respect for the land.

Apparently Maddy trusted me to find the truth about the maps, not only because I was an investigative reporter, but also because we had shared a mutual concern for the land.

My sense of responsibility had puzzled me from the start. I shook my head in wonder as I stared through the messy windshield, splattered with sand and slush, at the wispy cherry tree in front of me. I took a deep breath. It was a relief to solve the mystery of one of my reactions under the black spruce. The bonding between Maddy and me had registered in my subconscious. I'd had only a hint of it consciously until now.

It explained why I found myself moved by such passion to vow so optimistically, and even foolishly, that I'd find the person who stole Maddy's life. Maddy's note to me might actually lead to her killer or killers. I nervously tapped the note in my coat pocket, fearful that it might have disappeared.

I stepped out of the car into the cold and walked the few steps in the brisk air to the front door. The P&Z building seemed shrouded in grief as if all portals were draped in black. I pushed on the glass door. All of a sudden my knees turned wobbly, which surprised me. Maddy's dedication to the land most likely led to her violent death, and now whoever killed her might be after me. I was entering the building where perhaps it had all begun.

Twenty-Two
The Maps

A man was at the back files. He was dressed in overalls and a thickly lined wool jacket. I assumed he was a builder. I walked to the map files and glanced back at Maddy's empty desk. It seemed that she was right there with me. At least a part of her was. I tapped the note in my pocket while I paid her homage and expressed silent gratitude.

I searched for the H files and found them in the fourth drawer down. I pulled the drawer out and leafed through to the Holcomb Island maps. I tipped up the first map and saw three folded sheets of white copy paper tucked between the maps. I pulled out the folded copies and opened them up right under my nose on top of the cabinet, thereby shielding them from any passersby. It was a copy of the Stuart Island map dated 1955. It took three copy sheets to include the whole map. Attached was a handwritten note from Maddy.

"The November 1955 building permit application for a senior citizens dwelling was rejected by P&Z commissioners because of the wetlands and the Norwalk River flood way. The wetlands and flood way are clearly outlined on the site map.

"The selectmen rejected the application because of the October storm. The flooding destroyed buildings that were on the land, and the DEP frowns on building in the flood way. It doesn't want the land compromised by fill placed in this area. Fill would be necessary to mitigate the gallons of water that flow from the river during severe storms. Then the town frowns on building in the flood way because it leaves downstream residents and roads more vulnerable to flooding."

Construction in wetlands in flood ways proved perilous for a number of reasons, I recalled. If a building is built in a flood way, that in itself is considered hazardous. If it's built in a flood way on wetlands, it's a major risk. Buildings are far more likely to be damaged in a severe storm, and over years they sink and crack. This was the exact description of the land that the Stuart Island Condominiums were built upon, according to the original 1955 map.

The state doesn't prohibit, it discourages. The state DEP demands a permit and has the opportunity to reject it. It demands clean fill for wetlands. It also requires an Environmental Impact Study. If the building site impacts any watercourses or wetlands, a permit is required by the Army Corps of Engineers. The Corps could also reject the application. The costly red tape is to discourage building in wetlands and flood ways.

I swallowed hard and put the Holcomb Island map back in the drawer. I took the three sheets of copy paper with the map on them and slipped them in between the pages of my yellow legal pad. I proceeded to look for the questionable Stuart's Island map in the same drawer.

I pulled it out and laid it on top of the metal cabinet. The map was issued by Peterson, Myers, & Sheen, Inc. An official state seal stamped on the document proved that the local company was registered with the State of Connecticut. I saw the notes of a hundred-year flood line near the Norwalk River on the east side. Markings of railroad tracks indicated the railroad on the west side. Nothing indicated wetlands on the river's flood plains. Nothing indicated the flood way.

I didn't dare take out Maddy's copies of the 1955 map to compare. She thought there was a spy. After what had happened to her, why would I second-guess her?

The builder left the room. I went to the back file cabinet for the Stuart Island file, but first I laid down my yellow pad on top of the cabinet and jotted down some of the map's lines and markings. I opened up the S drawer and took out the Stuart Island file. My hands were trembling. I rifled through it as fast as I could, looking for specifics such as an Environmental Impact Assessment and Aquifer Impact Study. Stuart Island was close to the north end of the aquifer. My heart pounded in my throat. I expected someone to come up behind me and to ask me what I was doing, even though it was normal for me to be in the files.

The Aquifer Impact Study was there in a navy binder. I read part of it. The concerns were about the topography of the land where the rainwater would flow from the area northeast toward the aquifer. Any pollutant from the porous grounds would find its way into the aquifer.

In the comment section it was noted that a resident objected to the permit, referring to "the 1955 flooding." But his comments were dismissed by the Inland Wetlands Agency because the individual wasn't a "professional." The developer responded, "More accurate maps were drawn since the original map was done twenty-six years ago, and advanced techniques and materials would prevent degradation of buildings from flooding."

Other buildings in town off the island were severely affected by the 1955 storm, it was noted.

No EIS. No DEP permits and no Army Corps of Engineer permit for building near the Norwalk River and in the wetlands. No mention of the flood way in the wetlands.

Maybe there was another file?

I turned back to the file drawer for a second look, but there were no more files. This was all there was. I was a little nauseated when I slapped closed the files and jammed them back into the file drawer with my eyes dashing around the office. No one was in sight.

My emotions were roiling. Harrison knew. He was hired in 1955. If Maddy knew about wetlands, flood ways and the 1955 flooding, then he knew. Did Maddy die for this? Did she die so they could build one hundred seven condominium units on Stuart Island?

There's got to be more, I thought as I rushed out the glass door.

Twenty-Three
The Stuart Island Maps

I drove directly to the newsroom where calm had been restored, at least for the time being. The frazzled Susanna was eating her lunch at her desk. The phones were quiet. Evan, Dylan and Frank were at the noon conference, and everybody else in town was either glued to a TV or at town hall. The Chief was expected to announce the arrest of Richard Freemont any minute now. That would no doubt calm the raging waters of Wilton.

I took out Maddy's three sheets of copy paper with the original 1955 map from its hiding place in my yellow pad and spread it out half on the desk and put the rest on my lap. Wetlands in the "Norwalk River flood flow" were clearly indicated on ten acres of the fourteen-acre lot. Nothing of the sort appeared on the new map.

Five of the acres were designated wetlands in a flow zone in a flood plain. Three acres of the wetlands were in the area designated as a flood way. The whole building site was in a hundred-year flood plain.

Building on the land was an environmental hazard, I concluded. Stuart Island should have remained a nature reserve. Nothing should ever have been built on it. That damn Harrison.

Dollar signs started to click in my head. I placed my hand over my open mouth in astonishment as another theory occurred to me. Maddy's faith in Harrison had led her to call him to ask about the map discrepancy. I was as certain of this as I was that I was sitting in the newsroom. Her dedication to him would have led her to protect him at any cost. Never would she have uttered a sound about improprieties without his knowledge, or at least without warning him first.

She was probably on her way to the school to talk to him about the fraudulent map, thinking Harrison would solve all the problems, clear up the discrepancies. The betrayal seemed so hideous. Her devotion to him was the first thing I had noticed about her.

But did he actually pull the trigger?

Maddy flitted around the planner's office, involved in every aspect of the town's growth. During their watch an average home jumped from $57,500 in the 1970s, to $175,000 by 1980. Maddy's dark brown eyes lit up with hero worship when she told me this little bit of history.

Little doubt lingered in my mind that Harrison was at the heart of this environmental debacle and Maddy's murder. If he didn't hold the Glock to the back of Maddy's head, he certainly supplied the ammunition. As town planner he had to know that the new map was a phony. It was his business to know, and he sold out. He must have been paid under the table to go along, enough for a Bimini beach house.

My telephone rang, jarring me from my loathing thoughts of Harrison.

"Ms. Rossi, I'm Ann Bower, one of Maddy's friends," a woman was nervously saying. "We need to talk. I work at town hall. It's a circus here," she rattled as if she had to get something off her chest. "Three TV trucks just pulled up. The conference is about to start. Come in the back door and head downstairs. I do my typing in a room there. Nobody will see you. I just need a few minutes of your time. Can you come now?"

Twenty-Four
Ann Bower

I passed the TV trucks parked in the jammed town hall parking lot in the back of the building. I spotted a vaguely familiar woman waiting as I pulled up and parked illegally alongside the back door. The woman appeared cold, bundled up and troubled. She was middle aged, thin, with short, curly silver hair. Her black wool coat was almost to her ankles, and her black boots disappeared under her coat. As I hopped out of the car and approached her, she smiled as if she knew me. She was obviously grateful I had come immediately.

She held open one of the double doors that had windows on the upper half bedecked with evergreen Christmas wreaths. "There's a room downstairs where I do my typing, Ms. Rossi. We won't be bothered there."

We stepped into the entry hall. To the right was a hallway that led to the first floor offices. In front of us was a stairway to the lower floor.

"Ann, please call me Rossi," I said as I followed her downstairs. "I think I remember seeing you before. They keep you behind the scenes, huh?"

"Yes, lots of typing."

Glittering cutouts of white Christmas bells trimmed in red hung on the first office door to the right. We entered a small square conference room with a putty colored desk and no windows. A typewriter sat on the desk with a couple of wire baskets full of papers on either side. A Christmas wreath of pinecones hung on the outside of the desk. No doubt, the wreath was created by Maddy. A framed poster of an open field in the spring was on the wall that faced the desk, breaking the sterile office atmosphere. Two dark wood folding chairs sat in front of the desk.

"I know I can trust you," she began.

She sat in the far chair. I took the other and turned it slightly to face her. Ann seemed the type of person that Maddy would confide in. She stared hard at me, all business and clearly troubled, as she slipped out of her coat, folded it and placed it on a corner of her desk. I opened mine and took off my hat and gloves. I took a pen and yellow pad out of my satchel, rested the pad on my lap and gave Ann all my attention.

"Maddy spoke so highly of you and your concern for the environment." She stopped, her eyes filled with tears. "Maddy confided in me, Rossi. We were the best of friends." She hesitated and then said, "Somebody needs to know what I'm about to tell you, Rossi, but this needs to be off the record."

I didn't know if I could keep what Ann was about to tell me off the record, but I would try. I also calculated, observing Ann's state of alarm, that I'd change her mind if I had to.

"Okay, Ann, it's off the record."

"Maddy was trying to get to Harrison for two full weeks before she ... before that Tuesday. She was beside herself that the man would get into trouble. She found a discrepancy between two maps. She wouldn't tell me any more than that. She went back in the files to compare the two maps. She called me at home two weeks and a day before her death, that Monday, when she discovered that the new map was false. She said she never trusted the civil engineer who did the map. She had never seen him before or after."

Ann took a deep breath as if she were full of self-doubt but determined.

"Rossi, I think Maddy was murdered because she knew something about those maps. I've told the police that, too, and it's like I'm not saying anything. They say everything's fine at the planner's office. I even called Dominic, the Chief of Police, because he's a friend of my husband, and I heard he was questioning people at P&Z and Maddy's friends at town hall. He had the same attitude. So I'm turning to you to find the truth."

Ann peered at me with the eyes of a desperate creature being hunted down by her own thoughts.

"Ann, from the start my impression was that Maddy was executed, not murdered during a mugging."

She heaved a sigh and sat back in her chair. Her anxious expression changed to one of utter relief. "I knew I could count on you to see this thing for what it is. You know this town, Rossi. They don't like controversy. You know that better than most. They came after you at the paper a couple of times. The politicians in town wanted you fired."

"Yep, most of the board of selectmen came to the weekly office and told Evan to fire me. Evan told me that I must have done something right."

Ann's serious face cracked a smile for a second, but her light brown eyes were fixed and steady.

"I'm afraid the police won't do anything to find Maddy's murderer because they don't want to stir things up. It's more convenient to just call it a mugging and forget about it. I can't allow that to happen," Her eyes were still fixed on me. "I lost Maddy, but I won't lose our friendship. Do you know what I mean? I treasure that part of my life. Maddy would expect me to find the truth."

"Can you give me any more information, Ann? For instance, do you know why Harrison didn't call Maddy back for two weeks? Did Maddy say anything about that?"

She combed her fingers through her cropped hair, taking a minute to think.

"My impression at first was that he wanted to get a clean start someplace else. Harrison just wanted to have fun, enjoy his retirement. But then Maddy told me she was frightened, that she thought she was being followed." She shook her head as she relived that conversation with her departed friend.

"Is there something else?" I asked, noticing how nervous Ann was becoming.

"Then Maddy told me she told Harrison about the maps as soon as she discovered the discrepancy. That's when she started to be scared." Her nervousness increased as she spoke. She folded her hands to keep them from twitching.

"What are you not telling me, Ann? It's okay," I encouraged her.

"Maddy told me she thought somebody was following her those last two weeks," she said. "Then Maddy heard from Harrison that he'd be back here on Monday. He was supposed to meet her at Cider Mill on Tuesday. I guess Harrison didn't have a car. She told me she wanted to take him to Friendly's and talk to him about the maps over a cup of coffee. Rossi, that was the night she was murdered."

Ann had just confirmed my theory that Maddy had planned to meet Harrison at Cider Mill. I heard myself groan.

"Ann, I know Maddy told you this in confidence, but this is a fact that you must tell the police, that she was meeting Harrison at Cider Mill."

"I did," she said with bulging, indignant eyes. "I told the Chief, but he said it only proves that Harrison wasn't the last person to see Maddy alive. She never got to the school, he said. He promised to check it out, to find out if Harrison was supposed to meet her. But how? Maddy didn't tell anybody else. Harrison will deny it."

"Ann, are you afraid that Harrison came back here and killed Maddy?" I couldn't believe I uttered the words, but the question had to be asked.

"I think he might have hired somebody to do it." Her thin body was rigid as a pole. She stared at me and seemed the picture of sincerity. I had no reason to doubt Ann. She sighed and sat back in her chair, relieved that she had voiced the worst of her suspicions.

"Harrison changed over the years," she continued more calmly, "but Maddy lived in denial. Everyone heard Harrison gripe about the fat cats in town. That's what he called the Wall Street executives who had moved into town over the last fifteen years or so. He believed he deserved more money."

She stopped to stare at me for emphasis. "Then all of a sudden, Harrison is prosperous," she said. "He buys the beach house in Bimini. He didn't sell his marital home, even though he'll have alimony to pay, two of his four children are still in college, and he's about to pay off the mortgage for his wife. Maddy shared that with me. When she told me, she looked troubled. I ask you, where does a town planner get all this money, Rossi?" She raised her hands palms up in the air as she asked that question, her face distraught, as if this was incontrovertible evidence that Harrison was guilty of a crime of some kind,

As Ann talked, I started some retrogressive reshuffling. At the murder scene I thought Maddy had been assassinated. Then I believed her murder could be connected with the town planner's office. Perhaps Maddy saw or heard something she shouldn't have. Maybe it was some local investor who hired a professional gun because millions of real estate dollars were at stake. Then I learned about the questionable Stuart Island map, which seemed to justify my theory about its being a homegrown crime.

But seeing and hearing Ann describe Maddy's fearful state, I thought it had to be more than just a corrupt real estate deal. And no matter what illegal thing it was, why wouldn't Maddy have reported it to the authorities? There had to be more. For starters, if Harrison was paid off, as Ann suspected, who paid him off and why? Was he paid off to look the other way regarding the map? Or was there more? Obviously someone was tailing Maddy? Who? And why?

I heaved a sigh of relief, grateful I didn't need to pressure Ann to go on the record. I realized this investigation was just starting. I had too much to nail down before a story could be written.

Besides, the most important information Ann had to offer was that Maddy was to meet Harrison at Cider Mill School, and she had already told that to the Chief. The Chief brushing her off was interesting.

I hugged Ann goodbye, stared straight into her pleading eyes and promised to keep in touch. I fled out of the small room, up the stairs and out the town hall back door, anxious to get to my car to head off the traffic jam bound to occur when the news conference broke.

With one eye on the rearview mirror, looking for the black sedan, I drove down the town hall driveway and took a right onto Route 7. At the very least, Ann's information justified my loathing of Harrison and my theory that he was somehow responsible for Maddy's murder.

When I was back at my space for only a few seconds in the safe and secure newsroom, about to write about the 1897 murder, my phone rang. It was Jerry.

"I have some bad news."

My stomach dropped. My first thought was of Arabella.

Twenty-Five

Harrison Hayden

Jerry told me that Harrison Hayden was found floating face down in his pool in Bimini last night, Wednesday, December 16. He had been dead for three days, according to the coroner. His body was discovered by a young female acquaintance, Caroline Hill. The young woman had arrived for dinner at his new seaside home in Port Royale, South Bimini, at 7:00 p.m. and found Harrison's body floating in the pool. Drowning was the cause of death. Apparently, Harrison had been struck by a blunt object and pushed into the pool sometime Sunday night.

Jerry went on to say that the condominium had been ransacked. The stolen items included electronic equipment, appliances, and an uncertain amount of cash. The police reports declared Harrison's death a homicide that had occurred while a robbery was in progress. Jerry received the report of Harrison's death via telephone and fax from authorities in Bimini.

I was struck speechless. "Another respected Wilton town official murdered," I finally said, "both killed during a robbery and both working for the Town of Wilton in the planning and zoning department? Get ready for conspiracy theories. Is the Chief telling them about the murder of Harrison Hayden at the noon press conference?"

The Chief would announce it, Jerry revealed, because the Hayden family had been notified earlier in the day by the Bimini police, and it was bound to get out. It was just minutes ago that the Bimini Police had called the Wilton Police Department.

Jerry's voice was hurried, his normal speech pattern broken with sighs. "You'll be having a permanent guest until this case is closed, Ros," he announced after giving me the facts of the case.

"You won't get an argument from me," I responded. "Having you live with me is like the house wearing a bulletproof vest. Jerry, I think I'm suffering from a mild case of PTSD, but your hours are long now, and you've got the animals to worry about."

"It would be easier if you stayed at my place," he said. "The Bimini police declared Harrison's death a homicide that occurred during a robbery, but two robberies that end in death? Two people who worked in the same office. That's too much of a coincidence for me."

I didn't say I told you so.

"Jerry," I began, "I hope you'll direct your investigation toward the Planning and Zoning Department. Maybe Maddy's fears came from her discovery of illegal real estate dealings at P&Z. Multimillion-dollar commercial real estate projects depend on building permits, and Harrison was highly influential as the town planner. Need I say more?"

"First, Al wants me to go to Bimini," Jerry announced. "The Chief recommended it, and I agreed. Want to come? We'll go down Sunday, return Tuesday. Ros, I don't want you going there on your own, and I'm afraid you'll do just that. So this is a better plan for both of us.

"The police department is going to pay for this?" I asked incredulously.

"Well, they'll pay for me, and I'll pay for you."

Evan's approval for the travel time was required. He was on the phone, looking at me and shaking his head, and he was also receiving the news of Harrison's death from one of his contacts, no doubt. Since Harrison was the former town planner, and Maddy's murder might be tied to his, it was a local story. Leaving for Bimini on Sunday still allowed me to report on Maddy's wake on Saturday and to continue my investigation today and tomorrow. Since Jerry and I would pick up the tab, I considered this a done deal.

"I'm with you," I told Jerry. "Will the department have trouble with me traveling with you on official business?"

"They won't know we're traveling together," he said. "I, the department, or your editor, for that matter, can't keep you from independently going anywhere you want to go."

At this point I was thinking of traveling on a different plane so that Jerry would stay out of trouble with the Chief. "But what about the Planning and Zoning Department? Investigating that?"

"Al is going to search through Mrs. Trowbridge's files, but according to the Chief, everything's normal at P&Z. He questioned Timothy Esposito. Esposito says that Harrison and Mrs. Trowbridge left the place in perfect order, which is just what he told me."

"Right," I said. I recalled Ann's revealing comments about the Chief. Ann had confided in me, so I didn't feel free to tell Jerry right now. I also failed to understand the Chief's response to Ann's telling him that Maddy went to the school to meet Harrison. If I'd understood what Ann was saying, it seemed like the Chief wanted to give Harrison a chance to explain. And now Harrison was dead.

This was all too confusing. Let Jerry go to Bimini and see what he can find out about Harrison. One thing I was sure of, there had to be more to this story.

My investigation starts here.

Twenty-Six
Calling Arabella

I got to Orem's to call Arabella with the news of Harrison's death. The local diner was also historical, having been in business for several generations. The lunch crowd was dwindling down. At the end of the long, bustling counter was the door to the restrooms. I pushed it open and spun around to see if anyone was looking at me. Two quiet, closed telephone booths, perfect for surreptitious conversations, sat against the wall. I stepped into the first booth, dialed Alison's number and placed a quarter in the telephone. I was grateful to hear a young voice answer and asked Alison to get Arabella. I told her I'd call back in five minutes.

I stared straight ahead, waiting to see if someone had followed me in. My heart was racing. The death of Harrison didn't help. Whoever had killed Maddy wasn't finished killing people. Who'd be next? It was a logical question. While I waited to call back I could feel my stress level rise as if Harrison's death was finally becoming real. I was also planning on how I'd break the news to Arabella. I redialed Alison's number, and Arabella answered.

I kept talking to give Arabella a little time. I could hear her struggling. Her breathing was spasmodic and shallow and interrupted with heavy sighs.

She finally broke her silence. "I think Harrison called my mom on Sunday. Imagine, he called her on his last day, and it was two days before ..."

"I'm so sorry, Arabella."

"Mom seemed a little less tense the last couple of days. I meant to tell you that, Rossi. That's why I thought she talked to Mr. Hayden. He was her professional touchstone. If anything was bothering her at the planner's office, she'd always talk to Mr. Hayden, even after his retirement. I'm glad my mother didn't have to live to see this. She'd never get over it. To her, Mr. Hayden walked on water."

"I know. Arabella, right now my main concern is your family."

"Even my brother is jumpy these days. I told you how he rarely calls. Well, now he calls every day, asking if we're okay. Which is so strange."

"I think it's a case of conscience. It's a good thing. How's your father?"

"He's nervous, too. He's looking over his shoulder like my mother was. He tells me that it's nothing, but I wondered if someone contacted him or he saw someone following us."

"He may be frightened for you."

"You think my dad is afraid that we're in danger, too? Do the police think Mr. Hayden's murder is connected with my mother's? Are the Wilton police investigating Mr. Hayden's murder?"

"They initiated a wider investigation. Jerry Stevenson will be traveling to Bimini on Sunday. Arabella, I'm going to do some investigating regarding that note your mother left me." I hesitated. "I can't tell you what your mother wrote. The less you know, the safer you are. Also for your safety, let's not have any communication at all. Okay? I think I'm being followed."

"Can I make a suggestion?" Arabella asked.

"Sure."

"Call Mrs. Hayden. Maybe there's something among his papers. I've heard that Mr. Hayden moved out after a big argument. They were having marriage problems. There was a big blow-up when a woman called the house. Mrs. Hayden threw Mr. Hayden's clothes outside on the street when he was out. Then she changed the locks so he couldn't get back in. I also heard he wanted his business papers, and Mrs. Hayden refused to give them to him. So his papers are at the house, Rossi."

"Where did you get all this information?"

"Mr. Hayden's daughter Cynthia is a good friend. Now this. Cynthia loves her dad so much."

"I'm going to town hall regarding the note your mom left. Then I'll head out to the Hayden house."

"Rossi, I wouldn't wait. The police searched our house that Tuesday night. I was just lucky they missed Mom's note. They may confiscate everything at Mr. Hayden's house in the next hour or so."

"Right."

Twenty-Seven

2:00 Thursday: Sarah at the Assessor's Office

"Isn't it tragic? What happened to Maddy?" Sarah at the tax assessor's office asked when she saw me. She wore a shocked expression as she uttered Maddy's name and shook her head. She gazed down at the floor for a moment, as if to honor Maddy's memory in a moment of silence.

Then she rose and came to the glossy walnut counter where I stood. It was a relief to see her welcoming, kind face, even with its sadness. She was tall and in her fifties, seemingly contented and settled with her role in life. She was a little thick around the middle with soft brown hair and eyes that only added to her kindly persona.

I couldn't resist coming here before going to the Hayden house, despite Arabella's words still ringing in my head. His wife probably wouldn't want to show me their financial papers at any rate, and Stuart Island kept coming up. It wasn't only Maddy's note but my own decision to investigate the approval process at P&Z for illegal dealings, starting with the condominiums.

"What a shame," Sarah whispered. "Everybody loved her here. Maddy and I were good friends. We had lunch frequently and talked, you know what I mean? What I know about development comes from Maddy. She'll be remembered for her love of the town. I sometimes wondered how she held onto her job at the planner's office."

She gazed at me in silence for a second before speaking again.

"Maddy told me how things changed around here when the new Inland Wetlands Agency was established with the conservationists on it." She raised her eyebrows and leaned across the counter. "You don't hear that 'fill in the swamps' anymore. What you hear now is 'preserve our wetlands.' Your story helped out a lot, Rossi." She pursed her lips and shook her head. "Conservationists tried to get the land away from the developers for years. Everybody at town hall knows that. Your story split the thing wide open. That's why you're our hero."

I uttered a humble thanks and reminded Sarah that the story was only a catalyst. It was the people of Wilton who demanded change.

"Sarah, can you tell me who actually owns Stuart Island Condominiums?" I finally asked. I wore an innocuous expression. I needed to calm down. How could I doubt Sarah? But at the moment I suspected everybody at town hall, which was probably a good thing. "I'm doing a story," I explained.

"Of course," she said smiling good-naturedly. "That's easy, Rossi. Just see who pays the taxes." With that she went to the computer on her desk and in seconds brought Stuart Island up on her screen. "National Developers, Inc., a Miami company, pays the taxes."

I was stunned. An out-of-town company was involved with a Wilton project of this size, and I knew nothing about it? These kinds of things usually get around town, especially at the paper. Three years ago I was only a stringer; I didn't cover P&Z. Perhaps this was common knowledge. I'm relatively new to town. Perhaps out-of-town real estate investors are common.

"National Developers, hum," Sarah said, gazing at the document. "I didn't know anybody from out of town was involved in the condos," she said as if she could read my mind. "There was a time when everybody knew everyone in town."

She went to the file cabinets at the far end of the room and returned with a large manila file. She slapped it on the countertop and started to flip through it.

"Peterson, Myers & Sheen Development Corp. hired the builder, a Jack Manners. Both are from Wilton. It doesn't say anything about the ownership of the land. The building project was done through Peterson, Myers & Sheen."

"Can you look up the deed and find out who actually owns the property?" I asked, "because the people who pay the taxes don't necessarily own the land. So maybe National Developers doesn't own the land?"

"Rossi, you're so right," she said, smiling at me, impressed. "You always ask the right questions. It's typical for owners to pay the taxes, like I'd love someone to pay my taxes," she said jokingly and waited for me to grin back at her.

"Was it hard to get the condos built, Sarah? Did people in town object?"

"I remember a big fuss at the beginning," she said, knitting her eyebrows. "Nobody figured they'd be able to build on that land. I remember a hearing on that, before the Stuart Island Condominiums, that didn't get approved by P&Z. It seemed common knowledge that Stuart Island was filled with wetlands," she said, confusion marking her face. "Then there's the river, you know flooding happens every few years or so. There was a big flood at one time. People every once in a while talk about it."

She recalled the devastating pictures printed in the *Wilton Weekly* of the 1955 flood. "But the engineer proved everyone wrong."

"What did you say?"

"It seemed like Harrison didn't approve of the man. You could read it on his face," she said, leaning closer to me over the counter. "The civil engineer who drew up a new map of Stuart Island. He proved that they could build the condos on the land. I don't know the particulars. They were going to grade the land for possible floods, and there just wasn't all the wetlands they thought." She shrugged her shoulders.

"You know Harrison believed in taming the land," she continued. "You know, getting it to work for you." She gave me an insider's grin. "'Rescuing the land from nature,' he'd say. 'Fill in the swamps,' which we now know as wetlands so people can use their property. That's what Harrison believed. The DEP really allowed the town to do whatever with the so-called swamps.

"But when people realized that the swamps were wetlands, and they helped keep our well water clean, things began to change. Anyway, Rossi, you'll have to go down the hallway to the town clerk's office for the deed. You know Mary, she is usually there at the front desk. Just ask her to find the volume and page number for the deed for Stuart Island Condominiums. The deeds are stored in the adjacent room according to volume numbers. They have a copy machine there. You'll need ten cents for a copy of the deed. Do you have dimes?"

Town hall always seemed an oasis of calm and civility in an otherwise hectic and often rude world. I usually left the building grateful for the kind and patient help of those who worked there, but the information Sarah revealed only served to disturb me. Nobody in town owned the condos? National Developers, a Miami firm, owned them? For three years I, along with everyone else in town, thought they were built by the local developers, Peterson, Myers & Sheen.

What did it mean?

I walked back toward the front door and crossed the generous center hall. I took a left at the hallway that led to the town clerk's office. The ever-pleasant Mary served me with a smile, and I headed to the back room with Volume E687, page 38, neatly written in pencil on a piece of white pad paper. The four walls were lined from floor to ceiling with thick volumes that looked like oversized encyclopedias. Four oak work tables were in the center of the room. On the back wall on the bottom shelf, I found the Volume E687.

I brought the heavy volume to one of the worktables, my ears alert. I turned to page 38. The deed had been issued in November 1970 in the name of National Developers, Inc. of Miami Florida. They owned the land and the buildings.

I sucked in air. Orbiting in my brain was National Developers being from Florida and Harrison's dubious engineer who had drawn up the phony map. I made a copy of the deed. Then I returned down the hall for another gentle inquisition of Sarah.

"Sarah, what happened to that engineer? Do you know his name, the one who did the maps of Stuart Island?"

She tilted her head as if she were trying to recall his name. "The day he came in here with Harrison was the only time I saw him, but the local developers, Peterson, Myers & Sheen, they got the maps done. I'm sure their name is on the maps, and they're highly reputable. Everybody knows them. Been in town for years."

"Oh, I'm sure everything is on the up and up. I was just curious, you know me."

"We'll, it's your job to be curious," she said, her eyebrows knitted. "I like that you ask all those questions. We're depending on you to keep asking them."

I left the town hall, walking quickly to my car, anxious to get to the Hayden house and Mrs. Hayden.

Twenty-Eight
Mrs. Hayden's Home

I drove up Honeyhill Road, a quiet residential street in the western section of town. Christmas wreaths of evergreens with red bows adorned several windows of Mrs. Hayden's luxurious ranch home and the front door. I pulled up to the shoulder of the road several feet away from the house. It was 2:30 p.m. on the steely gray, cold Thursday.

The woman whose husband had publically betrayed her was most likely inside. Death by a thousand cuts, I thought as I sat in the car, preparing to go inside, and now here she is, Harrison's widow of only a few hours, and I'm trying to interview her. I wondered where my audacity came from, then reminded myself that reporters need a bit of audacity, or we'd never get the story. In this case, it wasn't even the story I was after.

Arabella and Mr. Trowbridge flashed across my mind. My promise to Maddy proved an adequate impetus to invade the newly widowed Mrs. Hayden's home. I got out of the car. All of a sudden I felt without a doubt that I was being watched, although I saw nobody on the street and no cars had followed me, no black sedans.

The white, ranch-style home was well kept. It sat on at least two acres of land and had a fenced-in swimming pool in the back yard. The areas free of snow revealed a lawn similar to that of a Florida country club, very unlike Wilton. I thought of the rocky soil at my house and how glaciers had long ago carried rocks and then melted across New England, leaving them to fill every inch or so of soil. I thought of the ubiquitous Stonehenge that marked boundaries no longer relevant, except that they reminded us of Wilton's history.

The Haydens' beautiful lawn, peeking out from under the tundra, was no doubt grown from very expensive sod.

The drapes on the large picture windows were drawn tightly as though they shouted, "Keep out." I prepared for full rejection and rang the bell. Footsteps approached the door. My heart was pounding.

The door opened, and I sucked in air. There stood a beautiful, regal woman. She was statuesque with short blonde hair, stylishly cut. Her sapphire cashmere sweater matched her glaring, questioning eyes. A delicate cold chain encircled her long neck, and her fair skin radiated against the blue sweater. Her beauty and posture were stunning, yet the lineaments of bitterness were the most impressive.

"Yes?" she inquired, her voice demanding and haughty.

"I hope I'm not disturbing you, Mrs. Hayden. I'm Carol Rossi from the *Wilton Weekly.* Do you have a minute?"

"For you, Ms. Rossi, I have more than a minute and a little information. Step right in." She swung the door open and stepped to the side to let me go by.

Stupefied by her reception, I walked into the immaculate house. "Oh, please just call me Rossi," I said.

The living room was to the right of the front door. White couches, white chairs, white carpet, white draperies, and glass and stainless steel-trimmed tables. Every piece of furniture appeared to be brand new. The house was so spotless that I wanted to seal myself hermetically before I stepped into the living room.

In the center of the hall was a decorated Christmas tree. It was an artificial white tree with tiny blue bells and white lights.

She showed me to a curved love seat covered by an embossed fabric of a floral design. Mrs. Hayden sat opposite me on a matching couch. Both couches were perpendicular to the huge picture window, the white drapes of which remained drawn.

"Mrs. Hayden," I began.

"Please," she said, obviously irritated by being addressed as "Mrs. Hayden." "Ellen is good for now." Her voice was smooth but tinged with bitterness. She gazed down at her graceful fingers and the tips of her nails, colored a deep white.

"Ellen, I'm so sorry about the awful news."

"You mean about Harrison's death. Yes, two police departments informed me a few hours ago." She folded her lips together, and tears filled her eyes. I held myself back from embracing her.

"I feel for my children, Ms. Rossi," she said as if correcting a false impression. "They lost their father. Now why are you here?"

She raised her icy blue eyes to mine. I caught my breath as they focused on me and told my racing heart to calm down.

"I'm writing a follow-up story on Maddy Trowbridge's death, ah, murder. Do you know if she communicated with Mr. Hayden recently?"

"I'm going to tell you, Ms. Rossi, what I didn't tell the police. Maddy was supposed to meet Harrison on School Road the night she was killed. Tuesday night. That's what you want to know, isn't it?"

I looked at her, stunned for the second time in seconds. "Why didn't you tell the police?" I asked, astonished, my mouth literally wide open.

"Because I just found out. I received a fax from him a few minutes ago. I turned off the fax machine weeks ago. I've no interest in it. Then this morning, it occurred to me to turn it on just in case there was a message from Harrison. We have the kind that stores messages. It's not totally turned off, it just stops printing. He said he'd be visiting the kids for Christmas. He expected to arrive sometime Monday. I'll call the police later, Ms. Rossi, and let them know."

My yellow pad was on my lap, and I was scribbling notes on it, not wanting to interrupt Mrs. Hayden. She paused, so I jumped in.

"Ellen," I began, but she interrupted me as if I weren't speaking.

"Do we agree that this is all off the record, Ms. Rossi?"

I found myself agreeing with a nod of my head.

"Maddy and Harrison were very close," she said, "but she was often lied to like the rest of us in Harrison's life. She wasn't in the loop," she said, gazing at me. "What happened in the planner's office wasn't her business. She knew the process, how things were done after decisions were made, but she only knew what Harrison wanted her to know.

"In the last three years Harrison seemed to have more cash," she went on, staring around the white room. "We redecorated the whole house and added the pool. You know a town planner's salary is modest, Ms. Rossi. The house is our main possession, and we still have a mortgage on it, but Harrison was not at all concerned about selling it before our pending divorce. He was to pay off the mortgage. He gave this house to me as a part of the divorce settlement and purchased a new condo unit on the beach in South Bimini."

She folded her lips and stared at the closed drapes, her mind elsewhere. "Harrison rarely had late-hour calls at home for the last twenty-eight years," she said, her eyes turning back to me. "It was only three years ago that the phone started to ring at two and three o'clock in the morning a couple of times a week. At first I thought it was one of his woman friends." She moved to the edge of her seat, still staring at me. "But once I saw Harrison get off the phone in a sweat and furiously angry. He was swearing under his breath. This never happened before, Ms. Rossi. A couple of times I answered the phone and heard a tough-sounding male voice on the other end."

She paused. "Every once in a while, he'd ask me if I thought anybody was watching me, following me. When I asked why, he didn't give me any answers. I know that in the last few years, Harrison didn't play by the book. He ruined himself," she said with sincere feelings for Harrison. "He was once an idealistic man. At least, I thought so. But he considered himself a failure for not being financially independent at his age. Some in town looked down on him. There's a lot of money in Wilton and a lot of snobbery to go with it, Ms. Rossi."

She stopped for a second, her eyes far away once again. "Alcohol grew to be the answer, his favorite companion. The three-martini lunches were followed by cocktails before dinner, wine during dinner, after dinner drinks and then nightcaps. No matter what I said, it didn't make an impression. Once he started to age, he began to seek young women to make himself feel young. At first, I thought it was a mid-life crisis ..."

She returned her gaze to me as if remembering that I was there.

"When you find out anything, please let me know," she said, cutting off her train of thought. She took a deep breath and returned to her former haughty demeanor. She leaned back into the cushion of the white couch, her silk sapphire blouse gleaming against the white. "Harrison once called you a tenacious reporter," she said. "He credited you for some significant changes in town."

"Let me make this clear to you, Ms. Rossi, I don't think Harrison killed Maddy or anybody else. That would take a spine." She was again sitting at the edge of her seat. "I'm fairly sure he was involved in something illegal and that it somehow cost him his life, but I'll be the last one to say anything about it." She stared at me.

"His reputation as a town planner was above reproach," she continued. "Nobody in town is inquiring about any malfeasance, Ms. Rossi, including me. I've got my children in mind. Harrison was a good husband to me for many years and a good father to them. I don't want them to think I betrayed him. For all I know, Harrison died to protect us."

I was again stunned by Mrs. Hayden. What did she know? What did she think Harrison was mixed up in?

"I have every intention of letting the police know about Harrison's plans to meet Maddy Tuesday night," she said with a shrug of her beautiful shoulders. "Everything else, Ms. Rossi, as we agreed is off the record."

"I understand, Ellen," I said. I waited for a second before I asked her the question that was most on my mind. "Have you ever heard of a Miami company called National Developers, Inc.?"

Ellen Hayden gazed long and hard at me. Then she shook her head from side to side as if to say she would not go anywhere near my question about National Developers. After thanking her and again offering sympathy for the loss of her husband, I let myself out of the Hayden household.

I rushed to my car, hell bent on finding out more about National Developers. They could be the lynchpin between the two murders. But once I got down to Route 7, I realized how hungry I was and recalled that Jerry might drop by. I decided to stop at the Village Market and pick up some Italian bread. Besides, I was sensing that it was going to be a very long day. After eating, I planned to write down some quotes from Mrs.

Hayden and Sarah, find out about National Developers, and then I'd go through the whole case thus far.

Go over everything.

Twenty-Nine
The Kiss

I pulled into the driveway and decided I wouldn't say anything to Jerry about Maddy's note and National Developers until I knew more. After all, I told myself, Mrs. Hayden promised to call the detectives about Maddy meeting Harrison at Cider Mill. The rest was off the record.

I got out of the car and unlocked the front door. Once inside I actually welcomed the knotty pine that covered much of the downstairs walls. I took off my boots and outerwear, leaving everything on the chair near the door, and rushed into the kitchen. I grabbed a stainless steel pot in the cabinet under the stove and a bowl of *pasta fagioli* from the refrigerator.

I placed a large wedge of Italian bread in the oven. As the aroma of the heating soup started to waft through the air, I heard a knock on the door. Jerry walked in and took off his boots. He greeted me with a big grin, as usual, as he walked across the living room. But then he shook his head in disapproval and mentioned that the door had been left unlocked.

"Guess I forgot in my rush to put on some soup for us. It's not automatic yet, locking the door," I said.

"You got *pasta fagioli* for me, too?" he said as he sat down with a big smile at the end of the dining table and shed his coat, hat and gloves. The savory smells of the light tomato sauce with the celery, cannelloni beans and elbow macaroni filled the air. On the sunless winter day, the soup seemed as necessary as an IV drip.

Ten minutes later we ravaged the piping hot soup ladled into deep white bowls set on saucers. We sat close together on the bench at the south end of the long oak table and dipped thick slices of crusty Italian bread into the hot soup. I was glad I had taken the time to pick up the fresh bread on the way home.

"This is so delicious," Jerry said as he placed a large spoonful in his mouth. "Glad you became a vegan," he added, smiling.

"Yeah, puts a whole new slant on getting to a man through his stomach," I said. "Don't forget, I was a vegetarian when you met me."

I was holding back the flood of questions until after lunch, but Jerry read my mind between spoonfuls of soup and bites of bread.

"At this point we need to establish a connection between Mr. Hayden's and Maddy Trowbridge's murders," he said, "in addition to the obvious fact that both victims were employed by the town and worked in the Planning and Zoning Department. That's our primary goal. Freemont still says he's innocent," he said between lots of "mmms" and digging in his bowl. "We offered him a reduced sentence if he talked, but he said he had nothing to offer. We've actually found no evidence to dispute his alibi or his story. We even found the shopping cart that Freemont claimed he had found the stolen goods in, and it had his fingerprints on it. I'm beginning to believe the guy. His girlfriend, Janet Goldridge, seems an honest person. Freemont is fortunate to have her backing him. She continues to swear he was with her at the time of the murder."

He went to the stove and helped himself to a refill. I was grateful that I routinely cooked on the weekend to have nutritious food during the week. If ever we needed good food, it was now, I thought, watching Jerry ladle out some more soup. Neither one of us was sleeping well or for any length of time. Again, my parents came to mind. I loved cooking for them, too, I thought, staring at Jerry eating. It was such a simple pleasure to cook for someone I cared for.

"We did get a ballistics report," he said, having filled his bowl to the top. "The bullet that killed Mrs. Trowbridge came from the Glock found in Freemont's apartment, but we've got no fingerprints except for Freemont's." Jerry shook his head in dismay.

My elbow was on the table, and I was leaning on my fist. My eyes grew heavy. My stomach was full. Why did I ever sit down and get comfortable? "Jerry," I said, sitting up straight and shaking off the tiredness. "Why aren't you going to Bimini today? I'm surprised Al isn't sending you there."

"That's the real purpose of this visit. I was hoping I'd catch you," he said, returning to the table. "The Chief wants me to leave tonight. He spoke to officials in South Bimini. There's a spirit of cooperation, and he wants me to jump on it before they change their minds. Can you get away?"

With the case unfolding as it was, I had no intention of leaving. "Well, that leaves me out. I'm convinced that I'm better off here right now," I said, thinking of researching the Miami company. "I also have to cover Maddy's wake." I studied his handsome face and wished Bimini had worked out. "Need a ride to the airport?"

"No, the department's taking care of that, but I'll miss you," he said, staring into my eyes to bring home his message.

"When's your flight?"

"At eight."

Jerry leaned over and kissed me on the cheek. "My little *cannoli,*" he whispered jokingly. "I was thinking of mixing some business with pleasure, but then, maybe a murder investigation might not set the right atmosphere. It'll be a hurried trip, but I'll miss you." He gave me another kiss, this time on the lips. "Delicious," he said.

"Vegans taste better," I said, repeating what he often said to me.

I looked at his thirty-six-year-old face and saw no signs of age, unlike those I saw on my own. "Jerry, since veganism makes you look younger, why don't you start eating meat again so that you can look older?" I joked. "I can continue eating vegan so I look younger, and we'll close the eleven-year age gap."

As I kidded Jerry about our age difference, I was considering all the things we have in common. It was the first time in my life I had met someone that I connected with on so many levels. That connection was obvious on our first date. I also thought that our age difference would not even be discussed if our ages were reversed.

He chuckled and put down his soupspoon. We were sitting inches from each other, but he put his face in mine. "Ros, you're beautiful, you know that. You'll stay beautiful, but did you ever think that someone could love you for more than your looks?" he said, staring into my eyes.

It was the first time either of us had mentioned the word "love."

Since our first date there had been strong chemistry, but it wasn't physical attraction that made me think we'd have a lasting union. It wasn't as though we had bonded or fallen in love at first sight either. We were in each other's element. We could do absolutely nothing, just sit on a couch together as we were doing now, and it was fun. We were sitting around, having a bowl of soup in the afternoon sun, and it was great.

I got up and put some Motown music on, keeping the volume low and soft. Stevie Wonder's "Key of Life" album filled the quiet air with its melodies as Jerry and I ate in silence. I thought of how Jerry had introduced me to *Saturday Night Live* and how we'd talked about the comedy of Mel Brooks, Gene Wilder and so many more entertainers during the last three months. We'd repeat iconic lines from movies. Dancing to Michael Jackson's music at a Stamford disco was a typical Friday or Saturday night treat I'd introduced Jerry to. That's, of course, when we weren't working on a murder case. As Stevie Wonder's music filled the room, I thought of the many artists Jerry had introduced me to, the Temptations, and the Dells, while I had always loved music from Elvis to Bach. We were both diehard Democrats, which was good for a lot of laughs, especially over Reagan's trickle-down economics. Our favorite authors, Gabriel Garcia Marquez and Tolstoy and many others, played roles in our conversations. And nature: the sunsets, the changing seasons, the birds and by all means the animals, not to mention Jerry's vegan food. Photographs of suffering animals in factory farms and labs had turned Jerry off eating animals and using animal products a while ago, as it had me.

It was a major relief and a near miracle to meet someone I didn't have to explain my beliefs to, I reflected as Jerry and I consumed the healthy soup. Once people know, once they see the pictures I saw as a reporter, read what I read, things would change.

"Okay," I said breaking the peaceful silence. "I see that my meat-for-aging theory isn't going anywhere. If the truth be known, you like looking younger than me."

"If the truth be known, I don't look younger than you, Rossi," he said shaking his head. "When I first met you I thought you were in your late twenties. Your looks belie your age."

"My vegetarian diet gave me back about fifteen years," I said without exaggeration. "Jerry, I might get sick, and that will be that."

"Ros, I might get sick, and that will be that."

That comment made me chuckle with relief, for there was so much truth in it.

Ten peaceful Stevie Wonder minutes later, we headed for the door. I couldn't wait to get to the newsroom and find the info on National Developers.

We stepped onto the cement landing outside the front door. I made sure the door was locked. I was about to wish Jerry a good trip to Bimini when he wrapped his arms around my waist and drew me to him. He leaned me back like a flower stem bent by the wind in a full-bodied embrace.

My arms went limp on either side of me as he leaned over me, crushing my body to him passionately. Then his moist lips were on mine, his eyes closed, our bodies folded into one another. When his lips parted from mine, Jerry placed me upright again and dropped his arms. He stared at me silently for a few seconds. Neither of us spoke.

We couldn't take our eyes off each other. I watched as he climbed into his truck and heard the engine start. He backed out of the driveway with his eyes still half on me, half on the driveway. He backed into the street and hesitated in front of the house, gazing at me intently for another second before he shifted into gear and drove off.

I was thinking of the many men I had known, only two of them seriously. Early on, I was betrayed, and trust got to be a lasting issue. Until now. Jerry was so good to the core. It was very possible that I could trust him.

Inside my own car, I stepped on the gas and backed out of the drive onto Sugarloaf, still preoccupied with the kiss. It was the kind of kiss that is acted out in movies by magnificent actors playing characters such as Scarlet O'Hara and Rhett Butler. It was a kiss depicted in paintings, like the one in which the handsome violinist steals a kiss from the beautiful pianist. What was that one called? Although Jerry and I had had our romantic moments, this one was a revelation. It was as though any guards he or I might have had up to that point to protect our emotions from each other had come crashing down with the kiss.

I took the left onto Olmstead Hill Road and then made the right onto Route 7, heading into the building traffic, his kiss still on my lips.

Thirty
National Developers, Inc.

Everyone was present, and peace was restored to the newsroom. Even the phones had calmed down. Wiltonians were either in shock from the announcement of Harrison's death, satisfied with the Chief's progress report, or didn't think Harrison's death relevant because he was killed in South Bimini.

I didn't have a clue.

I sat down and took another few minutes to meditate, to settle myself. I looked at the pine wood table. I gazed at Evan at his desk and at Frank and Dylan writing on either side of me to get anchored to my surroundings, to the present. They were all deadly quiet except for the tapping of computer keys. Tomorrow was Maddy's wake. I realized a pall had settled over the newsroom. They were bracing themselves. I heaved a sigh. Life as we presently knew it was rushing in.

I dialed information in slow mo, still reluctant to let go of the crystallizing, incredibly romantic moment I'd shared with Jerry. The truth was that I didn't know Jerry had it in him. He didn't seem very romantic. The kiss proved otherwise. After getting the Miami Realtors Association's telephone number, I dialed it, and a receptionist answered.

"I'm thinking of buying a condo, and National Developers owns the land," I said, my voice sounding like I was waking from a dream. "Do you have any information on them?"

"Of course. Where are you calling from?"

"Wilton, Connecticut."

There was a moment of silence. "That would explain it then."

"Pardon?"

"Well there's been a recent exposé in the *Miami Herald* about National Developers and Edgar L. DeMarco Senior. and Junior."

"Can you tell me, are they still in business?"

"Oh, of course. National Developers is a large company with real estate holdings across the country. They build condominiums and shopping malls."

"Then what was the exposé about?"

"Well, I'd rather just send you a copy. We have plenty on hand. In fact, we copied the article due to high demand. It's a service we offer realtors. I'd be glad to send you a copy. You're the first to call from out of town."

My feet were finally firmly set on the ground. "Can't you just tell me the gist of it?" I begged.

"We've been told not to repeat what's in the article, although this is a reliable and excellent newspaper."

Egads. "Okay. Well can you mail it ASAP?"

"I'll mail it this afternoon. You'll get it in three or four days."

"Okay. I might be dead by then, but go ahead. Really, thank you. You've been very helpful. You could have just told me zero. So thanks."

I was about to give her my address and hang up. "Oh, wait a minute. Can you tell me who wrote the article?"

"Sure, let's see. It's a Greg Himes."

After I gave the woman my name and address and disconnected, I couldn't dial Information fast enough for the *Miami Herald* number. My fingers actually shook as I dialed. I was finally fully engaged in the here and now. Greg Himes, however, wasn't in, but he would get back to me within the hour, I was told. I turned my attention to my stories and began writing.

At 10:00 that night, without a call back from Greg Himes, I drove home with my eyes once again on the rearview mirror, looking for signs of the black sedan. I needed to eat some soup in peace, relive the kiss once again and sit in my kitchen, dreaming of a life with Jerry. Fifteen minutes later I rushed back to the paper without the slightest chance of finishing up my stories.

At 11:30 I packed it in for the night, leaving my colleagues working. I was operating on fumes, but my eyes remained on the rearview mirror all the way home. I again entered a dark house, but at least the door had been locked. I locked the door now behind me. Then I took off my boots, hung up my coat, placed my hat and gloves on the shelf, rushed to the kitchen to the cutlery drawer and headed straight up the stairs to bed, locking the bedroom door. How strange that I felt I was going to bed alone, I thought. The house's quiet did feel a bit eerie. After uttering a few grateful words of prayer and asking for Jerry's safety and my own, I started to float off to sleep with the blissful remains of the day, the memory of the kiss, the warmth of the comfortable bed, the soft, chilly pillow—and the peeling knife I gripped in my right hand under the pillow.

Thirty-One
The Uninvited

The noise came from the back of the house.

My hand slid under the pillow to search for the knife. When I located it, I gripped the wooden handle as tightly as possible. I turned the light on next to the bed and snapped erect at the side of the bed, my heart pounding. I glanced at the round face of my clock. It was 5:30 Friday morning and still pitch black.

I got out of bed as quietly as possible and unlocked the bedroom door. I stepped into the dark hallway, where my toes brushed a hard object on the floor. I bent down.

It was a knife, one of my own, a duplicate of the one I held I my hand. It had been left at my door like a calling card.

With the two knives gripped in my left hand, I rushed down the stairs to the front door. I stood there and heard nothing but silence and sensed that the house was empty. I tried the brass knob on the door. It was still locked as it had been last night. I ran through the narrow hall to the back door off the kitchen. Still locked.

Then I headed downstairs to the basement, where I hadn't gone last night. There it was: one very accessible window. It was unlocked and faced the backyard. A dry well surrounded the window on the outside. Someone could squat down on solid ground, disappear from view and easily push the window in and slip into the basement. I turned on the basement lights and sucked in air while I closed the latch on the window and checked the others.

Back up in the kitchen I flooded the outside with lights but kept the kitchen dim. The knife left at the bedroom door was still in my hands. I wrapped the thing up in a paper towel to give it to Jerry as a coming home present. Maybe.

In an effort to regain some normalcy, I grabbed a pot from the bottom cabinet under the telephone and put water in it for oatmeal. Meanwhile, I was thinking, what do they want with me? How do I threaten them? What do they think I know?

I wasn't really frightened. I was numb. If anybody wanted me dead, they'd had ample opportunity last night. I grabbed the box of oatmeal from the cabinet, poured some into the pot and began to stir as I gazed out the back window. It was still dark. Even the car chase incident seemed to have been a scare tactic, since the man in the black suit and white shirt had never returned. As I poured the oatmeal into a bowl, my hands trembled. I did feel violated. Someone, maybe a hired gun, a hit man, had broken into my home. Maybe it had been the same person who killed Maddy and Harrison.

But I was not calling the cops. There would be questions, a report, and the whole morning or more wasted, and the violator would still be on the loose. I just didn't have the time. Jerry had told the cops to watch the house, and look what good that had done me. Besides, my thought process was still moving forward. This little scare tactic was just another element to consider.

Stalkers or not, I needed to slow the pace. I'd resume my daily run. A touch of normalcy was definitely required, and a run would help me think better.

The phone rang. It was Jerry's mother Lillian. She sounded so unnerved that I barely recognized her voice.

Thirty-Two
The Run

"Rossi, the neighborhood boy who helps Jerry take care of the animals, he's sick," Lillian pleaded. "He just called. You know, yesterday Jerry rescued two sheep? Two big friendly girls. I've got to clean their pen, lay some new straw and feed them. Then there's the goat and the three chickens, the rooster and the dogs."

"The chickens, the rooster and the two sheep?" I replied.

"He got the hens yesterday, too, on the way to the airport. They fell off one of those factory farming trucks heading to the slaughterhouse. Jerry says they're laying hens. My God, what horrible condition they're in. They don't look like hens, and one's a rooster. An officer brought them here after he dropped Jerry off at the airport. I never met him before, he must be new. Jerry's working twenty-four hours a day on this murder, taking a half-hour nap here and there, and still comes home with stray animals. I think he landed in Bimini a couple of hours ago. Hope he got some sleep on the plane."

"Lillian, I'll come over. I'll be there about 8:00 a.m." I wasn't going to give up my run.

"Rossi, don't tell Jerry this because, well, you know how he is. He'll worry too much. But I think somebody was moving around the place during the night. The animals were making all kinds of noise. The dogs inside the house were barking half the night, too," she sighed, indicating that she'd had little to no sleep. She hesitated a minute as if to rethink her remarks.

"You think maybe it was just that the chickens and the rooster are in the same barn with the sheep and a dog and a goat?"

I started to laugh with relief, thinking that the different species together in the barn probably had something to do with the ruckus. Lillian joined me.

Back in my bedroom I grabbed some old jeans and sneakers for the barn and put on my cut-off jeans for the run. Cut-off jeans offer me a sense of freedom, a much-needed sensation. Downstairs I slipped into my sky blue ski jacket, dark blue knitted hat and thick navy ski gloves.

I was definitely ready to feel some freedom, but instead of putting on my Saconys, I carried them and wore boots, determined to investigate the break-in. I made sure I locked the front door, then grabbed the brass doorknob and pulled on it to test it. I set my sneakers down on the cement slab at the front door and headed to the back of the house with a flashlight in hand. The basement window's half-moon well, about two feet deep, was covered with snow-laden leaves that had been disturbed by the intruder. I twisted to look behind me. The triangular light of my flashlight swept the thick woods behind the house, which was part of the nine-acre set-aside. There was a trail from the driveway to the house with indiscernible footprints, much like the trail at the murder scene on School Road. No fresh footprints were evident except for my own. The sandy road made it impossible to detect either footprints or tire marks leading to the driveway.

A heavy sigh escaped me as I picked up the sneakers and headed to the car. I was feeling like a sitting duck. My usual jogging routine on Pimpewaug, down by the train station, was out of the question—in fact, stupid. It was not only predictable, it was too dark and deserted at this time in the morning. DeForest Road off Ridgefield Road would be good.

The historic section of town would be safer and occupy my traumatized mind. I had slipped a steak knife into my pocket. I stored it under the passenger seat.

My eyes strayed to the rearview mirror all the way down Sugarloaf, Olmstead Hill Drive, and onto Route 7. I took a right onto Ridgefield Road by the village center. A few minutes later I took a left onto DeForest Road, continually glancing at the rearview mirror.

Meanwhile, I was thinking, what do they want with me? How do I threaten them? What is it they think I know?

I parked on the shoulder of DeForest Road, a half-block off Ridgefield Road. The roads were virtually empty. No sidewalks or curbs, of course. DeForest Road was also slightly covered with the clay colored sand left over from a recent snowstorm.

I got out of the car and put my foot against a tire to bend forward and stretch my calves and Achilles tendon. My body was still exhausted; the lack of sleep since Tuesday night was registering. Last night I had gotten a good five hours, but it wasn't enough. I cut the stretching short and started to run. Dawn was breaking, turning the clouds ahead gray. The invigorating morning air brushed against my legs and face. My thighs in the cut-offs were freezing and turning red, but that would change when the circulation started to flow. The temperature hovered around a chilly but bearable thirty-five degrees with no wind. It felt delicious. It felt like life. My blood was pumping. I was alone, at peace and jogging. I sighed with relief.

It felt great to get into the run, stretch my legs and feel the earth beneath my feet. My heart and body were soon pumping away. The fresh air brushing my cheeks continued to lift my needy spirits.

DeForest Cemetery was too far for this run, I told myself. I'd just do two miles, not four, I decided, gazing at the woods that lined the road on both sides. Eliud Deforest, one of the many members of the DeForest family, had purchased two hundred fifty acres on what is now called DeForest Road. A blue hydrangea bush, large and sturdy as a fruit tree, revealed the age of the cemetery. In summer the robust blue blossoms draped over the weathered, rounded gravestones of the cemetery, reminding me that everyone buried there had once been as alive as the bush. As I listened to my footsteps on the sandy road, I recalled how I had examined the gravestones one spring and read the dates and names that time had not erased. Some of the stones dated back as far as the late 1700s, at least. On close inspection I realized that too many small children had been buried in the DeForest cemetery, evidence of one of the greatest tolls on the early generations of Wiltonians.

A few minutes into the run, I thought I heard footsteps behind me similar to an echo. The steps were going at the same rate of speed as mine. I stopped and turned around but saw nothing but the sandy road bordered by snow and the woods. I resumed running. After a while I again heard the echoing footsteps.

I stopped running again, and they stopped. God, it had to be my nerves, I told myself.

I focused on the wood's understory, the feathery branches of leafless brushes in between towering bare oaks, maples, birch and evergreens. The tall tree trunks, one after the other, line up, and stretch deep into the woods. So peaceful, I thought, as I looked at them and listened to my footsteps. The first warnings of winter are always an autumnal fragrance in the air, nutty and sweet, followed by the fall of the magnificent leaves. Then during the long winters, the trees wait for spring like the rest of us. Again, I heard an echo, definitely an echo of my footsteps, I told myself, nothing more.

In about fifteen minutes I reached the crest of DeForest's hill. It led to a misty horizon with a hazy, light blue sky behind. It was like running into a dream. To my left stood a colonial house, hundreds of years old, white with black shutters and a three-foot picket fence surrounding it. It was painted by time, every slat tinted with history. It seemed like I had run back in time to Revolutionary days and before, when the house had been built. On Independence Day 1776, the house had been fifty years old with family members who served in the war for freedom. An American flag drooped lifelessly next to the front door. Although nothing but the haze was on the horizon, I peered ahead, expecting a returning Revolutionary soldier to emerge out of the morning mist, returning home from the war. My eyes refused to leave the front door as I jogged by. The date over it read 1726.

Jogging past the crest of the hill and heading downhill, I saw similar looking homes. About five hundred homes in town still survived the test of time. They never failed to transport me back to the country's beginnings with a glance.

I realized my struggles with the present made the quiet of the past inviting; its conflicts were already settled. I listened to the rhythm of my steps on the sandy road and realized that my legs were no longer cold. At the moment, I didn't hear the echo.

I recalled, in the quiet of the early morning, that Wilton had been one of the first towns to join and then lead the Revolution. The thirty-one petitioners for the Wilton Parish had been born right here in Wilton, and some of them had lived in these very houses.

Neighbor had turned against neighbor during the war, split by their different and passionate allegiances. Some of Wilton's few loyalists fled to Canada to escape retribution from Patriots, who could be their next-door neighbors. As I jogged past the historic homes, I recalled that some were burned to the ground in the heat of the Revolution. Some courageous former loyalists, however, returned home, successfully integrated and later ran for public office in Wilton, obviously forgiven for their lapse of judgment.

I couldn't stop thinking of the mystery of Maddy's death and why anybody would want to harm her. When her ancestor Jonathan Wood lived, the Meeting House of the Congregational Church was the place where everyone's lives intertwined. A common faith brought people together, and so did a common fear. Every town and parish in the Connecticut Colony had been required to form a volunteer army. Military training occurred on a regular basis. The militia's officers were considered some of the town's most revered citizens.

This early morning run was supposed to be my mental break, I reminded myself, but as I passed the historic homes I sensed that another kind of destructive force had moved into town the night we had found Maddy's body under that tree.

Whatever form it took, it threatened the town. It was threatening my freedom right now. I kept listening for the footsteps. I'm going to turn around and look once again over my shoulder, I told myself. Isn't that what Maddy had done for the last two weeks of her life?

Nobody.

I had to get back anyway. Jerry's brood was waiting, no doubt hungry and thirsty. I did my three-sixty and didn't see anything suspicious up ahead, and I heaved a sigh of relief. The sunrise was coloring the clouds an uplifting rosy pink, but I was unable to lose the nagging sensation that I was being followed. Was it the knife left at my door or the car chase?

As I jogged back down sandy and snow bordered DeForest Road, lined with tall bare trees and snow covered woods, I was grateful to spot my car in one piece, up ahead on the side of the road where I had left it. Another heavy sigh of relief escaped me, and I threw my head back, glad I had taken the run even if I had imagined someone following me the whole way. My body felt good, worked out, always a satisfying feeling. My legs were no longer cold. A run always jump-started my energy, never more so than when I was tired. I was even feeling a little relaxed for the first time since Tuesday night as I headed toward the driver's side of the car.

A thin black silk ribbon was tied to the door handle.

Thirty-Three
Friday Morning at Jerry's

I sighed with relief as I reached Jerry's long, narrow driveway in the Georgetown section of Wilton, again checking most of the way for the black sedan. Nobody was going to chase me down this road. My heart might even stop pumping like mad. My eyes flashed to the glove compartment, where I had stashed the black ribbon for safekeeping. A welcome home gift for Jerry, I thought.

I shook my head, thinking that when I had first spotted Maddy under that black spruce, I'd had the sensation that this was only the beginning of the nightmare. How right I was.

The driveway seemed like a long alleyway, because it was bordered by two solid fences. The quarry's solid, seven-foot-high picket fence was on the right side. To the left was Jerry's six-foot-high chicken wire fence, backed with thick woods.

Bumping along the graveled road with its share of holes and mole hills, I recalled Jerry's words, "Nobody will bother you at my house." I gazed with relief at his safe house. It was freshly painted, a gleaming white two-story with black shutters and doors. It smacked of days when life had been simpler. The small covered porch faced west so you could enjoy the sunset while sitting in a couple of rocking chairs. They just don't make porches like that anymore, I was thinking with my white-knuckled grip on the steering wheel. The porch also faced the new red barn about a hundred feet away. In the center were two giant graceful red oaks; it was pure Currier and Ives this morning.

Snow sat in the crooks of the oaks and the sugar maples and rested on the boughs of the evergreens that surrounded the house. The snow coated some of the wispy, leafless understory of sassafras, striped maple, junipers, hollyhocks and oleanders. I recalled Jerry telling me that red-bellied woodpeckers love oak woods. He had spotted the woodpeckers, but they are far from common in the area.

Jerry told me he called the huge evergreens that dotted his land "mother trees," for throughout the winter, red cardinals, sparrows and doves nested in them. Each had their own section. They were protected by the thick bows in severe winter temperatures and driving snowstorms.

It had been love at first sight for Jerry when he'd driven up to the place five years ago. The modest house sat in the center of eight acres of snow-covered land and needed a lot of work, which he knew he could handle. A small field in the back of the house to the east would be great for grazing, even during the winter when the snow melted in spots. The soil provided ample richness for summer and fall fruits and vegetables, and established apple, pear and cherry trees were on either side of the house.

He had fenced in all eight acres. Five years of his labor prepared the place for its new dwellers. It was perfect for his soul, he had confided in me, that part of him that wanted to see harmony on the earth. I could hear his voice as he told me that he was a vegan because he respected all living creatures. On this farm life for animals was exactly the way he wanted it.

I drove up to the end of the driveway and parked in front of the garage, a freestanding building to the right of the house. I figured that Lillian's car was parked inside. I stepped out onto the drive and slammed the car door harder than usual. I was tired and getting annoyed. The last thing I needed was to care for farm animals this morning on top of everything else. All of a sudden I wanted to smack Jerry in the head for rescuing animals while he was in the middle of a murder case and off to Bimini, even with that fantastic kiss still lingering on my lips.

The animals were restless inside the barn, and the dogs in the house had begun to bark as I drove up.

The gate of the chicken wire fence opened easily. Apprehensive about what I'd find in the barn, I walked on the shoveled cement walk to the front door, then headed across the front yard on the footpath to the barn. I remembered that under the snow was just a dirt path made by walking to and from the house to the barn because Jerry liked it. My eyes followed the path that circled around the oaks a tad and then straightened out again to head to the large barn door.

At the north end of the barn was the hay and grain, fenced in and protected by an overhead. I picked up a pitchfork leaning against the barn and shoveled grain into one of three metal troughs that sat about twenty feet in front of the barn, put hay in the next trough, then filled the last with water from the hose.

Now it was time to actually open the huge barn door. It swung open easily. Many sets of impeaching eyes welcomed me from the shadows, lit by the sun rays that spread through the barn from the east window. Barks, baas, and a chorus of other pleas spoken in several tongues reached my ears, all pitiful and each one louder than the other. I felt guilty for my run.

The eyes stared straight at me from the four stalls against the west wall. The terrified chickens and rooster at the northwest corner of the barn were to my left. They clucked freakishly and began to flit against the wall, hugging the wall, walking up and down and peering at me in their terror.

Lillian was right; they were pitiful. You had to stare hard at them to recognize that they were chickens. Their combs flopped and were white and bluish instead of the vibrant red combs of healthy hens. Bone showed through the skin of some of their featherless wings and I could feel tears sting my eyes. Their beaks were but snubs from being burned off and I wondered how they were able to eat and drink with them.

The shaggy, light gray healthy sheep in the first stall to my right made me smile with relief. At first sight, the names Gloria and Doris popped into my head. The two issued heartbreaking "baas." They looked so good natured, I thought. Their faces hung over the stall door. They were so large, they reminded me of ponies. Their sleepy, golden brown eyes trimmed in black begged me to come to them. No doubt they wanted to know what the heck was going on, wondering who I was and where was Jerry?

A strong desire to sink my hands in their shaggy coats took hold, but I resisted. Jerry had said they were large Katahdin ewes bred for meat. Jerry often helped out the local farmer who couldn't afford to keep them but didn't have the heart to send them to slaughter. No doubt the farmer's need was even more dire when he handed over his lovable one-year-olds to Jerry yesterday. If I remembered correctly, the transaction wasn't to occur until spring.

Nanny, the goat, and Oreo, an Australian sheepherding dog, were in the last stall to my left, on the southern end. They usually roamed the barn freely at night, but Jerry or Lillian had probably put them in a stall to keep them from the birds. Oreo was walking around in circles and jumping occasionally, issuing sporadic whines and spreading the straw that Jerry had scattered on the floor for hygiene and comfortable sleeping.

I released Nanny and Oreo first, then the sheep. Nanny headed straight out of the barn to the feeding trough, and the sheep followed while Oreo rushed to the house for his food after relieving himself by the convenient oak trees. The sheep ate, their long necks helping them to reach down into the trough, but when they chewed they periodically looked at me with what I chose to regard as affection and appreciation.

Bellies full, the sheep were now walking out in the open, and I decided that they reminded me of llamas, not ponies. Their thick, tall necks were fully stretched as they eagerly ventured to explore the acres of fenced-in frozen land. They walked slowly around the trees and then went past the house.

I realized they were walking east toward the morning sun. The dogs followed them respectfully, and I chuckled. Nanny and Oreo joined the six dogs that Lillian had just allowed out of the house, Max, Bella, Sam, Buddy, Tao and Lindy. The very tame pack of dogs, mainly medium-sized and smaller, didn't seem to present a threat to the sheep. Oreo heeded to his natural herding instincts and automatically adopted the sheep and took charge. The little pack of canines, their curiosity coupled with territorial rights, trailed, sniffing after the huge and tolerant sheep. The sheep gazed with respect at the watchful Oreo, who circled them while issuing the other dogs a warning in the form of stares and body language.

I returned to the barn thinking I'd better check on the terrified birds. They scattered frantically when I re-entered the barn, uttering comforting words. The corner door on the north end led to a fenced-in area for the birds with a wire fence overhead to prevent predators from climbing in and keep the birds from flying out. I walked out to the area that Jerry had shoveled completely. I filled a water tray and admired the thick, short cherry tree for perching. Jerry had thought of everything for the pathetic little things. Dust bathing and scratching for feed in the morning sun were available for the little hens and rooster if they could ever calm down. It was only last night that Jerry had found them on I-95 after they had fallen off a truck, I reminded myself.

Suddenly, I regretted wanting to hit Jerry in the head. He had prepared for the animals, and they'd actually fallen into his lap, according to Lillian's story. As for rescuing animals while being in the middle of a murder case and off to Bimini, I knew what he'd say: "It's never convenient."

I grabbed the rake standing in the corner of the barn and a plastic green garbage barrel outside and embarked on the morning clean-up. Lillian's tired eyes thanked me as she emerged from the house and handed me a cup of steaming tea. She grabbed another rake from a corner. A half-hour later we were done. I'd return at about sunset for the evening roundup and feeding, I told Lillian to her immense relief. She had left her own quiet little place to come to the farm here and help out her son, I thought, gazing at the exhausted woman. Then I recalled how Jerry looked after his mother and her property only a few blocks away.

"Let's hope there are no accidents in the meantime," Lillian said as she walked back toward the house. "With this many animals, there is always something."

Thirty-Four
Greg Himes

"Ms. Rossi?" Greg Himes asked. "What are you looking for?"

It was 9:30 a.m. I had reached my nice, calm space on the long table in the newsroom, refreshed beyond words by shoveling excrement out of the barn. The labor in the fresh country morning air, the thankful glances of the animals and the hens and rooster who had worked their way through their terror to the sunny area outside pushed fears of my pursuers to some far off silo of my mind. I didn't even look for the black sedan, much, on the way to work.

I told Himes who I was and what I wanted. "I'm waiting for a copy of your exposé," I further explained. "I'll fill in the gaps if you'll just tell me why you did an article on National Developers." As I spoke I withdrew my yellow legal pad from under a pile of folders and rested it on my lap, pen in hand. "They built the first condominiums in town," I explained. "I know nothing about them."

There was a pregnant pause. "I don't like talking about them over the phone," he said. "Where are you calling from?

"I'm calling from the newsroom of the *Wilton Weekly*."

"Have you written anything about National Developers yet?"

"No, but I think I know where you're coming from. I'm pretty sure I'm being followed. I've been in a car chase. And last night a knife was left at my bedroom door."

"Call me back on a public phone."

He hung up.

Thirty-Five

Bimini

"Establishing a connection between the two murders is the main reason for this trip," Jerry had told Rossi in a telephone conversation before he left for JFK. That mission was on his mind when he had finally arrived, exhausted and bleary eyed, at 6:30 a.m. that Friday at the South Bimini airport. Delays at Kennedy had kept him waiting for hours,

It was still dark. The temperature was seventy degrees but expected to climb into the low eighties, according to the congenial pilot. Jerry spread his map over the steering wheel of his rented Jeep, looking for the Bimini Sands Beach Club and then Hayden's house in Port Royale. At nine o'clock at Hayden's house he was to meet a Detective Tyrone Miller from the South Bimini Police Station. He heaved a sigh and put the map on the passenger's seat. He had plenty of time. He turned on his bright lights when he drove out of the air field and located the road that led to the west side of the island. He rolled down the Jeep window and took a few good breaths of island air. The headlights illuminated the overgrown tangle of low-growing native coppice that lined the road. The thickets of hardwood trees and bushes intrigued him, but it was the sight of the palm trees a little farther along that made his muscles relax. He instantly missed Rossi.

If the case had anything to do with the planner's office where Rossi was sniffing around, she'd be in danger. He sighed again.

It was seven-thirty when he and the rising sun arrived at Port Royale. He drove straight to the Bimini Sands Beach Club while the sapphire and turquoise water sparkled under the solar beams. He had an hour and half to kill, so he found something to eat and headed to Hayden's house a few miles away in the cluster of homes known as Port Royale. After a few turns he found Hayden's winding gravel driveway. It led to a modest white ranch house that looked like it sat on a builder's acre. In the back yard, facing the ocean, was the swimming pool. He heard the rumble of another Jeep coming up the gravel driveway.

After introductions, Detective Tyrone Miller walked up to the white front door with two small square windows at the top. He ripped away the crime scene tape with one hand and dug into his pocket for a key with the other. He mentioned that he was using the key that had been found on Hayden's body. There was another key, which fit into the lock of the garage on the south side of the house, but they could get to the garage from the house, he told Jerry.

"Since there was no break-in we think the garage door was left unlocked. We found it that way when we first arrived."

They entered the modest living room with Miller saying that there had been a rise in robberies since the severe recession hit the island.

"The recession made some people desperate," he said. "Our tourism trade suffered a severe drop in numbers this year. We think it is likely that Mr. Hayden's death is a result of a bad economy and robbers that panicked. Overall, our crime rate has risen in the last year. People like Mr. Hayden have become more of a target lately," Miller revealed, turning to look at Jerry as he showed him around the house that was torn with hanging wires and empty spots where appliances once were. From the sliding glass doors of the living room

Miller pointed to the sweeping ocean view and the swimming pool.

"We think Mr. Hayden returned home, walked around to the back and entered the patio that Sunday evening, surprising the robbers," Miller said as he followed Jerry outside. "We think someone acting as a lookout struck Mr. Hayden from behind. Our coroner said that he was near death from the trauma to his brain before he hit the pool. He could have fallen into the pool from the blow, but it is more likely that they threw him into the pool. We couldn't pinpoint exactly where the body entered the pool. Whatever the case, drowning was the cause of death."

He went on. "For many Americans this is a vacation home. We think the perpetrators thought the house was empty for the weekend. We recently had several homes broken into while people were sailing on the Royal Bimini Cruise Line. A few weeks ago an employee was arrested for selling booking information. Many homes were robbed while people were on cruises. In Hayden's case they may have thought he was also on a cruise. The perpetrators did, however, take the precaution to station someone on the outside of the house."

"Did his neighbors hear or see anything?" Jerry gazed at the ocean, then turned around to see nothing but the short island trees and shrubs. No other house was in view.

"No," Miller said. "As you can see, the house is hidden from the road.

While standing in Hayden's bedroom, Miller said that among Harrison's few papers had been a checkbook with a copy of a withdrawal receipt for two hundred thousand dollars from a Bimini Island bank, a branch of the Empire Bank and Trust.

"You'll be able to examine the few financial papers when we go to the police station," he offered. "The withdrawal slip is there. It shows a zero balance and is dated November of 1982. No evidence of another bank account was left among Hayden's belongings. The Bimini branch of the Empire Bank and Trust went out of business about a year ago, just about when Mr. Hayden withdrew his money," he said. "We could find no evidence of a new account in Mr. Hayden's name at the new bank, the Bimini National Bank. No cash and no lockbox key were found in the condo. I think it's safe to assume that the robbers stole any cash lying around. Everybody thinks Americans are wealthy anyway. The robbers would search for cash."

In the closet were several printed summer shirts, summer slacks and a white linen suit, all brand new. The closet's top shelf was filled with packages of underwear, handkerchiefs and golf shirts. Why were they left behind?

He thought of Mrs. Trowbridge's gloves being taken and Rossi's theory that the missing gloves were evidence of a cover-up.

They drove back to the police department at the airport to look at the files. The year-old Empire Bank and Trust withdrawal receipt dated November 28, 1982, stared up at Jerry. Harrison must have always carried the slip on him. A few sales receipts for the new clothes, the real estate papers on the purchase of the forty-eight-thousand-dollar home, built ten years ago, and the sales receipt for his Jeep in the amount of a thousand dollars were included in the case file. Judging from the withdrawal slip, Hayden could afford to pay for the house and Jeep with cash.

Again, Jerry became aware of his gut tightening. A newly retired town planner making thirty-two thousand a year with four kids to educate, two yet in college, and a home in Wilton with a mortgage to pay off doesn't have two hundred thousand dollars sitting in his bank account. He doesn't pay cash for a house.

Jerry couldn't help but think back to Tuesday night, standing out in the bitter cold on School Road. He found himself in a total sweat, remembering Rossi urging him and Al to investigate P&Z. Seeing the withdrawal receipt gave credence to the bribery theory. Images of Rossi leafing through files at P&Z made him sweat more.

What else did Hayden have to peddle but his influence at the planner's office? He had spent the last twenty-eight years at the job. He had been highly influential in town. In a way he had been more influential than the first selectman, who came and went with the political tide.

A payoff also supplied a motive for the two killings and the connections he was searching for. It was reasonable to conclude that the murders were not coincidental, that two people employed at P&Z had been eliminated because they were either connected to, or witnesses to, underhanded dealings.

He'd catch the first flight or boat out of Bimini.

Thirty-Six
Timothy Esposito

I was wishing I could be on the beaches of Bimini with Jerry as I drove up Route 7, heading to Johnson's Funeral Parlor and the grief that waited inside. The bright side was it was common knowledge that murderers often attend the funerals of their victims.

For some mysterious reason my mind focused on Timothy Esposito. I was determined to corner him and ask him a few key questions. Perhaps it was that the Chief seemed to accept Esposito's opinion that everything was perfect at the planner's office. At any rate it was one of those journalistic hunches I had learned never to question.

The white Victorian building with the wide gingerbread porch that wrapped around the house looked even more graceful than I remembered. It sat atop a slight hill surrounded by snow. I started to tremble. This isn't about Maddy, I thought. The place is too familiar. A wave of grief swept through me, surprising me with its intensity. I took a couple of deep breaths to meditate, then clutched the cold steering wheel as a young man handling the endless incoming cars directed me to a parking space. I grabbed my yellow pad and shoulder satchel and rushed toward the line of people on the Victorian porch. The silent mourners were being funneled into the second viewing room on the right, no doubt Maddy's. I jumped ahead of the crowd to take a peek at the room.

Timothy Esposito was seated in the last seat on the left in the second row. I retook my place on the long line. Finally in the room, I noticed familiar faces from Wilton and town hall. It was a community coming together in the face of tragedy.

The open coffin was at the end of the wide center aisle that had a burgundy runner to catch the slush, salt and sand carried in on the bottom of boots. Given the long line, people briefly knelt to pay their respects and moved on. After ten minutes of passing slowly through the full viewing room and acknowledging many familiar faces, it was my turn to kneel on the black cushioned knee rest before the open coffin. Maddy's French blue silk dress lay against the white satin casket lining. Her pretty face was framed in the familiar prim hairstyle. Her expression remained blissful, as it had been that night. I recalled Jerry telling Al and me that she looked peaceful, that he didn't think she had seen it coming.

My hands, however, started to tremble and my knees tighten from fear. I remembered the apocalyptic sensations I'd experienced under the tree and realized the haunting feelings would remain until we found her murderer. I was weak kneed when I stood up. The bereaved and exhausted family behind me sat in Queen Anne chairs.

Arabella's dark eyes were fastened on me. I walked straight to her and caressed her shoulders, forgetting my fears. I could feel her body collapse under my touch. I pulled away gently and gazed into her eyes to see the tears spill out. I mumbled condolences and moved on to Mr. Trowbridge, his son, his pretty blonde wife and their two grandchildren, about five and six years old. They shrank in the huge chairs and appeared dazzled by the sea of people honoring their grandmother.

I walked to the back of the room to the wall that faced the center aisle, my eyes fixed on the back of Timothy Esposito. At eleven o'clock the funeral director stood before Maddy's casket and called the room to order. An Episcopal priest approached and led everyone in several prayers as if Maddy had died of natural causes.

Finally Mr. Trowbridge, looking even frailer than he had two days ago, stood humbly before his wife's casket in his black mourning clothes. In a weary voice he addressed all of us as we collectively held our breaths.

"This is an extraordinary outpouring of affection for my wife," he acknowledged. "Her death is a tragedy for all of us." He stared straight ahead at his family. "Maddy was a loving wife, mother and grandmother. She was the sun that warmed and guided us."

He fell silent for a second, then lifted his eyes from his family and stared ahead at all of us. "In town here she was known for her patriotism. Maddy wouldn't want me to talk about her. She'd expect me to know that. So in honor of my wife I'd like to read the speech she delivered at every Veteran's Day celebration on the town green."

The speech covered all the wars, including some names of those who had sacrificed in 1745, when France declared war on England. Then he moved on to the Revolutionary and Civil wars, WWI, WWII, Korea and Vietnam.

"Each year Maddy paid tribute to the fallen heroes of Wilton. She lived her life in respect for those families who built this town and fought for our freedom." He hesitated. "My wife's honorable and fruitful life ended in violence. Like those Maddy honored every Veteran's Day, I believe her to be a hero for her country. Someday I'm sure we'll learn that Maddy sacrificed her life for her beloved Wilton and for all the values she held dear."

He gazed down at the floor for a second to gather himself, then turned to the coffin that held his wife.

"Maddy, the love of my life, will be buried in Hillside Cemetery next to her cherished veterans."

The sound of people gulping down sobs swept the crowded room of bowed heads. Brushing away my own tears, I followed Esposito after he paid his last respects to the family and managed to squeeze through the crowd to the door. Once outside, he strode toward the porch.

"Tim, can I talk to you a moment?" I said, trailing behind him. He stopped, turned and looked impatiently at me.

"Of course," he said, smiling politely. His green eyes, shadowed by heavy brows, stared at me with thinly veiled annoyance seasoned with curiosity. His hand clutched the steps' white wooden railing. As usual, he was immaculately groomed. He was well built, thirty-four years old and of average height. His hatless head showed a thick mane of dark brown hair.

"Do you know when Harrison's wake or memorial will take place?" I asked, studying his face.

He stared at me for a second as if it were a new thought. "We haven't been told yet," he said quickly. "We'll be honoring Maddy and now Harrison in January." He shook his head as if sincerely disturbed by Harrison's death.

"Harrison's death came as such a shock. He was murdered Sunday, and Maddy was murdered two days later, the two of them dying violently," he said as if moved, his voice trailing off.

"Don't you think there's a connection between these crimes?" I asked.

He folded his lips together. The sun was shining in his eyes, lighting his thick eyelashes. A group came out of the funeral home, and he moved to the side of the steps to let them go by.

"I'll let the police decide what happened. It's out of my league. It does seem more an unfortunate coincidence than anything else," he said, blinking nervously. He took a step down the stairs and turned to look up at me, his clear green eyes glowing with sincerity. "My wife will be with me tomorrow at the cemetery. She's pregnant, and I didn't want her to be exposed to the crowds here."

Interesting, I thought as I looked back at him. Why would the town planner explain his wife's behavior to me? I'm just a lowly reporter. A political thing, no doubt. With that, he rushed down the stairs and was on his way. I remained on the porch because I wanted to extract more quotes from exiting mourners. I got my camera out of my satchel and began snapping.

Esposito's words, "an unfortunate coincidence," were burning inside me. I realized his opinion that the two murders were nothing more than coincidental would be the company line, the politically correct thing to say. Ann's warning that there could be a cover-up gained more credibility with Esposito's comments. His every word had seemed guarded. What was the man hiding?

This thought clung to me as I drove out of the parking lot and made a left onto Route 7 to head to Orem's diner. Clearly, as a reporter covering planning and zoning, I had an obligation to find out. Timothy Esposito was our town planner. It was my obligation to cover him. I was beginning to believe that my instincts were right once again and he was somehow involved in this crime.

Since Tuesday night, three trying days ago, when I had identified Maddy's body, I had doubted that I should be playing the role of detective, but now, as I gripped the cold steering wheel, I realized that I was fulfilling my role as an investigative reporter.

Thirty-Seven
Greg Himes

Although it was 1:30 p.m., the lunchtime crowd still filled Orem's Diner. Greg Himes' telephone number was written on the top of my yellow pad. I pulled out change from my coat pocket. It clanked on the small shelf in front of me. I slipped in a quarter and dialed, and the operator instructed me to deposit the correct amount of change. The phone was finally ringing.

"Are you using a public phone?" Himes' voice was emphatic and husky.

"I'm at a local diner."

"National Developers, Inc. is owned by Edgar L. DeMarco, Sr., who is under suspicion of having mob ties." He rattled on as if he knew exactly what he'd tell me. "DeMarco, Sr. deals in developing commercial properties, purchasing land and the building and development of major shopping malls throughout the United States with the help of his son, Edgar L. DeMarco, Jr.," he said and then took a breath. "As far as Wilton is concerned, National goes into small towns like yours where locals are unaware of the family's reputation. The DeMarcos hire local developers to handle the job, but they physically oversee every aspect of the project."

My yellow pad was against the wall of the booth. I frantically wrote every word, but I didn't believe what I heard.

"Pardon me?" I asked.

"You heard me correctly. DeMarco, Sr. and DeMarco, Jr. were listed on the U.S. Justice Department's Organized Crime Principal Subjects List before it was destroyed." The reporter's voice became even more emphatic and husky. "It's fair to conclude that they're connected."

None of the fantastic information was really setting in. Organized crime happened in Las Vegas, New York City, Cuba.

"Greg, I'm going to ask a very stupid question, but this is too hard to believe. Could there possibly be two National Developers, Inc. in Miami?"

He chuckled. "I can understand your doubts. When I found out that DeMarco, Sr. owned the San Francisco 49ers, I couldn't believe it. That's when I began researching this issue. When I learned that he also owned a Miami business, National Developers, I decided to investigate the company for the newspaper.

"National Developers purchased its land in the early 1960s. So when DeMarco purchased the company from the original owner in 1965, all the land came with it. The company owned land throughout the U.S. In the 1970s DeMarco built houses in towns like Vero Beach, Jupiter, Orlando and other towns, large and small, on both Florida coasts.

"It doesn't surprise me that they're in Connecticut, Rossi. There is a mob boss in New Haven, for your general information. They're all over. DeMarco, Sr. handles construction projects like your condos and shopping malls. The company came under investigation by the feds during the late 1960s and '70s when it seemed that many of its lenders and clients were associated with Florida's infamous mobsters, like Meyer Lansky and Santos Trafficante.

"Is this really just about condos?" he asked in conclusion.

"Two people were murdered, Greg," I replied. "That's what this call is about. But the police are convinced that the two victims were both killed during robberies. One of the murder victims was Wilton's town planner. The other was the town planner's secretary. I believe the secretary was murdered because she discovered a fraudulent map."

A woman pushed open the doors to the alcove and passed by the telephone booth to go to the restroom. My heart stood still for a second.

"If exposed," I continued, my eyes on the restroom door, "this would cost National Developers millions of dollars in fines, and somebody would go to jail. Not only condos are involved. Greg, National Developers probably owns land in the village center, which is a prime location for a mall," I added.

"Ms. Rossi, I mean Rossi," he said with impatience. Obviously I was being naïve. "Let me explain how powerful the DeMarco family is. Meyer Lansky is the financial wizard behind organized crime. He's credited for organizing organized crime. When Lansky retired in '68, DeMarco, Sr. stepped into his shoes. These are big shoes," Himes said. "As I told you before, DeMarco, Sr.'s name appeared on the U.S. Justice Department's Organized Crime Principal Subjects List in 1970. It was basically a brochure of people who were suspected of having links to organized crime, but they were never brought to trial. His attorney objected to the inclusion of DeMarco's name on the list and the list itself. As a result, the list was destroyed."

With all the patience he could muster for this clueless reporter, Greg explained that Edgar L. DeMarco, Sr. had been born in Cleveland, Ohio, in 1916, received his degree in civil engineering from Notre Dame and made his fortune in the construction business, primarily as a builder of shopping centers. His son, Edgar L. DeMarco, Jr., age 30, joined his father as his construction business expanded to include condominiums.

"At least ten bombings occurred at National Developers' offices and various shopping malls between 1975 to 1980," Greg said. "No one was killed, and the crimes remain unsolved."

"Senior is a civil engineer?" I asked, still not believing all I was hearing.

"Yep."

"So he actually works up these construction sites, including drawing maps?"

"Yep. He takes pride in doing so," Greg said.

"So he probably drew this inaccurate piece of crap?" I asked, hearing my voice rise in anger and thinking of Maddy.

"It's a fair assumption," Greg replied patiently.

"And if a mall is built by National Developers, Inc., we might even experience bombings in Wilton?"

"If they have an office in the mall, that's another fair assumption The bombings came to an end three years ago, but I'm not minimizing the danger," he was quick to add.

Himes took a deep, nervous breath. "Bombings, Rossi, dead bodies, unknown and known, are part of the DeMarco history. Both father and son remove obstacles. They don't like losing money, Rossi. I can't emphasize this enough. Others have tried to nail them, but evidence gets lost. People refuse to testify. A smalltime local punk or a lesser OC member takes the fall. Or witnesses disappear."

"I think that's happening here," I said, thinking of Freemont. "The police arrested a man who has a record of nonviolent crimes. They're charging the poor sucker with the murder of the planner's secretary. Then the town planner, Harrison Hayden, was killed in Bimini. There, the police believe Harrison was killed in the course of a robbery. In both cases, I think, the robberies were staged just to cover-up a professional hit, but the authorities are buying it."

"Bimini, huh," Himes said. I heard him ruffle through some papers. "A Special Agent for the U.S. Customs service reported in 1981 that DeMarco, Sr., had control of some Florida state banks with branches in Bimini and the Cayman Islands," he said. continuing his search. "Here it is. There was a confidential report on one of the banks. It alleged that false loans were made by various corporations through Empire Bank and Trust of Fort Lauderdale. In other words they gave away the bank's money to their contacts. They never expected to be paid back. This was a banking institution whose majority stockholder was no other than Edgar L. DeMarco, Sr. This was reported by the comptroller's office of the Florida Department of Law Enforcement, the FDLE.

"The Racketeer Influenced Corrupt Organizations Act, or RICO, allowed crackdowns on organized crime," Greg continued. "It was passed in the early 1970s. It took ten years to work, but the crackdown on money laundering using RICO is pushing the mob out of Vegas.

"This is how it works, Rossi. OC takes dirty money from the sales of drugs, guns, prostitution, skimming operations and gambling, and they invest the profits into legitimate businesses. Like your condos in Wilton and shopping malls, hotels in Las Vegas, banking, real estate, dog and horse racing tracks, hockey, football and more."

Greg sighed and then continued. "I'm still astounded that DeMarco bought the 49ers, and the Justice Department couldn't do a thing about it. But as it was explained to me, it was a legitimate ownership. DeMarco, Jr., 'purchased ninety percent of the 49ers' stock for seventeen-point-six million. Do you know what he did with it? 'He gave the 49ers, a whole football team, to his father as a birthday present.

"Ten years after Edgar L. DeMarco, Sr. bought National Developers, a classified report from the Florida Department of Law Enforcement described him as a powerful, wealthy, highly influential person with connections to organized-crime in the state of Ohio." He paused for breath, and I jumped in.

"Let me get this straight, Greg, nobody can pin anything on DeMarco because he's actually doing legitimate business, even if it's to launder money? What about the bank and the false loans? And RICO?"

"The bank went into bankruptcy. They ran it right into the ground in no time, yet no one of significance was charged. They claimed their customers defaulted on their loans. The Justice Department is legally banishing OC from Las Vegas, thanks to RICO. It's enforcing regulations that keep crime families out and from flourishing, clamping down on skimming off the top. So it's being done, they're moving out. It just doesn't pay anymore.

"In your case, it could be that deals are being made with higher-ups, Rossi. Don't mess around with this. If I were you, I'd get in touch with the U.S. Justice Department and Fred Fitz, the Chief of the Organized Crime and Racketeering Section, OCRS."

"I don't know if I'm ready for that," I said a little too loudly. The woman came out of the restroom, passed by me and headed out the door and back to her lunch. "Greg, all I have is a phony map, but now that I know National Developers is mobbed up and owns the condos in town, maybe I can get the police chief interested."

"Don't get your hopes up," Greg said with a sarcastic chuckle. "You said the town planner and his secretary were murdered? That's two witnesses eliminated, and DeMarco has a team of civil engineers, any one of whom could take responsibility for the map. They'll go to prison, if required, and as convicts they'll be treated like royalty. Be careful," he cautioned, dropping his husky voice, "with whom you share your facts. Your suspicions are valid. Some of National Developers' sites are questionable building sites for malls or condos, but they manage to build anyway. Yours is not the first town planner to be bought off."

"They make them an offer they can't refuse?" I asked.

"Right." He took a deep breath. "For all you know your town planner could have been the most honest guy in the world, but they threatened him with his life or the lives of his family."

"There has to be justice somewhere," I said, thinking of Maddy and Harrison.

"Listen, Edgar DeMarco, Sr., let me say again, is replacing Meyer Lansky as the financial genius of organized crime. The Justice Department could never lock up Lansky for any length of time. He stayed on the job so long that he got old enough to become senile."

As Greg talked, I thought that Meyer Lansky and the DeMarcos, Senior and Junior, had evaded justice while being investigated by the Justice Department, the FDLE and Ohio authorities. What chance did we have?

"One more thing, Rossi," Greg continued. "My car was blown up. I wasn't in it at the time. If they had wanted me dead, we wouldn't be talking right now. But remember, I wasn't investigating a murder."

Thirty-Eight

Friday, 2:00 p.m., Jerry Calls

On my way back to the newsroom my eyes, more fervently than ever checking the rearview mirror, I picked up my pictures from One Hour Photo. I opened up the package in front of my computer. To my horror, in one of the photos I was looking at the man from the car chase. He wore a black overcoat and fedora and slunk behind a towering oak for cover.

My mouth went dry at the sight of him. How could I not have seen him? He was a menacing man in any clothes, and he was obviously still tailing me.

Greg Himes' warnings were echoing in my head. This was organized crime. Rules, humanity, all that goes out the window. Was this the fear that Maddy had lived with for the last two weeks of her life? Did she know?

I managed to write the description of the funeral and Mr. Trowbridge's remarks, then left for home, knowing I had to get to Jerry's. It was 5:00 p.m. and pitch dark when, with great relief, I pulled up my driveway to find my house in one piece. Since darkness, however, for good or for bad, it was hungry animals and not the underworld that drove me into a panic. I grabbed barn clothes and work clothes in record-breaking time.

The phone rang. I ran downstairs to the kitchen and picked up, saying, "Hi, Jerry. Are you okay?"

"Sure."

"Please don't tell me anything right now. The neighborhood kid called in sick. Your animals are waiting for food. I can't talk. If we start, I'll ask a million questions. Call me back in an hour or so."

"Thanks, Ros. Okay. I won't say anything except will you sleep at my house tonight?"

"Yes, of course," I said. "It's best for both of us. One thing, Jerry, the birds are so pathetic. I'm so grateful they fell off a truck." Before he could say another word, I hung up.

Jerry sounded worried, but I couldn't think of that. I rushed out of the house, tugging at the door to make sure it was locked. I looked up and down the block. That's when I noticed that a black sedan was parked a half a block down Sugarloaf. I sucked in the cold air. Nobody parks on the road; it's always the driveway.

With my headlights off and without turning on the motor, I backed down the driveway. When I hit Sugarloaf I backed into the middle of the road, turned on the ignition and took a right. I flew up the road, took the hairpin curve on two wheels and down the hill to take a left onto Olmstead Hill Road. Then another left onto Route 7, heading north to Jerry's. My eyes were on the rearview mirror, as usual. Ten minutes later, a little rattled but without an escort, I gratefully exhaled and pulled into Jerry's alley of a driveway with my high beams on.

"Oreo," I yelled, hopping out of the car in the dark and walking through the fence, being sure to secure it behind me. "Go get the sheep!" Oreo, no doubt just finishing dinner, emerged from the house. He took off as if he'd done nothing but sheepherding for his entire young life. Just minutes later, Oreo and the sheep and Nanny returned while Lillian and I stood at the door of the house, shaking our heads in awe. Our ability to handle Jerry's little animal sanctuary was enhanced by the very animals Jerry had rescued. Animal life seemed to develop its own order in the Peaceable Kingdom.

I grabbed the feed, filled the troughs and headed for the straw to line the stalls. I finally entered the house, depositing my sneakers and jacket in the bit of an entry area with a clothes tree and mirror. I avoided the mirror.

The openness of the first floor resembled a warm country inn. A roaring fire in the stone fireplace across the room and the aroma of vegetable stew and biscuits baking greeted me. I ignored the inviting couch that faced the fire and the two comfy chairs positioned on either side and headed to the narrow stairway around the corner from the fireplace. Admiring the wooden stairs and their wine-colored runner, I remember Jerry telling me that he'd bought the runner on sale and installed it himself. At the top of the steps and to the left was the bathroom with the shower I couldn't wait to get to. With a change of clothes in my arms, I realized I was becoming portable. I was sure my fellow tablemates at the newsroom would appreciate my hygiene.

One bathroom was typical of the houses built in the '30s and '40s, I thought as I undressed and piled my clothes on the black and white tile floor. Jerry had installed a small lavatory downstairs off the kitchen, an unheard of luxury back in the day. In only minutes after depositing my smelly clothes into a large plastic bag in the bedroom, I descended the narrow stairs with a towel around my head and wearing pajamas. The aroma from the stew and biscuits made my mouth water.

"Everything's ready," Lillian said. "You just sit down. You must be exhausted."

I walked through the living room archway into the kitchen. Lillian brought a large bowl of the stew and a basket of her biscuits to the circular pine table. It was surrounded by six barrel pine chairs and sat in the center of the huge, old-fashioned room. Double windows were on the three walls of the open room and allowed for plenty of daylight. Shades and yellow café curtains with a little white ruffle adorned the windows. The shades helped to keep out the cold. No doubt the cafés were Lillian's contribution. The lighting of the small brass candlestick chandelier, simple and colonial, was soft and a bit intimate. The small table lamp on a side bar under the south window offered another soft homey glow.

Once again I seemed to have stepped into a different world. Animals were in the barn, and the six dogs filled the kitchen, each on his or her own pillow and mellow with contentment. While Lillian silently served our dinner, Willie Nelson offered a laid back ambient sound. Every once in a while, one of the sheep or Nanny bleated outside. I sat down and took one deep breath, a breath so free of fear and stress it seemed I had entered a parallel universe where everyone lived safely and securely until they died of old age in their sleep.

Could this last? For at least the night, I hoped, brushing away thoughts of DeMarco and organized crime. I picked up my soup spoon and dug into the stew. While the savory flavors drove me into a swoon, I pulled apart a piping hot biscuit and gazed gratefully at Lillian seated next to me, just as the animals had gazed at me while eating heartily from their trough.

Lillian reached out and patted me appreciatively on the back, no doubt too tired for conversation.

Thirty-Nine
Conversation with Jerry
Early Friday Evening

Snug on Jerry's safe couch in front of the flickering fire, the dogs nearby blinking dreamily at me as they started to drift off, my heavy eyes were starting to close. Then the phone rang.

The anxiety in Jerry's voice made me sit upright and immediately shake off the cozy mood. He said he had come to share my theory that the murders were connected to P&Z, and he suspected Hayden was bribed and why.

"We're on the same page now?" I asked, alarmed but also relieved. "Did Al dig up anything?" My ears were alert, listening for strange sounds inside or outside the house.

"He's not sharing our enthusiasm that this case is directly linked to P&Z, but he's willing to investigate, question Esposito and employees at P&Z, and also Maddy's friends at town hall.

"Two of Freemont's friends had long rap sheets. No violent crimes, but they were both out of prison on Tuesday. They both have alibis. But Al's on it and thinks they're capable of committing murder. He'll be focusing the investigation on that angle.

"Freemont's criminal friends bolstered the Chief's theory that Freemont didn't find the stolen goods in a shopping cart on Elizabeth Street. He and Al are more convinced that Freemont is involved and guilty of some crime. He has no doubt that Freemont is withholding information, and it's only a matter of time.

"He considers the murder solved. Freemont's back in prison waiting to be tried for murder. If he's found guilty, he'll be in prison for life. It's Freemont's worst nightmare. He'll talk. That's the Chief's opinion."

Jerry had no idea about the significance of the Empire Bank and Trust withdrawal receipt, that it was a key piece of evidence that connected Harrison to DeMarco, Sr., and to National Developers. It gave good cause to believe Harrison was bribed and offered a connection between Maddy's and Harrison's murders.

"Jerry, take a seat. I've been doing a little investigating myself," I said.

"I expected that. Rossi, these people killed twice. They won't hesitate to kill again."

"Make sure you have a copy of the two-hundred-thousand-dollar Empire Bank withdrawal receipt," I plowed on.

"I have a copy of every damned paper in the file," he said with a little annoyance at the basic nature of my instructions.

"Maddy left me a note to check a map of Stuart Island. It's complicated. I'll give you the details when you get home," I said, sipping a bit of tea to let Jerry get his bearings.

"You withheld evidence?" he asked.

"Well, I only got the note on Thursday morning. I'm not a cop, Jerry, and neither you nor Al were too interested in my opinion."

"Okay, okay, just go on," he pleaded.

"Maddy found discrepancies in two maps drawn of Stuart Island. The recent one was to gain a permit to build condominiums on Stuart Island, the hundred and seven units. She questioned that map. I found out that the property is owned by National Developers, Inc., which is owned by

Edgar DeMarco Sr. And guess what? He is a known associate of organized crime and the greatest shareholder of the Empire Bank and Trust. So that's why the withdrawal receipt is so key.

"So, Jerry, to clarify, the Stuart Island Condominiums are built by an associate of organized crime, and Harrison might have been paid off to look the other way while they used a fraudulent map to acquire a permit to build. Ergo, the bribe. If the story about the phony map were revealed, the DeMarco family, through RICO, would pay the highest fines possible enforced by the Army Corp of Engineers, and one of the DeMarcos would do jail time. The DeMarco family would also lose the opportunity to build a mall on their land in the village center. There's about ten acres of prime real estate that I believe belongs to them."

I turned around to see what had thrown the dogs into a barking panic. They were jumping furiously by the front door. Must be a raccoon, I thought, dismissing it.

"As you know, according to Mrs. Hayden," I continued with my eyes on the canines, "and Ann Bower, Maddy's best friend, Maddy was supposed to meet Harrison at Cider Mill School Tuesday night. I believe DeMarco found this out and killed them both to silence them."

Jerry went quiet, so I continued. "Jerry, since Tuesday night I've been looking for a motive for Maddy's murder. I believe we have it, and if you need a reason for bribing Harrison, we've got that too."

There was complete silence at the other end of the phone. Jerry was so angry at me for withholding information that he wouldn't talk to me, I assumed.

"Hello," I said. Still silence. "Jerry, are you there?" Nothing. "Jerry?"

I tried to get a dial tone, but Jerry's phone was dead.

My eyes shot to the double-hung windows on either side of the door. The six dogs were still barking and milling around the door and windows. Maybe it's not a raccoon, I thought, hanging up the dead telephone receiver.

That old familiar chill shot through my veins.

Forty
The Barn

I told myself it must be ice that cut off the telephone wires, but it didn't matter. I realized I was being terrorized once again.

With jerky, nervous fingers, I slipped into my boots and jacket at the door. I trembled from head to foot at what I'd find, but I had to get to the barn. The dogs looked at me with concern as I uttered soothing words to calm them down. Lillian was dead asleep upstairs, and I didn't have the heart to wake her, although I wanted to. She hadn't slept at all the previous night. If this racket didn't wake her, nothing else would.

I remembered that Jerry had said the cops would patrol his property while he was gone, but waiting for the cops to show was impossible. The images of dead animals ran around in my head. I pushed the warm bodies of the dogs out of the way and yelled at them to stay so I could reach the door without their escaping. Then the doorbell rang.

Another uproar of barking ensued. I ran to the fireplace and frantically retrieved a poker from the stand. My heart pounded in my throat. Then I heard a familiar voice.

"Hey, Rossi! It's me!"

Dylan. I heaved a sigh of relief as I opened the door with poker in hand, so anxious to see a face I could trust.

"I just had to talk," he said. Vapor puffed out of his mouth from the cold as he spoke. He was all bundled up and rubbing his gloved hands. The cold turned his cheeks beet red. "This time I'm sober. Evan told me you were here," he added.

"Sorry, Dylan, but I need us to go outside right now." My fear for the animals was growing exponentially.

"Okay," he murmured docilely.

I rushed into the darkness, heading for the barn, and crossed the front yard in a growing panic. Dylan loyally trailed after me. Inside the barn, with the help of a nightlight, I made out to my great relief the appropriate sets of peering eyes. The animals were a bit unnerved. Oreo and Nanny were pacing around the barn. They others spoke nervously to us in their native tongues. The birds were in the last stall. I had coaxed them in there with feed earlier.

"It's okay," I said to everyone. I made the rounds, petting tops of heads and gazing assuredly into anxious eyes, including those of the typically laidback Doris and Gloria. I peeked at the birds, who were alert but not terrified.

Dylan looked dazed. He stationed himself by the barn door, ready for a fast escape.

"Who knew Jerry had all these animals?" he mumbled.

We trudged back over icy snow from the barn to the house and then checked the telephone wire on the north side with a flashlight. The wire hung suspiciously from the building.

"Looks like the telephone line is down," I mumbled in disbelief.

"Rossi, that line looks like it's been cut," Dylan said.

Back in front of the house, I peered down the empty driveway. Nothing but fences and darkness. It was just a quiet winter night except for the dogs that continued to bark. There wasn't a soul in sight, but I wasn't satisfied. I'd be sleeping outside the barn, protecting the animals from the OC pyromaniac who I believed had cut the line after talking to

Himes. There would be no barn burning tonight, I told myself.

Just then I saw the lights of a patrol car slowly driving up the bumpy driveway. A uniformed officer rolled down his window as he approached. "Ms. Rossi?" he asked with a smile. "Jerry asked us to check in on you. He said there was trouble with the phone. Everything okay?"

"Officer," I leaned over and read his name on the badge. "George Walters," I smiled "Thanks for coming over. I'm okay, but Jerry's telephone line isn't." I pointed a gloved finger in the direction of the telephone line hanging off the side of the house. "It's been vandalized. Is there any way a car can sit out here tonight, just until daylight? With this murder investigation going on, I'm a little jumpy. I have no way of getting hold of Jerry, so could you call and tell him I'm okay?"

"Jerry said to tell you he's catching a plane tonight and will be here early tomorrow morning, three or so. We can have an extra police car parked in the driveway, Ms. Rossi, until he gets back." He offered a concerned smile and radioed headquarters. "I'll sit right here until they get here," he said.

"Want a cup of hot chocolate?"

He picked up his cup of coffee and showed it to me but smiled gratefully at the offer.

I steered Dylan back into the house and to the fireplace, placing the poker back where it belonged. I told him to put on another log. Sleeping outside in the cold was going to test the waters just a little too much for my forty-plus body, which had been running on empty for a couple of hours now. I was grateful to be back inside.

"Hot chocolate or tea?" I asked. He chose hot chocolate, and I failed to inform him that I'd be using soymilk. He sat mesmerized before the fire as I headed for the kitchen.

"Okay, Dylan, you talk," I said, returning with two thick mugs of hot chocolate.

I was too exhausted to talk, but I knew Jerry's cut phone line, the black ribbon and all its implications, and my chat with Himes would keep me up until Jerry came home, even with the cop sitting outside.

I handed Dylan his hot chocolate and sat on the floor next to the fire, listening to its calming crackling sounds and staring at its yellow plumes.

"Ros, what's up with the cut wire?"

"It's a long story. Will you please go first? I'm so dead tired, I can't talk."

Forty-One
Dylan's Story

I listened as Dylan revealed that Maddy told him she was to meet Harrison at Cider Mill because the principal was one of Harrison's best friends, and he and the principal were scheduled to go out for dinner. He also revealed that Maddy had spoken to Harrison on the Sunday two days before her murder. She learned then that Harrison would arrive on Monday, and he would see her for an hour or so on Tuesday night. She was going to drive him to Friendly's for a long chat over a cup of coffee and give him his favorite Christmas cookies.

"Dylan, did you know that a senior center proposed to be built on Stuart Island was turned down because of the flood in 1955? It's in the flood way of the river," I said, my sleepy eyes on the fire, "and in a one hundred year flood zone."

He looked at me knowingly. "I covered that public hearing," he said. He took a sip of his hot chocolate and squirmed in his seat a bit, then looked at me with guilty eyes.

"Dylan, let me ask you a question," I said, sitting up and feeling life slowly return to my body. Maybe it was the caffeine in the chocolate. "Isn't it common knowledge that Peterson, Myers & Sheen, off Wolfpit and Route 7, own the condos and are the developers?"

"Of course," he said and took another sip of hot chocolate.

"Well, they're not. The real owner is a development company associated with the DeMarco crime family. Its name is National Developers, Inc. It's based in Miami."

Dylan sat back in the chair and gulped down his mouthful of very hot chocolate, his young face frozen in doubt and self-recrimination. I started with the RICO Act for Dylan and continued with the saga of organized crime that Himes had related to me, including the DeMarcos and their connection to the Stuart Island Condominiums. Excitement continued to rise in me as I mulled it all over with Dylan as if some important conclusions were germinating.

"Maddy's best friend, Ann Bower, who works at town hall, by the way, led me to piece together a sequence of events," I said."It supports the theory that Harrison realized Maddy's life was threatened. From all accounts I don't think he'd ever harm Maddy or go along with anybody else harming her. I never heard anything but sincere praise of Maddy from Harrison for the last two years. The two were so close that his wife was jealous of their relationship. I saw that when I interviewed Mrs. Hayden."

This conclusion about Harrison's affection for Maddy and his possible actions to protect her was an inchoate idea. I was grateful to be able to voice my theory to Dylan.

"But since Maddy continued to call him," I went on, "I'm sure DeMarco's thugs got to Harrison, warning him to keep this woman quiet. They probably tapped her phone and realized she was suspicious, or a spy in the office informed them of her discovering the fraudulent map. I believe there's a spy in the office, Dylan, but I don't know who."

Dylan was staring down at me from the couch, trying to take it all in and looking like he was having a difficult time of it.

"I think Harrison risked his life coming back here out of his love and respect for Maddy," I said as my thoughts came together, and I tried to speak more calmly. "Dylan, I believe he returned to Wilton solely to protect Maddy, convince her to play along and let the discrepancies between the two maps fade into the past. I believe Harrison did the honorable thing, and it cost him his life."

Dylan shook his head, indicating that Maddy would never play along.

"I guess the DeMarcos didn't like the odds either," I continued. "They got rid of one witness Sunday night, Harrison, but that still left Maddy. They must have tapped her phones to know that Maddy was going to meet Harrison Tuesday night."

"Rossi, why would the town planner approve this condo in 1980 when it was turned down by the first selectman in 1955?" Dylan asked.

He was feeling guilty, I thought. Since he had been the reporter covering this beat, he blamed himself for not smelling malfeasance. I realized at the scene of the crime I had felt some measure of responsibility, which had mystified me at the time. Here it is, I realized. Just like Dylan, shouldn't I have seen this coming?

"I even questioned Maddy about this permit," Dylan was saying, staring hard at me, his strawberry blond brows knitted. "I recall saying it was unsound land on which to build all those condominiums because of the possibility of flooding. I remember that at the hearing a resident questioned it, referring to the 1955 flood, but he was shut down by the commissioners because he wasn't a professional builder. They said advancements had led to more accurate maps and less harmful fill and other materials that wouldn't compromise the land, all that kind of crap." He looked far away, as if he were reliving the public hearing of three years ago. "Then the town planner left town just weeks before the project was completed. He left this mess in Maddy's lap." His eyes bulged in indignation. "He was paid off, he had to be. He probably lied to the commissioners while they were deliberating on this permit. Maddy lost her life so that Harrison could retire in Bimini," Dylan concluded darkly. "Harrison lost his life trying to fix screwing up in the first place. I don't think that's heroic, Ros."

I let a few seconds go by."I think Maddy sensed that a cancer had moved into town," I responded in a calm voice. "She probably noticed that DeMarco had undue influence on Harrison, or at least she suspected it." The fire crackled as a large log caved. Sparks and plumes sprouted up on each side of it, catching our attention. "I'm sure she realized that Harrison detested this DeMarco character. Harrison seemed to openly hate the guy, according to people at town hall. You know Maddy was knowledgeable. Nothing much got past her. Not unless she wanted it to, that is," I added.

"About co-writing stories," I warned, "you might want to reconsider. Two killings so far, and I believe I'm being followed day and night. Jerry's cut telephone wire is evidence of that."

He gazed down at me, his composure regained. "Hell, we're reporters, aren't we? This is what we're supposed to do," he said, his voice rising again in anger, and I knew he was thinking of Maddy."Have you told all this to Jerry yet?" he asked.

"Absolutely everything. In great detail ... over the dead phone."

Forty-Two
Early Morning Saturday
Jerry Comes Home

I heard Jerry walking in the door at 3:00 a.m. The police officer had guarded the house, and to my surprise I actually drifted off to sleep every once in a while for a few minutes. I could hear the patrol car rumble down the bumpy driveway in a rush to leave.

Next were Jerry's heavy steps as he climbed the stairs. I turned the light on, and Jerry shed his clothes, looking at me without saying a word. He crawled into bed, exhausted. He had heard most of the story before the phone went dead, he finally revealed, but he wanted a rerun to help him accept all the new information. I was grateful I'd had a few hours sleep so I could be coherent.

"You need to live here where it's safe," he said at last. His voice was so grave it moved me. I stared at his troubled and caring brown eyes. Again I saw a level of concern matched only by that of my parents.

I told him about the cut telephone wire. "So there are no guarantees, Jerry."

He replied in a quiet and patient voice. "I just checked the wire, Ros. Nanny did it. I think she's been chewing on it for days."

I laughed out loud, so relieved. "I love that goat."

"Ros, if what you say is true, you're better off living here. I don't think injuring a detective's girlfriend is good for the mob's business."

"That's true," I said. "Do you think the Chief was told to look the other way by higher-ups? He doesn't want to consider any other theories except that Maddy was killed during a mugging and Harrison during a robbery. Does he want to keep it a secret that organized crime is in town?"

"He thinks we got the right guy," he responded.

"Don't forget people like Bebe Rebozo, the friend of Nixon," I reminded him. "Remember Sinatra was building a special wing for JFK? I'm not saying they run the country, but winks and nods on occasion, yes. Don't forget the senator that was bought off in *The Godfather*. None of the Corleones were sent to jail," I joked.

I could see Jerry's smirk. Seconds later, I lay back down, and Jerry joined me. He put his arm around me and pulled me to him.

"On the plane trip home," he said in a soft voice, "I thought of a little Rossi running around the place, Nanny and the dogs following. I can't forget it." His eyes gazed straight ahead. "It was a vision."

"A little Rossi?" I asked in bewilderment. My childbearing days were close to over, but not quite yet. The thought struck me deeply. Was he proposing?

"This case complicates things, Rossi, I know. Your home is a perfect target. If you won't move here, I'll just move in with you until the case is closed. If organized crime is in any way involved in this ... it could be they aren't, but even on the chance that you're right, I think we need to live together, okay?"

I squeezed the hand that wrapped around my shoulder. Jerry was needed here to take care of his many friends. If anything, I'd love helping him. "I'll move in here tomorrow, bring some clothes over for work. The animals truly appreciate me, especially when I'm shoveling their poop out of the barn." I looked up at him. "I guess I can get used to living with a cop."

"Now, how do you feel about having a little Rossi?" he asked, raising an eyebrow at me.

I stalled for time. "You mentioned Nanny and the dogs, but what about Doris and Gloria in your vision?"

"Who?"

"Doris and Gloria, your two sheep."

He started to laugh with joy. "So you named them?"

"Yep, I named them at first sight, Doris and Gloria."

"Can you tell them apart?"

"Well, a gray swatch of hair sits on top of Gloria's curly head, right between her ears, and Doris is a bit more circumspect when she looks at you."

"Yeah, and she's a little smaller than Gloria too," Jerry added. "You're dodging the question about a little Rossi."

"It fills my heart so much that I can't think about it right now, Jerry. We need to get all this behind us." I had a plaintive note in my voice. I needed time to accept the death of my parents, too.

"Understood," Jerry said, pulling me to him. He looked at me with empathy as if he sensed my sadness. "And when you move in here, I'll be able to focus on the case. Worrying about you is preoccupying me and also taking years off my life."

"I still have to go to work, Jerry."

"DeMarco," he said, putting his head back down on the pillow. "I'll have a talk with the Chief tomorrow. This is a case for the Bureau," he said, referring to the FBI.

"I'd call Fred Fitz," I suggested.

"Who's he?"

"He's the Chief of the Organized Crime and Racketeering Section of the Justice Department," I rattled off. "Himes says he's the man to talk to."

Jerry gave me a squeeze. "You're good, Ros."

I gave him a body hug. "No, Jerry, you're good."

"We'll talk to the Chief tomorrow morning," Jerry concluded.

Forty-Three
The Chief's Office, Saturday Morning

It was a brilliant winter morning, and Jerry was optimistic as we entered the Wilton Police Department on Saturday. My optimism was MIA, which I attributed to our vast age difference and my healthy skepticism. He went directly to the Chief's office, while I headed toward his desk. It was one of four in a bank of desks forming a square in the center of the large room. About ten other desks, some occupied, were placed along the four walls. With my head down, I took a seat in a chair alongside his desk, willing to wait patiently in anticipation while I reviewed some notes on my yellow pad. All the officers, however, looked up to give me grateful smiles and then went back to their work.

Five minutes later the two entered the room. The Chief's disapproving expression quickly reminded me that I was the enemy, having supported his officers' successful strike for one more paid holiday and health insurance for the family.

I stood up. Jerry reintroduced me to the Chief, looking solemn. Then he sat down at his desk.

Chief Dominic Romano's deep frown transformed into his typical frown. I couldn't help but think of the lack of exercise and the excessive amounts of meat, heavy cheeses, pasta and wine that had produced his pasty pallor, swollen nose, puffy eyes and pot belly.

"Miss Rossi," he said in an authoritative tone, "please sit down."

He took a seat to my right in front of Jerry's desk, leaving both of us to face Jerry.

"I know the NFL didn't want Edgar DeMarco, Jr. to buy the 49ers for a birthday present for his father, DeMarco, Sr., but they couldn't stop him," the Chief began. He turned to stare at me as he dropped this bit of knowledge. I looked at him in utter surprise.

"Yeah, Jerry told me about your concerns. I know all about this," he said, waving his right hand in the air self-importantly. "Buying the 49ers was a legitimate business deal. The Justice Department couldn't do anything to stop it. There was opposition because DeMarco, Sr. owned racetracks, and he was tied to gambling, which was the issue here," he said. Thick, graying eyebrows hovered sloppily over his brown eyes. "'Anybody involved in gambling, legal or illegal, don't want the NFL games to look fixed.'"

He looked at me as if he were newly burdened with the task of cracking through my thick cranium. "If a game looks fishy, if there's too much money bet on the game, they just take it off the boards. The casinos and the bookies and the NFL lose. But the NFL and the Justice Department couldn't do a damned thing about the sale of the 49ers."

He stopped for a second and looked from me to Jerry. "Just like the NFL, we can't stop a legitimate business from building in town if the builders or developers have gone through the process and they've received a permit. Our town planner and a board of P&Z commissioners approved a building permit for the condos on Stuart Island. So they built the condos." He threw both hands up in the air, indicating that it was a done deal.

He turned to me. "We don't have any evidence that Harrison was bribed. We need proof of bribery to bring charges. That two-hundred-thousand-dollar withdrawal receipt was legitimate. It came from a legitimate checking account in his name, so the receipt in itself is not evidence of bribery. The account was honored by a legitimate bank, granted that it went out of business and it had mob ties.

"But Harrison withdrew his money a year ago. It could be part of his retirement account, for all we know. That's what he was using the money for. He talked about Bimini as if he lived there. It could be his return on investments over his lifetime. He did invest, so maybe he cashed everything in and put it in a checking account. So his wife didn't know about it. That's hardly unheard of, a husband hiding money from his wife." He sighed and continued, looking at his fingernails.

"Jerry will look into that a little more. I talked to Tim Esposito this morning. The condos are already built and being sold, so where's the motive to kill Harrison and Mrs. Trowbridge?" He looked directly at me. "Don't kid yourself, Ms. Rossi, that if a map missed a swamp, the State will make them pull down those condos." He looked at Jerry as if he expected him to agree.

"Tim told me they'll have to invest some money on fortifying the buildings, support the foundations for flooding. Even if the Town went to court, Tim said, they usually just attach a small fine and allow the builders time to fix it. It's common practice."

"What about the drawing of a fraudulent map?" I asked, my eyes darting to Jerry and then back to the Chief. "What about the Corps of Army Engineers?"

"The developer's engineer will say it's an honest mistake and create a new one," the Chief said, glaring at the ignorance of my question. "As far as a shopping mall goes, it's a legitimate business. DeMarco will go through the building process. It'll be up to Tim and probably the first selectman. I'm sure Tim and Hudson won't want to do business with the DeMarco family, but if the land belongs to them and the area is zoned for commerce, they'll have to consider it along with other options. Maybe the Town can buy the property from them."

"You mean, the Town can make them and offer they can't refuse?" I asked with a smirk.

The Chief continued as if I hadn't spoken. "Jerry was talking about calling the Justice Department on this, but we don't have evidence to connect either murder to DeMarco, so I don't see the point of having this town crawling with agents or ruining the name of a man who worked honorably for us for almost three decades."

He shot a hot glance at Jerry. "Whatever wrong Harrison did, I think he paid for it." He gazed down at the floor as if in sorrow. "A scandal will embarrass his grieving family for no reason. Harrison is not going to do this town any more harm," he said, lifting his eyes. "The Bimini Police Chief is satisfied that Harrison's death was a result of a robbery. Regarding Mrs. Trowbridge, I told Jerry that I think we caught the mugger's accomplice, and he'll eventually talk. Just give him some time in prison. Oh, and by the way, Janet Goldridge, the nurse, Freemont's solid alibi. She's disappeared."

"What?" Jerry jumped to his feet.

"I got the call this morning from the Norwalk police. She moved out of her apartment and quit her job. They think she left last night and didn't leave a forwarding address."

He smiled as if to say this was proof positive that Freemont was guilty. "She was a nice person. She was protecting Freemont. What else can you think? The woman didn't want to go to trial and perjure herself." He turned his palms up.

"So Freemont has no alibi," Jerry muttered, staring at the Chief, his hands on both hips.

"That's right." Romano stood up. "We just indicted several mob bosses in Connecticut. We've been able to infiltrate, go undercover, get a capo to wear a wire and go into the witness protection program."

He was quiet for a minute before deciding to continue. "In Las Vegas in the '60s and '70s, the Federal Government and the State of Nevada organized a campaign, spent a lot of money, to ensure that organized crime would exit Las Vegas and never come back. Then Howard Hughes purchased three hotels. That accelerated the whole process. The State wanted families to visit and feel secure in the city. The IRS, the Department of Organized Crime of Nevada State Police and the Las Vegas Gaming Commission created a web of laws. A system of audits and re-audits became the norm to make sure the mob didn't worm its way back in."

With that the Chief got to his feet and made his own exit.

"Jerry," I whispered as I shot to my feet. "Janet Goldridge disappears, and he doesn't think it's because the mob scared her off?"

Jerry shook his head. "I'll look over Harrison's financial records. Al said he'd check telephone calls from his house and from Maddy's phone for the last couple of weeks. We'll also see if Janet Goldridge has any relatives."

"The Chief was as much help as I expected," I said bitterly. "You've probably guessed what I'll be doing, not that I expect to find him in on a Saturday."

"They work crazy hours," he said encouragingly. "Be careful."

Forty-Four
Still Saturday Morning

I left Jerry at the police station and drove straight to the Wilton Library. I decided I needed more information before I called my pal Fred Fitz.

Was Himes right about organized crime infiltrating New England? The question nagged at me as I drove. Even some cops didn't think the Mafia actually existed. Jerry had mentioned this to me a while ago. What existed, they believed, were pockets of local mobsters with influence over corrupt politicians, not a crime syndicate.

The key strategy of the Mafia, it appeared, was to remain below the radar and not bother the cops.

I entered the spacious, airy building that morning and peered around to see if someone had followed me in. I requested a stack of newspapers from the accommodating librarian at the front desk, along with an autobiographical book written by an ex-member of the Mafia, Vincent Teresa. I found *Wiseguys: A Novel* in the card catalog along with several magazine articles. I piled all the material on a table situated against a long picture window.

"Raymond Salvatore Loreda Patriara was the undisputed boss of the Patriarca family," I read. The Patriarca family was the most powerful organized crime family outside of the five New York City crime families according to several accounts. Patriarca was a member of the Mafia commission and operating right here in the Northeast.

The Patriarca family's initial wealth and power had come from bootlegging, loan sharking and illegal gambling. The organized crime syndicate was known to be in Providence, Rhode Island, and Boston, Massachusetts, part of *La Cosa Nostra* or the Italian American Mafia.

Apparently, New England was divided among the five New York crime families like bounty. I read that since 1954 the Patriarca crime family had controlled the criminal activities on the east side of the Connecticut River. Carlo Gambino took control of Fairfield County and the west side of the river. The Genovese family also dipped into Fairfield County's nefarious activities.

Violent assaults, extortion, loan sharking, union embezzlement, illegal gambling, trafficking in stolen property, drugs, prostitution, counterfeit goods and mail fraud were all common business practices.

I sat back for a moment and considered. If a Mafia commission exists, isn't that proof that there is a Mafia? Would it be possible to find justice for Maddy and Harrison? Were mob leaders so powerful that they could evade justice as Himes proclaimed? The New England Mafia was started sixty-seven years previously by Gaspare Messina, who was followed by Phil Buccola. He rose to power during the prohibition era, and in 1932 Buccola was accepted as the Boston boss by the national Mafia commission.

If Maddy had suspected that organized crime was moving into Wilton, she'd think it her obligation to her ancestors and part of her job to pursue the corruption and get to the bottom of it. Her only restraint would be her conceived obligation to Harrison.

As a reporter, I couldn't help but compare the nefarious occupations and businesses of organized crime with those of Wilton's original settlers and those who had further developed the Connecticut colony. They had included violent assaults, extortion, loan sharking, union embezzlement, illegal gambling, trafficking in stolen property, drugs, prostitution, counterfeit goods and mail fraud.

I recalled that in the early nineteen hundreds, the town's people were mostly artists, musicians, tradesmen, craftsmen and laborers.

I kept reading. Raymond Patriarca, Sr., called "the toughest guy you ever saw" by Boston police, had helped make organized crime invisible by maintaining a low profile until a 1957 raid. More than sixty powerful crime bosses met in Apalchin, a small town in upstate New York. Raymond Patriarca, Carlo Gambino, Vito Genovese, Joe Bonanno and many others were arrested. Officials ardently and successfully pursued Patriarca from that time. Then in 1961, when Robert Kennedy was appointed Attorney General, the Mafia was infiltrated. The witness protection program, part of RICO, worked as a place to turn to for those in the Mafia who believed they were threatened from inside the Mafia or by the government.

Patriarca was no longer under the radar after this debacle. Patriarca's story ran like a crime family soap opera with a series of arrests and betrayal starting with Patriarca himself. He failed to bail one of his hit men out of jail. Consequently, the hit man put on a wire for the FBI, which eventually led to Patriarca being charged and arrested for two murders. Patriarca was then charged with the murder of his associate, Robert Candos, who he believed turned FBI informant.

I stopped reading for a second to digest the information. If Patriarca, the architect of organized crime in New England, had been vulnerable to arrest, then there was every chance of apprehending Maddy's and Harrison's murderers.

The FBI had shut down a cocaine operation on the campus of Norwalk Community College just last month. The story was buried in a Norwalk daily. "As sure as the sun's coming up tomorrow" someone will take his place, the FBI agent said, referring to the cocaine dealer. "This is not the end of organized crime in Connecticut." But the agent admitted that the Mafia was weakened after ten years of RICO. I found this and others articles buried in the local newspapers. The various towns, including Greenwich, Stamford and Norwalk, obviously wanted to avoid being associated with the Mafia. They didn't want the stigma, and they didn't want the infamy of Las Vegas.

It finally dawned on me that for all I knew, the powerful Gambino family could be behind Maddy's and Harrison's murders. They apparently operated on the west side of the Connecticut River. The man in the black suit could be a Gambino hit man.

God, what was I thinking? I was sitting in the cozy library in secure and wholesome Wilton, Connecticut, on a bright winter morning, in Ethel Hart's library, Wilton's first librarian, on the job for fifty years of her life. Yet I was reading about a real life Corleone family with the name of Patriarca, and I knew that the Mafia might be infiltrating Wilton.

Read on, I told myself, and returned to the next newspaper in the stack before me. Meyer Lansky died on January 15th, one month before Maddy's death. Funny Himes never mentioned his demise. Lansky no doubt was the organizer of organized crime in Himes' part of the world, notably in Florida and Cuba, with ties to Las Vegas's illegal operations and to Carlo and Tommy Gambino in New York.

Lansky had a dream, I learned in my reading, to bond the two worlds, organized crime and the United States, together so that one could not survive without the other.

The English settlers' dream was for land and freedom. Again, I couldn't help but compare the two worlds.

I sat back, grateful that on January 15th of this year, death had deferred Lansky's dream, hopefully forever.

While glancing suspiciously around the library, I ran off copies of several articles. I thrust the copies and my yellow pad into my shoulder satchel, remembering the knife at my door, the car chase, being stalked. I headed for the door feeling far less secure than I had when I entered. I surveyed the library once more before leaving, certain I was being observed. I didn't see anybody, I just felt eyes on me.

I thought of Maddy.

Forty-Five
Fred Fitz

Fred Fitz of the Justice Department was not only in, he was practically waiting for my call. "DeMarco, Sr. has a one-hundred-thousand-dollar line of credit at Caesars Palace in Las Vegas," Fitz revealed. "He's also the owner of the Pittsburgh Penguins of the National Hockey League and the Pittsburgh Civic Arena. The family has a lot of political influence. They wanted to buy a baseball team, but the other team owners managed to block the sale. It's very well known that National Developers builds shopping malls across the country. DeMarco, Jr. claims that's where he made his money. He's a civil engineer."

Himes was so right on that score. I took notes as Fitz talked. "I believe that two people in our local government were killed over a real estate scheme," I told Fitz. I explained the facts as I knew them.

"From what you've just said," he responded, "and a little chat I just had with Chief Romano, it sounds as though the man responsible for the condos being built, Harrison Hayden, is dead as a result of a robbery. There's another person under arrest, Richard Freemont, as an accomplice who will be charged for the murder of the woman involved, a Maddy Trowbridge. He's expected to implicate the killer."

"Mr. Fitz, I believe that Richard Freemont is a fall guy for the Mafia," I said with the most authoritative voice I could muster. "I believe he was set up. He's a petty crook. How can you accept that Harrison Hayden was also killed during a robbery?"

"I'll give the Bahamas police a call," Fitz said, "but your police chief is satisfied with the South Bimini Police Department's conclusion that the Hayden murder occurred during a robbery. They are going forward with their investigation under that premise."

"Mr. Fitz, as an investigative reporter working for the *Wilton Weekly,* I believe that Harrison Hayden and Maddy Trowbridge were executed by Mafia hit men. We have a bank withdrawal receipt that links Harrison with the now defunct bank in Bimini, Empire Bank and Trust, for the amount oftwo hundred thousand dollars. The bank was proven to have strong ties to organized crime. The money came straight out of Harrison's checking account. I believe that money was given to Harrison as a bribe for a building permit for one hundred seven condominium units built in town and further, that the money was put into Harrison Hayden's checking account by the owner of the now defunct bank, Edgar DeMarco, Jr."

"Can you prove Harrison didn't deposit that money into his own checking account?"

"No, but I don't think he had that kind of money given to him by the town of Wilton when he retired. Harrison may even have deposited the cash, but he got it from the DeMarcos. His wife told me that in the last three years he had money he'd never had before. She made me promise this information was off the record, Mr. Fitz, but it was exactly three years ago when the Stuart Island permit application was approved. Harrison didn't have to sell their marital home in order to buy a house in Bimini. Where did all of his money come from?"

"But from what I understand from your Chief, there is little evidence that organized crime is in Wilton or that your two victims were mob executions."

"I realize that the Chief doesn't want to soil the pristine reputation of Wilton with connections to organized crime," I shot back. "Mr. Fitz, if the Mafia didn't want the new town planner, Timothy Esposito, to think that the mob or their associates, Edgar L. DeMarco, Sr. and Jr., owners of National Developers, had a hand in the murders, wouldn't they stage the murders to look like robberies to cover them up? So they can build this damned mall? On their damned land here in town?"

"I'll send a couple of agents out," he said. His tone changed. "Ms. Rossi, let the agents and the local police handle this from here. If you're right, you don't want to be the next victim. Remember, Ms. Rossi, there's a certain amount of revenge shown those who dare to interfere. It's not good for business."

"Mr. Fitz, I think Maddy's and Harrison's murders are evidence of that."

Forty-Six

Saturday Afternoon, Four Days since the Murder

A couple of hours later Jerry called and revealed that Harrison's modest financials fit the profile of a pubic servant until the two hundred thousand dollars magically appeared. I sat in front of my computer, again taking notes on my yellow pad.

"We're building a strong case on circumstantial evidence," Jerry said. "His wife knew nothing about the money in the Bimini account.

"Hayden's income of two thousand a month includes proceeds from the town's retirement plan, Social Security and dividends on his investments of about sixty thousand," Jerry said as I scribbled down the information. "Two accounts remained at the local First National at the Village Center, ten thousand in a savings account and another twenty-eight hundred in a checking account."

Maddy's desperate, unanswered telephone calls to Harrison had been verified by New England Bell records. She had called all times of the day and night for the last two weeks of her life, four or five times a day. The calls abruptly ended on Sunday.

Harrison's phone records, prior to his retirement, revealed frequent calls to National Developers in Miami. The telephone number led Jerry to DeMarco's lawyer, Albert Basille. He had already offered him all the company records regarding National Developers, Inc.

The building permit for the condos had been approved through a municipal process, Basille reminded Jerry. Harrison received the particulars when he met with the builder and DeMarco, who was acting as the civil engineer for the project. He reviewed the site map and plans, and the project continued through the normal municipal channels.

"Basille actually apologized for mistakes on the map," Jerry said. "They are in the process of creating a new map and contacted DEP and the Army Corps of Engineers to mitigate any environmental problem and secure the buildings according to town regulations and to federal codes. It's expensive, Ros. Since the condos are already built, the State will give them a small fine and ask them to do a little work and let it go. I've seen this before."

"I know. They probably counted on that."

"The Chief thinks it's a waste of money for me to fly to Miami to look for a money trail to Harrison's two hundred thousand dollars. I do, too. Harrison most likely deposited the money into his own account. Where did he get the cash? I believe we can establish a direct connection between National Developers and Harrison. We've got the Empire withdrawal slip. A substantial amount of money appears from out of nowhere. There's the faulty map, which in my mind any lawyer could convince a jury was not just an honest mistake, but a huge benefit to National Developers. Then there's Harrison's approval of the condos, which is out of sync with his twenty-eight years as town planner. Then there are Maddy's calls to Harrison for two weeks, when she seems to be in a panic about something, and all of a sudden the calls stop."

Jerry continued. "Why? We know why. Then Ms. Hayden has Harrison's fax, saying he was going to arrive in town on Monday. In addition, there's Maddy's note to you marked private and urgent. Then Maddy and Harrison are killed during robberies. Both of them?"

"But Jerry, what does this actually prove?"

"We're proving that National Developers would profit from having Maddy and Harrison dead. Edgar L. DeMarco, Sr., in particular, who is actually the owner of National Developers, has everything to gain. The District Attorney must be convinced that there's enough evidence to issue an arrest warrant for him for second-degree homicide charges for the contracted murders of Maddy Trowbridge and Harrison Hayden. A pre-trial hearing will follow. A judge will decide if there's enough circumstantial evidence to go to trial."

I briefly recapped my conversation with Fred Fitz. "He's sending two agents even after speaking to your Chief."

"They'll find the link we need between Harrison and National Developers and the Empire Bank, if anybody can," Jerry said, "and the Chief will take the credit for solving the case in the end. At the same time I think the Chief's thinking that since RICO, the government is legally cleaning up Las Vegas. Nixon is quoted saying he didn't want to send agents into Las Vegas and ruin everybody's fun because they were already taking Vegas back from the mob. Ros, I think this is why the Chief is dismissing so much of this case."

"They don't hang out in casinos anymore. Now it's strip clubs. Jerry, I just learned about two of them right in Stamford. There's this businessman, Larry Madison. He owns the two strip clubs, Larry's Place on the West Main and Twirlers on Orchard Street. According to the prosecutor, Madison's businesses were legitimate. A little problem with the State Liquor Commission, but nothing serious. Just lap dances and legal drinking. No history of prostitution fights or other goings-on, right?

"Then one night five guys walk in, a Gambino capo, Jimmy Citani and some enforcers from Long Island. Citani makes an announcement that they're taking over the whole east coast. Then he demands two thousand a month protection money from Madison.

"Since Madison didn't have any problems, he didn't understand what he needed protection for. Citani told Madison that he'd had a free ride all these years, and it was time he started paying. Then Citani tells everybody he owns the clubs, invites his friends, all on the house, and turns the strippers into prostitutes. Citani threatened Madison if he didn't leave the so-called grocery money each month.

"The surprising thing is that Madison didn't fold; he instead contacted the FBI. That's why they've made so many arrests in Connecticut recently. It was this Madison guy going under cover."

"I wasn't aware of all this, Ros. We get legal notices from the prosecutors, but if you're out of the station at the time, you might never hear about it. The communication sucks."

"I didn't hear about it either, Jerry. I found these stories buried on the back pages of local newspapers. Just like the Chief here, no town wants to advertise a Mafia infiltration, even when we know two strip clubs and a Greenwich restaurant are paying protection money. How many more? We have no idea."

"So Madison paid protection money for two years while he wore a wire recording everything for the FBI. The FBI heard them force Madison to install poker machines, which are highly profitable for the mob. The syndicate offers high odds. It doesn't collect taxes, and people don't have to leave their neighborhoods to play. One poker machine could net ten thousand a month. Madison set up drug buys. He observed the gambling business and other criminal activities such as prostitution and loan sharking in Norwalk where a reputed loan shark demanded a hundred dollars per week interest payments on loans and gambling debts of as little as a thousand. A former used car salesman was indicted and sent to prison for thirteen years for a bulk cocaine sale outside Casey's Diner in Stamford in a set-up organized between Madison and the FBI.

"Thanks to Madison, the FBI got an inside look at the Mafia workaday world. Mob business meetings were held during walk-talks and in coffee shops and diners, anyplace that protected them from being bugged. Tefano and others made millions of dollars, it was revealed, during the last decade from loan sharking, union embezzlement, illegal gambling, racketeering including violent assault extortion, trafficking in stolen goods, drugs, counterfeit goods and mail fraud. All this condemning information was revealed by one guy, Tefano.

"Jerry, do you know any correctional officers up in Sing Sing?"

"I'm ahead of you there. I called a prison guard I know. He's going to call me back at about five o'clock. If we can connect DeMarco with Freemont, we have our circumstantial case locked down. It's over."

"You're good, Jerry."

"Thanks, Ros, but it's just standard police procedure."

Forty-Seven
Later Saturday Afternoon, Telling Evan

The pouring rain was hitting the porthole of the window in front of me. I checked my watch. It was just about noon. The temperature had risen above freezing, and the rains came as predicted. I recalled the radio announcer telling us we should be grateful it's not snow. As I sat there I had to think of how I would tell my exhausted editor about organized crime moving into Wilton. It was just four days after he had been hit with the first murder in town in eighty-six years.

In ordinary times, before the murders dominated our lives, an avalanche of words would have hit Evan's ears regarding this possible sensational exposé. It would have been an exciting and challenging time for the newspaper. But under the circumstances, I needed to be certain of the facts of the story before I laid this on him. As I followed the path of the raindrops traveling down the window, I realized there was one more rock to look under before I went to Evan.

I reached for my phone and dialed a familiar number. To my relief, Timothy Esposito picked up. It wasn't unusual for the town planner to be working on Saturday, but I think I caught him off guard when I inquired about the possibility of a new mall to be built in the Village Center.

"Nothing concrete," he said and chuckled. "Pardon the pun."

I laughed good-naturedly. "But the idea of a mall is being discussed?"

"I can't officially say anything about it right now."

"Would National Developers, Inc., which owns the Stuart Island condos, be the builder?" I asked.

There was silence for a second. "I'm not sure. Of course, the prospects are wide open," Esposito said finally.

"They would build it on the land they owned in the Village Center, is that right?" I pushed.

"Well, yes, they own a substantial amount of land there," he replied.

Bingo.

"We'll be going through the public hearing process," he was saying, "and there are other possibilities."

"But a new mall is part of your town plan?"

"Let's say it's a possibility," he replied. "We're just considering it. We think there's enough volume for a mall. Super Stop & Shop is interested, so we'll see."

We said our goodbyes.

Translation: "There's something unofficially going on regarding a mall, and most likely a mall is part of the new town plan being considered by the new town planner, Timothy Esposito. It is subject to public hearings, and National Developers has sufficient land to build the town's first mall."

More grist for the mill.

With the yellow pad in hand containing Esposito's quotes, I travelled to the far end of the attic and the next step of this investigation. I sat in the chair to the right of Evan's turn-of-the-century desk and relayed my story to him. His steady eyes bored into mine for a few seconds as he thought it out. Then he instructed me to write only the basic facts, such as that National Developers, Inc., and not Peterson, Myers Sheen, Inc. owned the Stuart Island condos. That Edgar L. DeMarco, Sr. owned National Developers, and he and his son, Edgar L. DeMarco, Jr., had been on the Justice Department's Subjects List as principals associated with organized crime, before it was destroyed. He told me to check with the Justice Department to confirm that information, which I had intended to do. I was to include Esposito's quotes about National Developers as possible builders of a new mall in the Village Center. I was told to wait to read the copy of Greg Himes' exposé to write about the mall bombings.

"And look up the deed to find out how much land they actually own there."

Then I was to offer whatever update I had on the murder investigations from the official report from the police, which, of course, didn't yet link the murders to National Developers. The story would not include Maddy's note about the map.

Evan reminded me that Maddy's note was crucial evidence in a murder case. I was to copy it and the maps and Maddy's other note and turn them over to the Chief. I'd write about the inconsistencies in the maps and question all the proper authorities, Timothy Esposito, the DEP and the Army Corps of Engineers.

I was not to mention the link between Empire Bank and Trust and Harrison's suspicious two hundred thousand dollars. Yet.

"We'll sit on that for now," Evan said with fire in his eyes. "That information, I hope, will come from the police. If it doesn't, then we're on it."

I returned to my desk. Seconds later, Evan was at my side, looking down at me. "Rossi, you have the best nose for news I think I've ever seen in a reporter. How did you get from Maddy's note to National Developers?"

"Seeing Maddy's body lying under that tree," I said. "I felt I owed her. I started to dig after the discovery of her note. I called the Miami Board of Realtors for information on National Developers after I went to town hall and discovered that they owned the Stuart Island condos."

He gazed at me with intense eyes set a mile deep in dark sockets. "Be careful, Rossi," he warned. "This is unknown and dangerous territory for us, but it is our job. I'll gladly take over this story from here."

"Don't worry, I'm not about to be whacked," I joked while realizing the last thing I wanted was to have this story taken from me. "I'm now living at Jerry's." A blast of wind and rain hit the side of the building and the little window facing me so hard that it drew our attention to it. "I've read that organized crime stays under the radar of the local police," I continued, my eyes back on Evan. "If that's correct, they'll never invade a police officer's home or kill his reporter girlfriend."

"That's a big 'if,' Rossi."

Forty-Eight
Saturday Evening

I checked my watch. It was 7:15 p.m. I had finished what I set out to write, and it was time to go home. As I got into my Nissan, I realized I wanted my home, not Jerry's, even after all I'd said to my editor about living at Jerry's. Sometimes you need to go home, and tonight was one of those times, I thought as I drove down Route 7. Nothing but my own bed would do. Writing the exposé had put me under the black spruce in the darkness once again.

At the sight of my modest home, set back on a slight hill graced with giant oaks, I issued a sigh of relief. I pulled up the drive and parked, leaving my gray Nissan outside. Not a good idea, I told myself, but I was not just exhausted as usual. I was beyond that. It'll be okay, I assured myself. The temperature had dropped in the last couple of hours, turning the rain to sleet. As I stepped inside, the house seemed chillier than usual.

In the kitchen I called Jerry. He would be over in an hour or so. He'd sleep a couple of hours and head back to work again. There was a ten o'clock meeting at the station with Al, the Chief and others involved in the investigation. He wasn't thrilled with my choice to sleep at home.

After putting my things away I turned the thermostat up and heard the oil heater kick on, but I decided that the damp evening called for a nice, roaring fire as well. I grabbed several sheets of last week's Sunday *Times* in the brass newspaper rack on the floor next to the couch and rolled them into thick wads to use as kindling. After repeating the process several times, I thought it safe to lower the thermostat, but even the thick logs sitting in a pile on the hearth were still cold to the touch. I interspersed the logs and the wads of newspaper on the fireplace rack to create the necessary draft.

I squatted in front of the fireplace and pulled out a long wooden match from the box on the mantel. I struck the match and was reaching over to ignite the newspapers when the peaceful night changed into bedlam. An explosion shook the house to its foundations. The window near the driveway was lit up with flashes of red. It was as if a bomb had been dropped.

I rushed toward the door. Did the underground oil tank near the front door explode? Through the side window I saw plumes of yellow and red flames roaring from my car and lighting up the tall trees.

The words of the Miami reporter came rushing back to me with momentum. "One more thing, I'd be careful. My car was blown up."

As I opened the front door the heat that charged the air hit me. I stepped back behind the door and squinted at the conflagration. The shooting sparks died on impact with my rain-soaked house. I slammed the door and ran to the kitchen to call the fire department, my legs weak under me. I grabbed the phone and leaned my forearm on the countertop to hold myself up.

A fire engine was on the way, I was told, thanks to several calls from concerned neighbors. I got on my coat and stood right outside the front door, holding onto the doorknob to steady myself. I watched the flames light the night air, and send sparks everywhere, including into the surrounding soaked forest. Thank God, my neighbors' homes were a few acres away.

But why had this happened? Didn't we know everything by now? I was already writing the story. The organized crime people, the DeMarcos, the Gambinos or whoever had to know that. Blowing up my car as a scare tactic just didn't make any sense. The story would be written.

"Be careful. This is unknown and dangerous territory for us," I could hear Evan's words. I covered my nose and mouth and stepped outside to stand on the cement landing. The burning rubber and oil polluted the fresh air.

I peered north and south for suspicious vehicles. What are they afraid I'll uncover? I asked myself. What intelligence don't I know? When will this end? I recalled Himes hanging up on me.

Now I understood why.

Forty-Nine
The Police Chief

Only a few minutes later, at exactly eight o'clock, fire engines and an ambulance screeched up Sugarloaf escorted by two police cars. The volunteer firemen scrambled to pull the hose off the truck parked in front of the house to douse the raging conflagration. The concerned neighbors huddled together, freezing, to view what looked like a death scene from a distance, obliging firefighters by staying on the opposite side of the road.

I waved to them to ease their minds. Then Jerry parked behind the hose truck and ran with jacket open in the sleeting rain over the slushy lawn, his wild eyes lit by the fire. I called out to him, and he shuddered with relief.

Not caring what the bevy of young uniforms thought, he grabbed hold of me and held me to him. I felt his cold, wet nylon ski jacket against my face and the intense beating of his heart, and for a second I collapsed in his arms. He pulled me away to scrutinize me, his brown eyes examining my face, "Are you okay?" he asked, his voice deep.

"The Chief must keep Maddy's and Harrison's cases open now."

"Please go in the house," he said, sighing. "Keep warm. You look like you might be suffering from shock."

A few minutes later the Chief himself showed up and entered the living room with Jerry at his heels. I leaned on the chair by the window.

"Are you okay?" the Chief asked. He was dressed in his uniform and a dark blue overcoat. I pushed myself away from the chair and managed to stand on my own two shaky feet as I invited him to come in. He walked a few steps toward me and waited for my reply to his question.

"Yes, I'm okay, but I'm nervous. I now definitely feel like a target, and I have no idea why."

"We won't be able to tell until it cools off," he muttered, almost to himself. "Right now all we smell is gasoline as if there was a gas leak that somehow got ignited." He strained his neck to look around me and gaze at the window.

"What, another coincidence?" I asked, astounded. I put my hands on my hips, preparing for a verbal battle.

"There is no obvious evidence that an incendiary device caused the explosion, that's my point," he said. "It's a suspicious fire, but we can't rule anything out at this point."

"Chief Romano," I said, stupefied. I was dressed in my usual garb, a black knitted pullover sweater and jeans, but all of a sudden I was in a sweat. I was going to explode from his lame response. I forced myself to calm down.

"I'm in touch with another reporter at the Miami Herald who wrote an exposé on National Developers," I said civilly. I lowered my hands from my hips, attempting not to look battle ready. "His car was blown up, too. Don't you think this is more than another coincidence? The reporter strongly warned me, telling me he had no doubt that his car was set on fire as a warning for him to back off the story, and he added that he wasn't investigating a murder at the time. In other words, Chief, I can expect even more." I truly couldn't believe this guy.

"Until we've investigated this incident thoroughly," the Chief said, turning toward the window and the view of my burning car, "we have no idea what occurred here tonight,

Ms. Rossi, but I'll keep a car patrolling your block periodically for the next couple of weeks."

He pulled out an official complaint sheet and handed it to me, then turned to leave. He hesitated in the entryway and stared back at me. "It's of course up to you, Ms. Rossi, but right now we have no evidence that organized crime is doing anything illegal or legal in town. You could scare your neighbors by making spurious charges in your stories."

"Spurious?" I was about to lose it. Jerry gave me a warning glance. "My car was just blown up, but let me assure you, Chief Romano, I just report the facts. Neither I nor my editor, Evan Hillcrest, would have it any other way. We have confidence in the intelligence of the people of Wilton. They'll draw their own conclusions."

With that, the Chief walked out the door.

Fifty
Back at P&Z

The temperature was in the low forties Monday morning, and it was sunny, but the mild weather had little effect on my spirit. In fact, the glare hurt my eyes. I had to admit to myself that I was still shaken by the second attack on my home on Saturday night. I had the feeling that the car explosion had blasted me and my lovely memories of my parents right out of the house. I could even hear my parents urging me to move out.

I was grateful I had spent yesterday leasing a new car and moving a few things into Jerry's. It was good feeling having transportation, even though the reason for blowing up my car was still evading me. Going through my notes and reconstructing the case on paper hadn't lead to any new conclusions. It seemed as though we knew all the aspects of the case.

I told myself to think on the bright side. I was still alive.

Also, Jerry and I did have a definite future, and the murder case appeared to be accelerating it. Jerry was having visions of a little Rossi, and I was moving into his home. I had been as comfortable Saturday night and yesterday as if Jerry's home were mine.

The steak knife stored under the passenger seat of my new silver Nissan was another comforting thought.

As I got closer to town hall in the ebbing rush hour traffic, I realized it had been six days since Maddy's murder, and I was adhering to my usual work routine but dreading it. I was going to collect the information for Wednesday night's public hearing as I did every Monday. My eyes, however, were harnessed to the shiny new rearview mirror, still looking for the black sedan or any other suspicious vehicle. I parked in the small annex parking area and climbed out of the car into the sunshine. I pushed open the glass door of the Wilton Planning and Zoning Department. My eyes went directly to Maddy's empty desk, and my heart sank as if it were the first time I'd seen it.

Her Christmas decorations and pictures on the wall had been removed. Nobody yet occupied her prestigious space. No doubt, a little depression was setting in. After all, it was the season of good will. Christmas, I realized at this moment, would never be Christmas again if Maddy's murderer wasn't apprehended. I missed my parents, in particular, at Christmas. I realized how my mother, with all her personality problems, had been the spirit behind Christmas in my childhood years. Why hadn't I mentioned that to her?

Tears sprang to my eyes as I viewed the stack of the official public hearing notices that sat on the empty desk like any other day. I gulped down a sob, thinking of life's injustices and how all of a sudden any person can disappear forever from the face of the earth.

My fingers gathered a copy of the public hearing schedule. I reluctantly but quickly glanced over it. A notice about Stuart Island and the underground oil tank was included. They were pouring concrete for it and installing it this week. Also listed were a couple of permits for new spec houses in the east section of town. I would have to get to those sites, I noted. I realized that as usual, thinking about my work was having a calming effect.

Tim Esposito stepped out of his private office in the alcove across from Maddy's desk and seemed surprised to see me. Wordlessly, I waved the P&Z public hearing schedule at him and smiled. He nodded knowingly. The routine was obviously still new to him. Dressed to perfection as usual, he wore a navy blazer and steel gray pants. Without speaking, he continued down the hall, headed to the Public Works Department, leaving the scent of mint aftershave in his wake. He wasn't my favorite person, but I was relieved to see a human being walking around the place.

A dark-haired, middle-aged woman typist sat at a new metal desk set up along the south wall, no doubt picking up some of the slack. She continued typing as if I were invisible.

Drawn to the old familiar map files in the center of the room by instinct, I bent down to view the S file drawer to find the old Stuart Island map, just to look at the cursed thing one more time. For what reason, I don't know, maybe just to see if it was still there. Maybe to return to the beginning.

I never challenge such instincts. It struck me that I wasn't afraid anymore as I had been Thursday, two days after Maddy's murder. Strange, since they'd blown up my car Saturday, and it was only Monday. But I simply didn't care if a spy was in the office and observing my actions or not. I was already a target.

I found the new map and placed it on the top of the file cabinet for the whole world to see. I rifled through the many other maps filed in the S drawer, but I couldn't find the original 1955 Stuart Island map.

I tipped the drawer down so I could slide my hand into the square metal space behind it to see if anything had slipped out. The drawer was at least a yard wide and two feet long to accommodate the large maps. My arm, up to my elbow, disappeared into the cavern, and my fingertips felt a slender object, no doubt a pen. I pushed it, and it rolled out and a burgundy-colored pen dropped to the tile floor at my feet.

I bent to pick it up just as Esposito walked back up the hallway to return to his office. "Oh, there it is," he said, smiling at me. "I was looking for that." He took it from my right hand as I was rising. I found myself gazing at several pens of the same burgundy color that crowned the top of the breast pocket of his blazer.

"A gift from my wife for landing the job," he explained.

He's thinking I had found the pen on the floor, I thought. Then his eyes darted to the Stuart Island maps set on top of the cabinet. They cut back at me, glaring with condemnation. Irrefutable recognition by both of us was taking place, the simultaneous understanding that I knew he had removed the missing map.

Fifty-One
Lunch at Home

I threw open the glass doors, anxious to get to the safety of my car. Once inside, I slammed the car door and locked it. My heart was pounding in my chest as I drove out of the parking lot and headed to the sanctity of the newsroom.

I asked myself if Timothy Esposito was the spy in the office. Was he a plant for organized crime? Was he an associate or a mob boss? An underboss? A capo? I had caught Timothy Esposito, or he had caught me. It had been both. I saw emptiness when I looked into Esposito's eyes, no life at all there.

Was the new town planner's connection to organized crime the fact I was not to discover? Was he the reason they had blown up my car, to scare me off?

Settle down and attempt to define what just took place, I told myself as my cold hands gripped the steering wheel. It seemed perfectly clear that Timothy Esposito was involved in some fundamental way with the murders of two employees of the Planning and Zoning Department, Maddy Trowbridge and Harrison Hayden. Well, if Esposito was connected, as town planner he'd be a great influence for the Mob in Wilton now that Harrison was dead.

I couldn't wait to make the turn off Route 7 onto Ridgefield Road. I parked in the parking lot, and in seconds I was charging up the steep steps to the newsroom. I dashed to my spot, slamming my yellow pad on the dark pine table, and picked up the phone to call Jerry. No one was in the newsroom, but Evan would be coming in any minute now, I told myself.

Jerry was out and would get back to me, I was told by the sergeant at the front desk. I banged down the phone, took off my coat and hat and sat down. I took a couple of deep breaths. Focus, I told myself. Focus on the work.

I gazed at my blank computer screen. The writing on the murder seemed infinite at this point. There was the police blotter of my exploding car, which I had forgotten to pick up. Of course, I had yet to get to the sites of those buildings under consideration by the P&Z commissioners this week.

My damning moment of clairvoyance regarding Esposito puzzled me. I was stunned into inaction, numb. I continued to sit at my desk and look at the empty screen. I rubbed the rough surface of the battered old library table just to feel something. What a relic of a thing it was. It had received so much abuse, and had no doubt seen some fairly brilliant reporting, over the years.

I was stuck. I couldn't think. Esposito's psychopathic eyes were right here in my head, crushing me, staring at me.

It was all catching up to me.

I watched the Christmas shoppers through my little window, but it didn't help. I sat back in my chair, closed my eyes and meditated. Immediately, I recognized the blinding fear I had been busy suppressing. I took a couple of deep breaths and was able to clear my mind of all troubling thoughts, including Esposito. I breathed free and clear of terror for several seconds.

I opened my eyes and began to write the description of my exploding car. I'd get the police blotter later. Maybe the fire marshal had reached a conclusion regarding the origin of the blaze and decided if it had been just a leak in my gas tank that mysteriously ignited itself, as the Chief had implied.

By noon my urge to go to my parents' home was irresistible. I'd eat a healthy portion of the home-cooked spinach soup I'd made yesterday in between reading my notes, and I'd feel better. Italians maintain their appetites during a crisis. It's one of the characteristics that keeps us strong, I thought with a smile. We go on. I was grateful I had dropped the soup off at the house in the morning just in case.

Evan hadn't arrived yet, which didn't help, and there was no call back from Jerry. My heart was pounding again when I hit Sugarloaf Drive. My eyes had been on the shiny rearview mirror, as usual. I was ambushed again by the charred driveway. This morning it hadn't bothered me, but now the explosion ignited once again in my memory.

It was the Esposito encounter that triggered this fear, I told myself as I got out of my car, post-traumatic stress. I started to doubt my impressions as I walked in the bright sunlight to the front door and fumbled for my key. Maybe Esposito had just been annoyed that I was at the file again. He probably got a call from the Chief asking pesky questions and was annoyed that I was still drumming up trouble. I stepped into the vestibule and unlocked the vestibule door.

My house smelled of burning rubber and gasoline. Would I ever feel completely safe here again? I slapped my things down on the corner chair by the door and rushed to the kitchen to get the large bowl of spinach soup out of the refrigerator and attempt to quiet my nerves. I got the bread from the fridge, too, and set both on the countertop next to the stove. I found a pot and turned on the oven to heat up the bread.

But every petrol-tainted breath I took in the process reminded me of my exploding car, the impact on the house when I lit the match and the racket of the rattling windows and doors. My life and my emotions were absorbed by old, new and potential threats. I grabbed the sickly greenish-yellow wall phone, which suddenly seemed so very unattractive. I'd never noticed just how ghastly a color it was until this moment. And how in the world had my mother lived with all this knotty pine?

I dialed the Chief's direct number, my eyes riveted on the picture window opposite me that overlooked Sugarloaf. I did admire the Chief's knowledge of organized crime. I slid my hand over the smooth, cold Formica countertop as his phone began to ring.

"Chief Romano," I began, my voice sounding near hysteria. "I need to report something to you." I described my revealing pen encounter with Esposito that morning.

"Well, he didn't deny it was his pen," the Chief responded, "and why wouldn't he be in those files? It's his department. Ms. Rossi, you know I've been talking to Tim. I followed up because of your questions about Harrison's business with National Developers and the maps used to get the building permit."

"You have?"

"Yes. More or less, it's for the record," he said, filled with self-importance, "but Tim more than cooperated. He's also going to cooperate with DEP to bring the condominium buildings up to code. Regarding the map, he says honest mistakes were made.

"Now as far as this morning, Ms. Rossi, there are better ways to start a new job than having your whole department under investigation by the local newspaper and the police department."

"But why remove the 1955 map? That map is evidence."

"No, it isn't, Ms. Rossi. We've never connected Mrs. Trowbridge's murder to the Stuart Island condominium project. We've arrested a man, a convicted felon, with her stolen belongings along with the murder weapon, and now Freemont has no alibi."

"But if you were to investigate this whole affair, the map would be evidence, I must remind you. Chief Romano, I believe I found Timothy Esposito with his hand in the proverbial cookie jar, and he knows I'm the one who found him. I don't feel safe right now. Suppose he's connected?" I yelled, my eyes still on the window and Sugarloaf.

"You're obviously still upset by the fire, but listen," he said, showing concern. "Don't worry. I have a patrol car circling your area several times a day. The officer should be there in a few minutes. I'll tell him to park for a while."

"I'll be leaving for the newsroom in about a half-hour, so that'll be a help. Thank you." I exhaled again.

"About the cause of the fire, our fire marshal found no incendiary device in your car," the Chief went on, "but he deemed it a suspicious fire anyway." I thanked the Chief, but I knew that Jerry, Al and I would be solving this crime without his help. The phone rang as soon as I hung up.

"Sorry, Ros, couldn't get right back," Jerry was telling me. "Gloria had an accident. Some idiot left a steel jaw leg-hold trap on the property, probably years ago. She was hurt. Oreo came back to the house to get help. Luckily, Mom was there and managed to free her from the trap, but Gloria didn't want to walk. She just sat down. I drove the truck over for her."

"Is she okay?"

"Yep, she's got mean cuts, but I don't think her ankle is broken. She let me clean it and wrap it up. After that she limped back. She's okay. She's sitting on a bunch of straw in the barn, looking dazed. The vet's coming over this afternoon to give her a shot. Oreo won't leave her. He's in the barn, too."

"What a dog."

I told Jerry about my brief encounter with Esposito, and it concerned him.

"I'll be over in about ten minutes. This is not good, Ros."

"No, don't come unless you want some spinach soup. The Chief is sending a car. It's going to park here for my lunch. He's humoring me, but I don't care. I'll be over tonight after work, okay?"

I heard Jerry take a deep, troubled breath. "Ros, leave right now, and don't go back there in the dark. If you had been living here, you'd still have your old car."

"I moved into your house yesterday, Jerry, but I needed some soup."

"Leave now, Ros."

"Okay," I lied. I was thinking that the Chief was right, I was suffering from PTSD. Maybe Esposito wasn't connected.

"I was in the middle of questioning some of Janet Godbridge's friends," Jerry continued. "Seems nobody knows anything about her move. I'll get back to work, if you're okay. Come to the house tonight straight from work, no stopping, okay?"

I promised. Then I allowed myself to cling to a basic Italian staple, good food. I placed a healthy piece of Italian bread into the oven. I scooped some soup into the pot to heat up, trying to get as much spinach as possible into the ladle. I noticed the mailman drive up the street and stop to deliver a package. He shoved it into my mailbox.

I grabbed my coat and rushed out into the damp, cold air. I waved hello to the mailman. It was a nice, ordinary, non-PTSD thing to do. Then I ran back into the house, clutching the package from the *Miami Herald.* It put a big smile on my face. I couldn't wait to read the stories.

Still in my coat and sopping wet shoes from the slushy driveway, I stood just inside the entryway, facing the living room, and surrendered to my curiosity. For the first time since Maddy's murder, I allowed myself the excitement of a promising story.

I tore into the oversized brown envelope and pulled out three issues of the *Miami Herald* which contained the three-part series on organized crime and National Developers, Inc. A picture of the New England Mafia leader, Jake Delipanti, and the owner of Green Acres Racetrack in Vermont, Ronald Puchi, were on the front page of the last of the three issues.

I felt a chill running through me once again. Ronald Puchi was the spitting image of Timothy Esposito. I was sucking in air at the sight of him. I recalled Himes telling me about the New England mob, thinking I had no knowledge of mob ties in the area. I stood stunned, paralyzed by the resemblance. I couldn't pull my eyes off the photo and its revelation. Puchi was definitely an associate of organized crime, and Timothy Esposito had to be a relative. Therefore, he had to be connected.

I felt a draft and turned to my right, thinking I had left the door to the vestibule open, my eyes still glued to the traumatizing picture. Something ripped around my waist like a restraining bar. I felt hard metal pressing against my right temple and realized it was the muzzle of a gun.

With my eyes still fixed on the damning picture, I felt the newspapers slip to the wooden floor.

Fifty-Two
"The Bull"

He turned me around and pushed me up against the closet door, my back hitting it hard. I was staring into the grinning face of the man in the black suit. He was wearing a long black overcoat over his suit, and his shaved head was bare.

Up close for the first time, his battered face looked like that of a former pugilist who had fought a few too many bouts. One of his thickened eyelids hung lower than the other. His misshapen cheeks were swollen with permanent lumps.

His eyes shone with emptiness, so lacking in human compassion that my knees buckled at the sight of them. His blank expression and his body strength seemed to sentence me to immediate death.

He is going to kill me. He is the last person I'll see in my life, I thought, trembling. I also realized that I was probably looking at Maddy's and Harrison's murderer. Anger surged in me as I stared back at him.

"You're number thirty-one," he was saying, as if reading my mind. "Couldn't scare you off, huh?"

His eyes lit up with his evil humor. He shook his head, a wide grin still on his face and his foul breath of cigarette smoke and coffee pouring down on me. It seemed that only in killing was he in his glory. He stared at me with apparent contentment that I was giving him an opportunity to kill again.

"Did Tim send you here?" I demanded, my anger driving me. "Did Harrison and Maddy get in the way? Did DeMarco want me dead, too? What are you, his capo?"

I was actually sticking my Italian chin out, getting closer to him. My heart was pumping out of my chest. His grinning face was two inches from me. His foul breath was getting thicker, and his breathing was quickening.

"That Hayden guy was number twenty-nine," he told me in his gravelly voice. "His secretary, number thirty."

The banality of evil, I thought as I watched and listened to the man who numbered his murders as if they were professional accomplishments and who was now counting me as another one of them. The man who had stalked me. No doubt, the man who had blown up my car and left a knife at my door.

He twisted my right arm hard behind my back and pushed me ahead of him toward the door to the vestibule. Tears of anger filled my eyes. I was about to start sobbing from my helplessness against his physical strength when I remembered my father's words: "The bigger they are, the harder they fall."

"They tell me you'll be writing a goodbye note, you're movin' away," my assailant taunted me. "You're too afraid to stay on the job, afraid you'll get whacked like the other two." He laughed heartily, actually getting a kick out of the idea of the phony note.

I was struggling, just to loosen his painful grip on my arm. We were now in the vestibule and facing the front door.

"We're gonna take a little ride in your new car to the condos," he said. "You should thank me for your nice new car." He laughed his evil laugh. "They're pouring cement today, and you're gonna be part of it. It was Tim's idea to put you in it. Good one, huh? Whaddya think?"

My God, they were pouring the cement for the underground storage tank today. That's what he was talking about. They would never find me. He must have parked down the road and walked. If I got into the car, it would be all over.

"You killed Maddy at the school," I said in an attempt to distract him. I needed time to think. My heart was pumping in my throat. He gave me a shove through the outside door.

"She fell right down. One shot. She slid like a sled over the snow."

He laughed again. His hand tightened on my arm, twisting it like he wanted to break it off. I was in pain, but anger controlled my thoughts.

My car was unlocked with the keys in it. I looked down the road. Why had I told Jerry I was leaving? The police car was supposed to come up the road any minute, but there was no sign of it. I couldn't get in the car. It would be over if I got into the car. I started to flex my leg muscles, feeling like a trapped rat, but then I remembered that trapped rats attack. Trapped rat, trapped rat. The thought came to me like a bridge to salvation.

He thrust me toward the door on the passenger side. I looked up and down the street for my neighbors, for Jerry, for the patrol car. Nothing, nobody. But then I told myself, that's okay, and felt my muscles flexing. My body was readying itself to take action. I knew that I would rather die in my driveway in a struggle.

I had little chance of survival, but I could choose my murder scene. Let my executioner shoot me right here, and then the evidence would be indisputable. The Chief and every member of the force would know I'd been murdered. Then Jerry would make sure someone paid.

The calmness that came over me was as deep and still as the waters of a summer pond.

I had decided to die trying to escape, yet, I hadn't totally given up. Four ounces can deflect a thousand pounds, I reminded myself, thinking again of my father's words. I will take his overpowering strength and use it against him. The bigger he is, the harder he falls. Shift your weight to your left leg. Then knee him in the groin with your right knee. With any luck the door will close on him. You know you almost got knocked out once when that happened to you. The door always closes if you don't hold it. The driveway's on a hill, remember? When the door closes, it'll clip him.

He won't expect it from you.

You have the element of surprise.

I twisted before the car door he had opened as if I were preparing to slide into the passenger seat, as if I were cooperating. He misread my calmness as acceptance of a hopeless situation. The stupid smile was still on his face; he thought I had surrendered. He allowed his grip on my arm to loosen. It was then that I saw the pale wooden handle of the steak knife sticking out from under the passenger seat next to the door.

The ominous weight lifted from me. The weapon changed the odds. I dipped down to slide into the seat, my heart hammering in my chest. His crotch in the black machismo pants that hugged his muscular body, was facing me like the perfect target. I grabbed hold of the knife, my eyes on the target, and slashed hard, upwards into his crotch, twice.

He bent forward, horrified and screaming. He backed away from the door with both hands on his crotch, still clutching the gun. The door closed and clipped him in the head, and he dropped the gun. Blood spit at me from the split in his forehead. He and the door fell toward me. I shoved him away with two hands.

He fell back and then folded onto the ground. I stepped over him as he screamed, writhing in pain, still horrified and looking down at his pants that were filling with blood. His gun slid under the car, and the door slammed shut.

A black sedan pulled into the driveway. Had I really thought he worked alone? I fled up the driveway to the hill in back of the house and started to scramble up the slushy hill on all fours, still gripping the knife in my right hand.

I hear a vaguely familiar voice calling out to me. "Ms. Rossi, it's okay!"

Still clinging to the earth, I turned my head to see a tall man standing outside the car, his face unfamiliar.

"I'm Fitz from the Justice Department. We talked, remember? You called me?" He was walking toward me as he spoke. "The Chief called. He told me about the car explosion. I came over to talk to you."

I recognized his voice at once. All the tension left my body. I began to slide backward down the slushy hill on my hands and knees, but my eyes were on the man with Fitz. With a gun in his hand, he approached the bald man on the ground. He had stopped screaming and lay twisted, his back to me.

The strong hands of Fitz were on my shoulders, helping me up. "Come on, Ms. Rossi. It's okay. You're safe."

Fifty-Three
Justice

All charges against Richard Freemont were dropped, Jerry informed me on the phone several days after I was attacked. I sat at my desk at the *Wilton Weekly*, writing up the sensational news story. Jerry was at the station where he was still spending most of his time, mopping up the investigation and preparing for a double homicide trial.

"The U.S. Army Corps of Engineers, under Section 404 of the Clean Water Protection Act, can enforce its highest civil fines," he told me. "It requires a permit for activities involving the discharge or dredging or fill material in all waters of the United States including navigable waters, inland rivers, lakes, streams and wetlands. I'm reading this, Ros," he added. "Basically the Justice Department is putting National Development out of business."

Using RICO, the Justice Department collaborated with the Army Corps of Engineers to charge National Developers the highest civil fines possible, twenty-five thousand dollars per day of violation, and also criminal fines of twenty-five thousand dollars a day, Jerry explained. Since the wetlands on the bank of the Norwalk River had been filled for two solid years, the total fine amounted to thirty-six and a half million dollars, which meant bankruptcy for National Development. Edgar L. DeMarco, Sr., as the owner, could face a year's imprisonment for each day of violation, or seven hundred thirty years. Also, the Connecticut District Attorney charged him with two counts of second degree murder and one count of second degree kidnapping.

Timothy Esposito was charged with second degree kidnapping. Mario "The Bull" Magalino was charged with the murders of Maddy Trowbridge and Harrison Hayden, and my attempted kidnapping.

Magalino and Esposito never implicated the Gambino family. Both men kept the Omerta rule, the Mafia code of silence. The number of arrests and the sensational *Wilton Weekly* exposés, however, generated coverage by the major television networks. Evan splashed the stories across the front page of the *Wilton Weekly*. The Mob was far from under the radar.

"It's fair to say that organized crime was weakened by the arrests," Fitz had told Jerry. What worked in Las Vegas to get rid of the Mob was working in Wilton, I thought.

"Freemont will be out in six months," Jerry continued. "I did a lot of talking, but Freemont's patrol officer was also influential. His opinion was that with the help of his girl friend Janet and the promise of a job, Freemont had a good chance for a productive life.

"I've invited Freemont and his girlfriend over anytime. I told him that shoveling manure would help him heal all wounds."

Fifty-Four

February 1, Georgetown

It was still dark when Jerry I were awakened by the weirdest pathetic sound. I opened my eyes and thought, it's the first day in February and my first day at a daily, *The Norwalk News.* I sat up and realized that the strange sound was coming from the barn. I listened a little harder. It was definitely a rooster call.

"That's our rooster," I announced. "The vet says the birds' respiratory systems are getting better. I guess so." I lay back down.

"They're still leery of us," Jerry mumbled, half asleep.

"But they love Arabella," I retorted, and he turned over to go back to sleep for another few minutes.

Arabella was like our very own Dian Fossey. I recalled how she'd spent a couple of solid days and nights with the birds. She slept in the barn with them and followed them outside, giving them names. After that Jerry told her he expected more birds to fall off a truck any day now.

I realized that Clifford now visits us almost on a daily basis, coaxed, no doubt, by Arabella. He goes off for a healing walk, surrounded by dogs, while the winter sun is setting and before one of Lillian's incredible vegan meals. I was grateful she cooked for us during the week. It was our turn on the weekends.

We were able to convince Arabella to continue her schooling by promising to watch over her dad.

I sighed. Life was changing. Again.

I slipped my arm around Jerry, thinking that *The Norwalk News* might not be *The Boston Globe,* but Jerry and his Peaceable Kingdom weren't in Boston. I wondered how Dylan was getting on there. Besides, at the moment I was three chapters into the writing of my first novel. Most of the story was about keeping my promise to Maddy, granted I did it with a lot of help from my friend.

I put it all out of my mind by hugging Jerry tighter. He also helped to warm me under the covers. The single-digit winter air manages to creep through the walls of the sturdy wooden house, even with the near constant hum of the faithful furnace. My cheek rested against Jerry's back. He turned around and wrapped his arms around me. Yes, life is changing once again, I told myself, and I could feel my parents' happiness for me.

In Jerry's embrace, I closed my eyes and drifted, drifted in the bliss.

Author's Note

This is a work of fiction, but two of my characters, Edgar L. DeMarco, Sr. and Edgar L. DeMarco, Jr., are based on real-life criminals known to have Mob ties, who engaged in practices similar to those of my characters.

Dan E. Moldea, a courageous investigative reporter who has been writing about organized crime since 1974, was the inspiration for my Miami reporter, Greg Himes. Himes' experiences belong to the fictitious character, but the information he provides comes from Mr. Moldea, whose book *Interference* provided the lion's share of the facts on organized crime. Other sources include *The New York Times*, 9/30/04 article written by Alison Leigh Cowan, and Greenwichtimes.com, *Police eye restaurant*, by Eve Sullivan, which addressed more recent Mafia crimes in Connecticut.

The history of organized crime in New England and New York and its activities is based on reported organized crime events published in Moldea's book and articles in countless respected newspapers, including *The Hartford Courant*, Edmund H. Makoy's 4/4/2006 article, and information on several websites.

Wilton historian Robert H. Russell, in his amazing book *Wilton Connecticut*, and G. Evans Hubbard's history books of Wilton provided the town's historical facts. Hubbard, Wilton's first historian, was the inspiration for my character, S. Gilbert Taggard. I give credit for all the recorded history of the town, from the purchase of its land from Chief Mahackemo to the information about the names of early settlers on the road signs today, to Mr. Russell and Mr. Hubbard. I didn't include the 1911 and 1929 murders for dramatic purposes so that the murder of Maddy Trowbridge, my character, could be the first since the 1897 David Lambert murder some eighty-six years previously.

The Wilton Town Hall and Planning and Zoning Department provided information regarding wetlands, condominiums and site maps in their public files. Be assured that the forged map and the illicit permit to build a condominium complex in my story are fictitious.

The *Wilton Weekly* is loosely based on *The Wilton Bulletin* and my work there as a planning and zoning reporter. Of course, no murders were committed during my tenure there, and all the newspaper characters are fictional, although the editor in my story has some similarities to Greg Bartlett, who was my excellent and patient editor at the time.

I take full responsibility for any mistakes on all scores.

I thank my editors, Arthur Hayes, Theresa Crusius, Mahie Galvin and James Tyler Coon, who kept me and my characters on the right path. My proofreaders and morale builders were Lenore Cereghini and Lisa Lersner. A thank you to my sister, Carol Coon, who listened to my complaints and allowed me to use her first name for my main character along with my friend, Carol McConway. My fellow writers in Sisters in Crime provided cogent direction and inspiration along with CAPA, the Connecticut Association of Publishers and Authors. A big thank you to WomenofMystery.net and CriminalElement.com that provided on-line exposure.

Finally, to my parents, Dorothy Reid Phillips Davino and Anthony Davino, who taught me that I could do anything if I put my mind to it: Thanks Mom and Dad.

Respectfully submitted,
Dorothy H. Hayes

CPSIA information can be obtained at www.ICGtesting.com
Printed in the USA
BVOW041032040313

314473BV00001B/1/P

9 780988 194496

Meet Author Dorothy H. Hayes

Dorothy Hayes, a graduate of Western Connecticut State University, taught Language Arts in Connecticut schools for three years. She was then a staff writer for *The Wilton Bulletin,* and *The Norwalk Hour* and received an honorary award for her in-depth series on Vietnam Veterans from the Society of Professional Journalists.

Dorothy also worked as a staff writer for a national animal protection organization and wrote *Animal Instinct,* published by IUniverse in 2006. She lives in Stamford, Connecticut, with her husband Arthur and is the proud mother of four, the happy mother-in-law to three, the grandmother of fourteen, and GN to Bella. She also writes for Womanofmystery.net and CriminalElement.com. Visit her at DorothyHayes.com.